"Ms. One-Name," he said quietly, intimately, while sliding his fingers down her arm.

He grabbed her hand, then looked down as his thumb skated over her rings. He released her. "Sorry. You didn't seem...taken."

"I'm widowed." She said it breathlessly, hungrily. Stupidly. What was wrong with her? She'd just met the man, a man who was obviously a player, given the way he'd come on to her.

"Dating yet?"

"I...no."

"Can I give you my number for when you start?" His deep blue eyes lured, enticed.

"I...I have your number." She stopped, flustered by the sparkle in his eyes. Oh, he knew how he affected her. Liked it. Flaunted it.

Oh, yes, she had his number indeed. Womanizer. In it for the game, the fun. That wasn't her style.

Or was it? Who said she couldn't have that kind of life?

Susan Crosby

Susan Crosby has enjoyed every stage of her life, from childhood to middle age, a stage she expects to stay in for at least another fifty years. Along the way she's done a lot of the usual things—married, had children, attended college a little later than the average coed and earned a B.A. in English, then dived off the deep end into a full-time writing career. She wrote twenty romance novels before venturing into women's fiction, and will always believe in happily ever after.

More can be learned about her at www.susancrosby.com.

The Merry Widow's Diary

SUSAN CROSBY

THE MERRY WIDOW'S DIARY

Copyright © 2006 by Susan Bova Crosby

isbn-13: 978-0-373-88108-6
isbn-10:   0-373-88108-8

All rights reserved. Except for use in any review, the reproduction or utilization of this work in whole or in part in any form by any electronic, mechanical or other means, now known or hereafter invented, including xerography, photocopying and recording, or in any information storage or retrieval system, is forbidden without the written permission of the publisher, Harlequin Enterprises Limited, 225 Duncan Mill Road, Don Mills, Ontario, Canada M3B 3K9.

All characters in this book have no existence outside the imagination of the author and have no relation whatsoever to anyone bearing the same name or names. They are not even distantly inspired by any individual known or unknown to the author, and all incidents are pure invention.

This edition published by arrangement with Harlequin Books S.A.

® and TM are trademarks of the publisher. Trademarks indicated with ® are registered in the United States Patent and Trademark Office, the Canadian Trade Marks Office and in other countries.

TheNextNovel.com

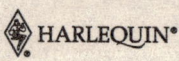

PRINTED IN U.S.A.

If you purchased this book without a cover you should be aware that this book is stolen property. It was reported as "unsold and destroyed" to the publisher, and neither the author nor the publisher has received any payment for this "stripped book."

From the Author

Dear Reader,

The average age a woman in this country becomes a widow is fifty-six. Surprising, isn't it? I was younger than that, as is my heroine, Jill Townsend. What she and I learned is that we all grieve and recover differently, but recover we do.

So this is a story about reinventing yourself out of necessity, about finding a new path when a landslide blocks your old one. It's about letting new people into your life, people who make you laugh, who make you glad to be alive, while never forgetting the ones you've lost.

Some of Jill's experiences are my own, some came from people I met after I was sent down the other path, and some I created just for her. I'll leave the fun of separating fact from fiction to you.

Susan

For all of you who are reinventing yourselves—
this one's for you.
For Melissa Jeglinski, who encouraged me to reinvent
myself as a writer—thank you.
For Robin Burcell, who has aided and abetted all my
reinventions—thank you, too.

CHAPTER 1

Jill Townsend spied the city limits sign then glanced at her dashboard clock. It was eleven twenty-three? Already? The last time she'd looked, it was ten o'clock. She must've been driving by rote since then.

Trying to be more alert, Jill sat up straighter. On this late summer evening, the community of Darien, Connecticut, slept. Lights were out, the roads almost clear of traffic. She should probably wait until morning to return the borrowed Suburban to her next-door neighbor.

By the time she came to that conclusion, however, she'd driven past her house and found herself at the entrance to Alan Haggerty's long driveway. She eased down it, rolling to a stop in front of his garage. A light shone in his upstairs office, which probably meant he was working, not entertaining. She didn't want to disrupt his creative flow....

Which was a lie. She was stalling, plain and simple. Tonight, tomorrow morning—what did it matter? The SUV had to be returned, and she had to face reality. She would be going home to an empty house. At forty-five years of age, she was facing her first night of living alone. Who would be in a hurry to achieve that milestone?

She pushed Alan's garage-door remote then maneuvered his big Suburban inside. She hesitated then, her fingers on the key, delaying the end of her life-changing journey. For just a little while longer she wanted to ignore the fact that her already turned-upside-down world now spun on a completely different axis.

She switched off the ignition, silencing the engine and Norah Jones's smooth voice on the CD. Quiet. Such extraordinary quiet.

"Okay," she said aloud, gripping the steering wheel. "O-kay."

She climbed out of the car then opened the door leading into Alan's kitchen. "Anybody home?" she called out, in case he did have company.

"In my office," he shouted. "Come on up."

Jill jingled the keys as she climbed the stairs. After Alan's wife left him three years ago, he'd redecorated and remodeled, removing all trace of her. The more contemporary style suited him, all sleek lines and modern art, a cool look that fit his post-divorce years.

She rounded the corner into his office. "Hi," she said with ridiculous cheerfulness.

He typed for a few more seconds, then looked over the top of his glasses at her. Anyone who didn't know he was a bestselling author of horror novels would never guess by looking at him that his imagination ran down such dark and twisted paths.

Her cheeks froze as she held the stupid smile.

"Home from the wilds of Boston, I see," he said, tossing

his glasses onto the desktop before drilling her with his perceptive gaze.

Don't ask me how it went. Please don't.

"My car still in one piece?" he asked.

The knot in her stomach eased. "Except for the bashed-in passenger door."

He leaned back.

She tossed him the keys. "All tucked away, in the same condition I got it. How's the book coming?"

"I'm about to murder someone." He rubbed his hands together in gleeful anticipation.

"I'll leave you to your mayhem. Thanks again for the use of the car. I would've never fit all Tori's stuff into mine."

"You don't have to go."

"Yeah," she said against the hot lump in her throat. *No sympathy. Please, no sympathy.* "I do."

He didn't try to stop her. She scurried downstairs and out of the house, then cut across his yard to hers. She envied him having work to keep himself occupied. Even when he'd been devastated by his divorce, he'd had deadlines to meet, which forced him to keep going. She didn't know what she would do now.

Why hadn't she planned for this day? She, the world's all-time champion planner, had not planned for this huge life change. Why not?

Oh, yeah. She'd been busy grieving.

She unlocked her back door and made her way through the dark house and up the stairs to her bedroom.

Her answering machine blinked, a welcome diversion. She pushed the message button.

"Hi, Mom. Just wanted to let you know I'm thinking about you. I know this is a tough day, but you'll be okay. Love you. I'll call you tonight."

Sweet Shanna. Jill smiled at her older daughter's upbeat voice. She glanced at the clock and decided it was too late to call Shanna back. Then her gaze shifted to her day planner/diary lying facedown on her bed, where she'd left it after writing her daily to-do list. She picked it up.

Wednesday, August 22
1. Clean out Wade's closet and office.
2. Drive Tori to college. Try not to cry in front of her.
3. Skinny dip.

The first item had headed her list for months, transferred each day. She drew a line through the second item—mission accomplished—then tapped her pen against the third, added hastily that morning, anticipating being alone tonight.

Alone. Wade should've been there, helping to take their younger daughter to college, as they had with Shanna three years ago. Jill had never driven into Boston before. The trip had been doubly hard because of the pressure of driving in new territory in an unfamiliar and larger-than-she-was-accustomed-to vehicle. Wade had always done the driving out of the immediate area.

But you did it, said a proud little voice in her head. The achievement ranked high on her list of accomplishments.

She set down her pen and rubbed her face. What now? She couldn't go to bed. She would only lie there, thinking. She needed not to think.

3. *Skinny-dip*. Okay. There was a good reason why she'd put it on her to-do list this morning. Wade had tried to talk her into skinny-dipping for years, and she'd always resisted, afraid one of the girls would catch her. He'd sworn again and again to be her lookout. Finally, last year, he'd outright dared her, and she'd promised him that when Tori left home, she would take the plunge, naked. It was supposed to mark the date when they returned to a household of two, like newlyweds.

But Wade had died almost nine months ago, on New Year's Day, one day after their twenty-third anniversary. And today her last bird had flown the nest. With the house finally free of teenagers who never went to bed, Jill no longer had an excuse.

"And I promised you, didn't I, babe?" she said aloud, as if Wade were watching and listening.

She stripped, leaving her clothes on the floor, something she never did, then slipped into a short silk robe and sandals. She headed downstairs and outside, talking to Wade the whole way. "If I can drive a car bigger than a tank into Boston, I can skinny-dip, right? I'm keeping my promise. Now you keep yours. Be my lookout."

She inched open the French doors leading to the backyard. The moonless sky and surrounding greenery offered her all the privacy she needed. Yet when she touched the gate latch of the fence guarding her swimming pool, she hesitated, her confidence slipping. A gust whipped around her, parting her short robe. She clutched the edges and tightened the sash.

She debated with herself, rationalizing a way out. Just because she was a compulsive list maker didn't mean she had to follow through. After all, who would know?

"I would," she whispered into the night. "A promise is a promise." That was reason enough.

She pulled on the latch, the metallic sound seeming more like a fanfare announcing to her neighbors what she was about to do. Which was ridiculous. She was the middle-aged mother of two college coeds. Who would care? Summer would fade soon, and she wouldn't have many more opportunities to swim before the weather turned.

Her pulse beat a quick cadence as she sat on the edge of the pool and set her feet on the first step. Cool water nipped at her toes and ankles. After scanning her surroundings she untied her robe and let it drop to the deck. Her breath caught as she slipped into the water then pushed off from the bottom step to glide underwater, not coming up for air until she was more than halfway down the pool. She finished the lap, her head up, straining to hear—

Stop. Just stop worrying. She grabbed the tile overhang and pressed her forehead to it. *You're alone and you're safe. Wade is watching over you. He promised....*

Her eyes burned, but not from the chlorine. She hadn't

known how like silk the water felt against bare skin. She let her mind go deliriously blank as she propelled herself through the water, lap after lap, until she couldn't lift her arms anymore. She rolled over and let herself drift, her hair floating around her, a reminder that she hadn't had it cut in months. There was something satisfyingly sensual about the feel of it now, undulating in the water.

A noise intruded. She moved quickly and soundlessly to the side of the pool, pulling herself close to the edge. The gate opened and closed. In the darkness she saw a man stop next to her robe and stare at it. He bent to pick it up.

Jill groaned silently at the irony of getting caught the first time she dared to skinny dip on her own. What were the odds? "Come here often?" she asked.

"Jill?"

"No, it's Elizabeth from next door, looking for a place to meet single guys."

"I'm sorry," Alan said. "I'll go."

"What are you doing here?"

"You told me I could use the pool anytime."

He sounded uncomfortable, and she realized her sarcastic tone had put him off. "And I meant it, Alan. I'm just curious as to why now?"

"I was having trouble sleeping. Murder does that to me."

She laughed.

He turned toward the gate. "I'll leave you alone."

"Nonsense." She'd swum long enough, anyway. Maybe

her mind hadn't quieted enough to sleep yet, but she could let him have the pool. "I'll just—" She started to climb the stairs, then realized her dilemma. "I can't get out. I'm, um, naked."

Crickets chirped in the ensuing silence.

"So, this *is* the place to meet hot singles," he said, his tone light and flirtatious.

Jill had never thought of him "that way." He'd become a buddy, that was all. They'd known each other for fifteen years. He'd been Wade's best friend, and Barbara, his exwife, had been Jill's until Barbara had walked away from her marriage.

Alan dove in before Jill could say anything, apparently taking her silence as an okay to join her. She'd seen him in a bathing suit plenty of times. He was shorter than Wade, but still close to six feet tall, and with a broader chest and wider shoulders and more chest hair. At forty-seven, he'd aged well. His temples were graying, but his dark hair was otherwise thick and wavy.

She hung in a corner as he swam the length of the pool again and again, as she had done. After a while he came toward her.

He flashed a grin. "You've got that deer-in-the-headlights stare. Don't worry. I won't look."

They had never teased each other sexually. Never. Friends, and only friends. She tried to smile, if for no reason than to show she wasn't bothered by his presence.

"You don't trust me, Jill? After all these years? Why would I ruin a good friendship?"

She wished she could come up with something witty to say, but he moved a little closer and no words found the path from her brain to her mouth.

Apparently he realized that the whole situation was making her uncomfortable, because he said, "So, you didn't say how the drive to Boston was for you."

She didn't really want to talk about sending her daughter on her own into the world, but she grabbed hold of the change of subject with relief. "You know what it's like, leaving your kids at college. You've been through it."

"For Barb and me, it was just more freedom to argue." He flicked some water at her. "Are you sure you don't want to get out of the pool? You look cold."

He was right, but she wasn't about to admit it to him. "I think you're projecting," she said.

He grinned. "Maybe I am a little cold now that I've stopped swimming."

"Wimp."

"You have more layers."

"What's that supposed to mean?"

"Well, it's a proven fact that women are able to…keep out the cold better than men."

"You brat!" Like she needed him to tell her that she needed to lose weight.

She lifted her arm to splash him, but he sank beneath the surface, his laughter leaving bubbles. He was teasing her, but he was also right. She'd avoided exercising to the extent that she hadn't even put it on her to-do list, hadn't wanted the sympathy she would encounter at the country club. Or that was her rationalization, anyway.

"I'll head home," he said.

He climbed the stairs. Jill watched without thinking, her gaze fixed on his shoulders, then on the water dripping down his back, revealed inch by inch as he mounted each step. His swim suit clung to his wet body like a second skin, albeit one with lightning bolts printed all over it.

I need to find a guy with a butt like that....

He turned around, catching her eyeing him. She sank underwater, the water cooling the heat in her face. When she came up for air, he was gone. What had he thought of her? That she was pathetic? Or weird? He'd be right. She was those things these days. And more.

She made her way into the house, took a warm shower then climbed into bed, trying to find a new focus for her thoughts. Maybe it was time to make changes in her bedroom, make it more feminine. Hers. She could have a lace dust ruffle and pillows. And a lavender-colored comforter...

Which would mean painting the walls and getting new window treatments. And daintier furniture instead of the large pine pieces. No. She would stick with the country look for now.

She snagged her diary from her bedside table and opened it to the current entry. She drew a quick, satisfied line through *skinny-dip*.

Her phone rang. She grabbed it before the second ring. Was Tori homesick already? Did she need her mother?

"Hello?"

"Hi, Mom."

Not Tori, but that was okay, too. "Shanna, hi. Sweetie, it's one-thirty in the morning."

"I've been calling every so often. I was worried."

"I'm fine. Everything is fine." Well, not fine, but at some point it would be.

"I know this is a big change for you, Mom. Your first time alone."

"Really, I'm okay." And then, just to prove her words, added, "I even went skinny-dipping."

"What? Mom! What if the neighbors saw you?"

The prudish shock in her daughter's voice made Jill smile. Shanna had always been the conservative one, in that sense like her father in most ways.

"You have a reputation to protect, you know," Shanna added.

"Don't worry. Only one neighbor dropped by," Jill said in a tone that implied she was joking.

"Okay, I get it. It's none of my business."

"I understand you don't want my reputation tarnished, but I promise you no one can accuse me of being a merry widow."

"I know, Mom. I do know." She yawned. "Well, I've got to be up early for my first class tomorrow. Love you."

"I love you, too," Jill said, missing her daughter so much as she hung up. She stared out the window, not really seeing anything through the blur.

She settled into her pillows and pulled up the sheet,

proud of the fact she'd survived one more day without cracking up or breaking down. One more day of grieving.

One more day of not having fun, she thought. Then she considered Shanna's shock at Jill's having gone skinny-dipping. Had she broken a rule of mourning? It wasn't like they taught classes on this stuff.

Maybe writing it down would clarify it in her mind. After all, it wasn't as if she hadn't learned enough on her own to teach a class herself. She picked up her pen.

> How to Mourn 101: Learn the best way to deny, rail about, bargain over, wallow in, and finally accept the death of your husband, father of your children, gainfully employed life partner.

Who swept you off your feet at first sight, she added mentally, and who defended you to his noses-in-the-air parents, and who made love to you like there was no tomorrow.

But tomorrow had come, followed by almost nine months of yesterdays. If she didn't turn around and look toward tomorrow again, she would fall into an even worse routine now that she was alone, without any reason to get up in the morning.

The loneliness hit her full force. She'd gone from living at home with her parents, to a college dorm, then to marriage in a linear path, never living on her own. Never wanting to.

She turned out the light, rolled onto her side and

closed her eyes, but the bombardment of thoughts didn't abate. Coloring everything was her being alone. Then she thought about Shanna, a senior at Wake Forest, who'd always been solid and stable, and who'd confided in Jill, but now kept her grief at bay rather than dealing with it. For the first time, Shanna had stayed at school during the summer break.

Then there was Tori, Daddy's girl, emotional and dramatic, making another huge transition, this time to college.

Alan. Jill hoped she hadn't messed things up between them by him catching her admiring his body. She would hate to have their relationship change. She needed him.

She flipped back to face the ceiling and blew out a breath. It was stupid to worry about it.

And it wasn't like she hadn't seen a man's butt before….

Just not for a very long time.

CHAPTER 2

Thursday, August 23
1. Clean out Wade's closet and office.
2. Get a dog—they're noisy and fill up space.
3. Start the starvation and torture plan.

Jill's bed looked like something out of *The Princess and the Pea*, discarded clothes creating layers stacked high. Her handsome late husband had defined the term *dress for success*. It hadn't hurt that he'd also been graced with a GQ-cover face and an athlete's body. Sports were his passion, an arena to drive relentlessly toward goals, like climbing Mt. McKinley when he turned forty, and Mt. Everest at forty-five.

It was on one of his extreme ski trips—helicoptered into a pristine and remote mountain in Canada—that he'd suffered the heart attack that killed him, a fifty-two-year-old man in top physical form. If only he'd been home, within range of immediate emergency help....

Except she'd been told that his heart attack was massive and his death instantaneous. She wondered whether doctors just say such things to the family as a way to offer comfort.

Wrapped in Wade's bathrobe, Jill hugged herself. After a minute she stretched out on top of his clothes, sinking into the fabric that breathed his scent and told stories of his life. The CEO suits. The four-handicap-golfer khakis and knit logo shirts. The at-home-husband-and-father comfy sweaters.

What was she going to do without him to shop for her? She had iffy-at-best taste in clothing, as he'd pointed out, kindly but honestly. He used to surprise her with new garments that always fit perfectly and looked classic. He used to take her on whirlwind shopping trips, used to arrange for a personal shopper at Barneys....

Used to.

She squeezed her eyes shut. Giving away his clothes was so much more than a physical act. It signaled yet another stage of acceptance and finality.

Determined to cross off the long-listed item from her to-do list, Jill hauled the first batch of Wade's clothes downstairs to the mudroom. He had so much, she needed to borrow Alan's Suburban to deliver them. And she needed to get them out of the house today, not wait for a truck to come pick them up.

Except for Wade's bathrobe and a couple of his T-shirts, she would donate everything. It seemed easier emotionally than to stretch it out over months.

She shut the door on the empty cavern of his closet,

grabbed an armload of suits and headed downstairs. Forty minutes and nine trips later she pushed open the door to Wade's home office, the next item on her list. She hadn't been inside for months, since their longtime accountant always handled the bills.

Still being taken care of.

The disloyal thought startled her with its truth. She'd wanted to know about and understand their finances, but Wade had never included her, assuring her that there was plenty of money. He'd not only earned a good living, he'd had a substantial trust fund that allowed them to live above his salary.

He'd never even put her on a budget.

If that is the worst thing you can say about him...

She plopped into his big leather desk chair and opened the drawers, poking through the contents. The bottom drawer was jammed with greeting cards, apparently every one that she and the girls had given him through the years.

She sat back in amazement. She'd never considered him sentimental. He'd always been even-keeled, except when it came to sex. Only in bed had he opened up and shown her how he felt, their sex life phenomenal from the beginning. Even through all the normal ups and downs of marriage, they'd enjoyed each other physically.

"Jill?"

Cards scattered and fell to the floor as Alan stepped into the room, surprising her.

"Sorry. I brought the Suburban," he said. "I knocked

a few times. Your car was in the garage. I was worried, so I used my key."

"I got lost in memories. I didn't hear you." She helped him pick up the cards from the floor. "I'm finally clearing things out. Look," she said, sweeping her hand over the desktop, scattered with proof of Wade's surprising sentimental streak. She pulled one from the pile. "I remember when Shanna made this. She was just learning to write, and she started over several times until the lettering was exactly how she wanted it. A perfectionist even then."

Happy Father's Day was printed on the outside, and I Love You Soooo Much on the inside. Stickers and glitter dressed it up. "Have you kept your cards?" she asked Alan.

"I have sons. I get phone calls." He sat on the edge of her desk, close to her chair. "Plus Barb wasn't one for doing crafts with the boys, as you probably know." He crossed his arms. "So, how about if I load up the clothes and take them away? You don't need to be part of that."

She considered then rejected his offer. More than ever she needed to stand on her own two feet. "I'll do it. But thanks. You don't need to bother."

The air vibrated with sudden, intense silence until Alan spoke again. "He was my friend, too, you know," he said in a tone she'd never heard him use.

Caught off guard by his low, angry voice, she hesitated, finally saying, "I know he was."

He spread open his arms. "So, why won't you ever let

me do anything? I miss him. I need to do something." He laid a fist against his chest. "You know, I would've driven you and Tori to Boston. All you had to do was ask." He clamped his mouth shut then shoved himself away from the desk and strode to the window, his back to her. "I feel helpless. It's the worst feeling."

"I didn't realize, Alan. Why didn't you say something before?"

"I figured you would ask. Aside from using my car, you never ask."

"It's hard, asking for help." The hardest. It was horrible having to depend on someone else. She had an accountant, the gardeners and the pool service but otherwise managed on her own. "I'm sorry. I didn't have any idea you felt like that."

He didn't respond right away. "I've put on weight without him dragging me to the handball court," he said finally, changing the subject, his tone softening although still tight.

She studied his body, looking for proof. Her face heated, embarrassing her, catching her off guard. Since Wade's death she hadn't been able to imagine herself with any other man. Now her body was imagining without any help from her mind.

"I went to the gym at the club this morning," she said to end the silence.

He turned to face her. "Oh?"

"After your comment about my extra layers last night, I decided it was time to get back on the treadmill."

"I didn't—"

She held up a hand to forestall his words. "No, you were right. I've let myself go."

"You look fine. I was trying to distract you. You were uncomfortable being naked—"

"I know," she interrupted in a hurry, not wanting to relive that moment. "Anyway, I went really early so I wouldn't run into too many people."

"I'll bet you turned some heads."

"As a matter of fact—" she picked up a rubber band and toyed with it "—there *was* a guy there working out with weights who seemed to notice me. A *young* guy."

"How young?"

"Midtwenties." She looked up at him, aiming for nonchalance. "He was…ogling me."

Alan's mouth tipped in a half smile. "Ogling?"

"There's no other description that fits. Every time I looked his way he was staring at me. I can prove it. They have security cameras, you know."

"Were you wearing your contacts?"

"Alan!"

"Well, maybe he was just staring at that spot on your chin—" he squinted "—of whatever it was you ate for breakfast."

She ran her fingers across her chin, just in case. "He was not."

Alan smiled. "I told you. You look good."

"You said I look fine, which is vastly different from good." She fired the rubber band at him.

He ducked, avoiding the shot. "Did the ogling Adonis talk to you?"

"He started to come over, but I left. I mean, he was, you know, young. I like my men with experience."

"Ah. But, after the fact, are you sorry you didn't talk to him?"

"Nothing to be sorry about. He didn't give up. He was waiting when I came out of the locker room."

"And?"

"And he was an old friend of Shanna's from high school. He wanted to know how she was doing."

"Ouch."

Jill returned his grin. She admitted to herself that she was flattered and even a little stirred up when she thought the guy was interested. Who wouldn't be?

Silence settled again between her and Alan, not uncomfortable but not as comfortable as usual.

He laid a hand on her shoulder. "Let me take the clothes away for you."

"No, I—"

"Then let me go with you."

She should accept help from friends, all the grief books said so. He needed to give help, and she should let him. She could be independent another day. "Okay. Thank you."

He stood. "I'll load the car."

"Can I buy you dinner tonight as a thank-you?"

He hesitated at the door. "I've got plans."

"Okay." She straightened the desk pad, aligning the corners precisely. Of course he had plans. He dated a lot.

It's just that it had never bothered her before.

* * *

After Alan dropped her at home later, Jill grabbed a load of sheets from the dryer and carried them upstairs to Tori's bedroom. She sat on the bed, hugging the still-warm linens. The room had been stripped of Tori's essentials—computer, television and other electronic necessities. Her closet door gaped, revealing clothes still on hangers and jumbled on the floor. Not long ago posters decorated the walls, but Tori had ripped them down one night in a grief-filled rage and had never put anything up in their place. Torn corners, still stapled into the walls, were all that remained.

She'd even taken her pretty yellow-and-green quilt off her bed and tossed it in the back of her closet, replacing it with a heavy black comforter, completely at odds with the white provincial furniture, plantation shutters and pale yellow walls. When Shanna left home three years earlier, she'd left her room spotless. But then, the sisters had always been opposites.

Jill crossed the room and opened all the shutters and windows, something Tori had stopped doing, living in a cave instead. The windows faced the street at the end of their winding, tree-lined driveway. Had she stopped looking out the windows because she knew her father wouldn't ever come through that iron gate again?

The same night Tori had torn down her posters, she'd removed a cherished, framed picture of her with her father that sat on her desk. Jill hadn't seen it since.

Tori was too young to lose her father. Shanna, too. And Jill was too young to be a widow. Not for the first time she wished she'd had another child or two. Why had she and Wade decided against having more? She liked her nest feathered, not empty. Since her graduation from college and immediate marriage thereafter she'd never worked outside the home, had made a career of being a wife and mother, and she'd been good at both jobs.

The phone rang. She shot off the bed, grateful for the interruption.

"Hi, Mom," came the welcomed voice.

"Shanna, hi," Jill said cheerfully. "Thanks for calling last night. It helped a lot. How was your first class?"

"Killer. They're all killer. Mom, I realized after I hung up that I forgot to ask how little sister did yesterday."

"She couldn't wait for me to leave."

"I remember the feeling," Shanna said.

"Really? You didn't show it."

"I know. It doesn't mean I didn't love you."

Jill smiled. "I never would have thought it. But I remember my parents leaving me in my dorm, too. It was exciting. An adventure."

"And scary."

"That, too. You'll call Tori occasionally and check on her? She'll talk to you in a way that she wouldn't talk to me."

"Mom, I promise I'll call her, but you know she doesn't talk to me, either. Or at least she doesn't confide."

"I wish you'd been home this summer. I think you could have helped each other."

The phone line filled with static in the silence.

"Are you there?" Jill asked.

"We've been over and over this, Mom."

Yes, they had. Jill had ached to have Shanna home for the summer, had thought they all needed each other, but Shanna chose to stay away as her way of grieving.

"So, have you been dating anyone special?" Jill asked to change the subject.

"No."

Jill worried about that. Shanna hadn't had a boyfriend in high school, or now through three years of college. Concentrating only on her education, she'd never been a worry as a teenager, but Jill wanted her daughter to have fun, to experience life. A 4.0 GPA shouldn't be the sole focus of a college education.

"Are you really doing okay, Mom?"

"Don't worry about me. It's just so quiet. The house seems to have doubled in size."

"I'll bet. What are you going to do now?"

"I thought about getting a dog."

"Don't dogs have to be walked a couple of times a day?"

Jill heard laughter in Shanna's voice. "You read my mind. So then I figured maybe a cat instead. They're easier." But still company, someone to talk to.

"Good idea, Mom."

Maybe. "It was a fleeting thought. I did start back at the gym. Oh, do you remember Darryl Michaels?"

"Why?" The word came out cold, hard and fast.

"I ran into him at the club. He asked about you."

"You didn't talk to him about me, did you?" Faster, harder, colder.

"A little." Why wouldn't she? "He knew you were at Wake Forest. He seemed concerned about you, that's all, you know, since…"

"Don't talk to him about me anymore."

"All right." Curiouser and curiouser. Shanna had always confided in Jill, at least until the past nine months. Or so Jill thought. Was Shanna's contempt a carryover from high school? Darryl would've been two years ahead of Shanna. Had there been a relationship that Jill wasn't aware of?

"I've got to get to class, Mom. Talk to you later."

"Call—"

"Tori. I know. I will. Mom, find something to do, okay? Something besides skinny-dipping. Something the neighbors won't be talking about. You can't sit around obsessing about Tori and me. Bye."

She hung up before Jill could respond. *Find something to do.* She was doing something. She was clearing off her to-do list so that she could start fresh. That was big.

She finished cleaning Tori's room, then poured herself a Chardonnay and sat by her pool until the mosquitoes began to feast on her. She ventured back into Wade's office after dark, determined to finish the job she'd started earlier, determined not to transfer the task to her diary the next day.

She set the box from Wade's Manhattan office on the desk, her last item to sort. Although he'd been the CEO of GlobalJet Airlines for the past ten years, the contents of the box were strictly personal—framed photographs of her and the girls, and one of his parents, whom she realized she hadn't talked to for a couple of months, although they called Shanna and Tori frequently on their cell phones, keeping Jill out of the loop.

She reached for a bubble-wrapped object and found a small bronze sculpture of a climber planting a flag on a jagged mountain peak. His wall art had been delivered months ago, but Tori had claimed them, although she hadn't hung them on her walls. Maybe they were shoved in her closet, which Jill hadn't touched, figuring Tori would be furious at the intrusion into her privacy. The paintings weren't particularly valuable, but pieces he'd bought in galleries from local artists, art that had moved or excited him.

Jill flipped through a small, black address book, stopping to run her finger along the handwritten entries. She lifted out a bottle of his favorite aftershave and opened it. He was there with her again.

She was about to take the box to the trash when she saw a tiny manila envelope caught in one of the bottom flaps. She slipped it free, opened it and tipped the contents into her hand—a key chain holding two keys and a tag. On one side of the tag, in Wade's handwriting, was a woman's name, Ilene Stillings, and a phone number. On the other was an address in New York City, where he'd commuted each day.

She flipped the tag over and back several times. Wade hadn't kept secrets from her....

Yet he'd kept the keys in his office, not at home, which meant...what? Something. A key signified *something*.

Jill glanced at the phone. As Wade's best friend, would Alan know? She lifted the receiver then carefully set it down again.

Find something to do. Shanna's words whispered through the confusion in Jill's mind. She didn't need Alan's help, not when she was perfectly capable of learning the explanation herself.

She stared at the keys for a long time, but the decision, in the end, was simple. Tomorrow she would go to the city and find which doors the keys fit.

Tomorrow she would *do* something.

CHAPTER 3

Friday, August 24
1. Get a ~~dog~~ cat—they're much less work.
2. Do something—find the doors that the keys fit.

Jill waited until after the commuter rush the next morning to take the train into the city. At 10:00 a.m. it was already muggy. She should've worn something lightweight instead of tailored pants and a jacket, but she'd felt the need for some kind of armor. She didn't know what she would find, had tried all through her sleepless night not to dwell on the possibilities. She had loved Wade, had trusted him, with good reason. Jumping to conclusions was foolish, although, without answers, conclusions had jumped on their own all night.

She'd looked up the address online and had decided to take a cab from Grand Central Station to the TriBeCa location, an area close to Wade's office, and one of Manhattan's hottest and priciest neighborhoods. She'd attended parties and business functions in some of the luxury condos and lofts in the area.

Her mouth went dry as her cab driver maneuvered through town, then paralysis almost set in when they stopped in front of a six-story building. The lump in her throat burned and throbbed.

"You gettin' out, lady?"

She dug some bills out of her purse, shoved them at him and climbed out. She stood in front of the building, one of many converted warehouses for which TriBeCa was known, and realized she'd attended a Christmas party in a third-floor apartment last year. It had been an elegant occasion, and Wade had bought her a gorgeous, forest-green, floor-length gown with black trim and a black velvet bolero. She'd had gold highlights woven into her then chin-length chestnut-colored hair. He'd teased her about looking like a college girl again.

He'd been unusually attentive all evening, and had taken her afterward to the Grand Hotel for a sexually adventurous night and a leisurely breakfast in bed before heading home. The memory warmed her as she headed to the front door then came to a sudden stop, wondering how she was going to get past the doorman. The keys alone wouldn't be permission enough—

Then she remembered. There wasn't a doorman, but a video intercom. And she had two keys. One was probably for the front door.

She studied the list of names on the panel beside the front door. She didn't recognize any of them. Two were blank.

Please don't let me run into anyone, she prayed as she

tried one key, then the other, which turned. Whose party had it been last year? Someone connected to Wade's business, but who?

Her heart pounding, she moved to the elevator, her legs shaky, clothes glued to her sticky body, sweat beading her brow. She kept her eye on the front door as she waited for the elevator to descend to the first floor, then she rushed inside. The tag on her keys said #601, so she pushed the button for the sixth—and top—floor.

She let out a slow breath when the doors opened without making a stop on any other floor, without encountering another person. She took quiet steps down a long, narrow hallway. The top floor appeared to have only two units, dividing the floor squarely down the middle. On the left side was #601.

At the door she listened but could hear only relentless thundering in her head. She'd concocted a story in case someone answered the door. Beyond that she could only react to what she found. If anything.

Jill rang the doorbell but had no idea if it worked. She couldn't hear tones from within. After about ten seconds she knocked. Waited. Knocked again. Waited. The key seemed to catch fire in her hand, searing its imprint into her palm. She had to hold one hand still with the other while she aimed the key into the lock. She turned it, felt the lock disengage.

She put her hand on the doorknob. The fact there was only one lock made her hesitate. Would she trigger an alarm when she opened the door? She glanced toward the elevator. It was still on the sixth floor. If an alarm sounded, she could make a run for it.

She turned the knob, then stopped and studied her surroundings again, looking for security cameras. Either they were well hidden or they didn't exist.

She nudged the door open a fraction. No alarm screamed. She peered through the crack, allowing it to widen a bit at a time, revealing the interior, but all she could see was a wall. Nothing adorned it, no photographs or art or mirror.

She stepped inside. Beyond a short hallway she could see a huge, unfurnished room and a bank of windows as tall as the ceiling, eighteen feet or so. She tiptoed farther, noting an overall industrial look to the space, including metal stairs that led to a partial loft, probably a bedroom, with a catwalk bridge that angled to a space near the front windows, an area big enough for a small home office and guarded only by railings for safety, not walls.

On the first level, in the middle of the floor, sat a toolbox, with a circular saw, hammer and measuring tape beside it. The air smelled of construction, the distinctive scents of glue and sawn wood. She turned and spied a gorgeous kitchen, large for a city loft, with a center island and stainless steel appliances.

If not for the tools she would've said no one had been there for months.

Who owned the place? The same person as nine months ago? The Ilene Stillings whose name was on the tag? Wade must have visited often enough to need a key.

Except...not overnight. He'd come home every night. Almost every night. Sometimes business kept him in town late, but it was rare that he didn't come home.

He'd been quieter, though, in the months before he died. Distracted. Less attentive. They hadn't made love as frequently, which was why the night after the party last December had been especially important to Jill. She'd thought he'd recovered from whatever had been bothering him. Work, he'd explained when she'd questioned him, a buyout he was trying to pull off that would open up new European markets for the airline. She'd believed him, had no reason not to believe him.

But now... Now Jill was standing in a newly remodeled loft a few blocks from Wade's building, having used a key he'd hidden in his desk at work, a secret he'd kept from her. Who owned it? What was Wade's connection?

Jill eyed the metal stairs leading to the loft. She put her hand on the railing, climbed the first step, weighed down by the horrible, disloyal thoughts running through her mind. Her stomach churned. Nausea threatened. She turned around, rushed toward the kitchen sink, her hand over her mouth.

The front door opened. A twenty-something man entered, his tuneless whistling announcing him. He wore torn jeans and a seen-better-days T-shirt, and carried long planks of wood molding.

They both jerked to a halt. She swallowed and lowered her hand, the nausea startled out of her.

"Yo," he said. "Didn't know anyone was here."

"I just—"

"No sweat," he interrupted, bopping into the room and setting down the molding with a clatter of wood on wood. "I did the floors yesterday. I'm supposed to put up the floorboards. Okay?"

"Sure." If he wanted to assume she had permission to be there, who was she to argue? "Are you the contractor?"

He gave her a what?-are-you-crazy? look. "I'm union. I do floors. You're lookin' for Bobby."

"Bobby?"

"Link. The contractor." He cocked his head. "Right?"

Her stomach settled. "Yes. Do you have his phone number?"

With a weary sigh, he pulled out a cell phone from a hip clip and scrolled, then turned the screen toward her.

She dug into her purse for a pen and paper, found nothing but her checkbook. She wrote the number on a deposit slip. "Thank you."

He grunted.

She started toward the front door, glad to escape. "You'll lock up?" she asked at the door.

"It wasn't locked when you got here?"

"No, it was. I mean yes." Her head was spinning. "I mean—"

"Okay." He dismissed her by turning his back on her.

She pulled the front door open.

"You can catch Bobby on the third floor, 304. He's bidding a job."

Why didn't you say that in the first place? she wanted

to scream. But she muttered a thanks then headed toward the elevator, trailing the wall with her hand, keeping herself steady. Her heart had never pounded that hard for that long. The workman hadn't questioned why she was there or how she got in. Why not?

She punched the third-floor button and mentally geared up for round two: Bobby Link, contractor.

A few seconds later, the doors opened. Before she could step out, a man entered, a very attractive man in his early forties, maybe, tall and broad shouldered, with supershort blond hair. He wore khakis and a moss-green shirt with the sleeves rolled up a few turns, and he held a measuring tape and clipboard. He had a woman-killer smile that announced his self-confidence and awareness that women found him attractive, even a gym-denied, widowed suburbanite. Her gaze drifted down him without thought to his taking note of her appreciation of his fine form.

"Going down?" he asked.

There was a hint of mischief in his eyes when she quickly met his gaze. Her face heated.

"Um, are you Bobby Link?" she asked, ignoring his double entendre.

His brows lifted. "Yep. And you are?"

"Jill."

"You're so famous you only have one name?" His smile was crooked.

"Your flooring guy on six told me I could catch you on three."

The elevator had arrived at the ground floor. He

leaned against the open door, letting her walk past him into the tiny lobby, where they stopped.

"You a Realtor?" he asked, giving her the once-over, not quite a leer but certainly admiringly.

Jill welcomed—and was appalled by—the way her body reacted to his appreciative inspection. "I'm trying to track down the owner of the loft upstairs."

"I don't think it's for sale."

"Who could I talk to about it?"

"Rafael D'Amato, probably."

"The architect?" Even she knew of D'Amato. If she could just remember why…

"He's who hired me for the job."

He would be listed in the Yellow Pages, so she didn't ask Bobby for a phone number. "Thank you," she said, then started to walk past him. He cupped a hand above her elbow, stopping her.

"Ms. One-name," he said quietly, intimately, while sliding his fingers down her arm. He grabbed her hand then looked down as his thumb skated over her rings. He released her. "Sorry. You didn't seem…taken."

"I'm widowed." She said it breathlessly, hungrily. Stupidly. What was wrong with her? She'd just met the man, a man who was obviously a player, given the way he'd come on to her.

"Ah. How long?"

"Since New Year's Day."

"Not dating yet?"

"I…no."

"Can I give you my number for when you start?" His deep blue eyes lured, enticed.

"Start?" she repeated.

"Dating."

"I...I have your number. Your floor guy—" She stopped, flustered by the sparkle in his eyes. Oh, he knew how he affected her. Liked it. Flaunted it. "I need to go."

"Call me," he said to her back.

She escaped into the muggy streets, struggling to breathe in the thick air, her flattered hormones compounding the problem. Imagine that. A man like that finding her attractive. Imagine.

And she had his number. Oh, yes, she had his number, indeed. Womanizer. In it for the game, the fun. That wasn't her style....

Or was it? Who said she couldn't have that kind of fun? Maybe not yet, but someday. When she found her stride. She could be anything she wanted to be, couldn't she? Her role as wife was over. Her role as mother had been altered forever.

Find something to do. Shanna's words didn't whisper, they shouted.

Well, Jill thought with a grin, she didn't think her daughter meant she should date the first gorgeous lumberjack to come along.

But it was a nice fantasy.

Jill remembered why she knew of Rafael D'Amato. He'd attended the same Christmas party last year, in the building she'd just left. She even remembered the name of the party giver. She figured her chances of catching Mr. D'Amato in his office were slim, but better if she showed up in person rather than calling, so she tracked down his address and took a chance.

She pushed open the heavy glass door of his fifteenth-story office. A starkly contemporary reception area greeted her, all ebony wood and deep jewel tones. Framed photographs of his work lined the paneled walls, mostly interior shots, each lit by a tiny spotlight.

The young and hip receptionist, her nose stud twinkling, smiled at Jill. "May I help you?"

"My name is Jill Townsend. I'd like to see Mr. D'Amato."

The young woman consulted a sheet of paper on her desk. "I don't see your name on the appointment list."

He's in the office. "I didn't call ahead. Would you tell him I'm here? We met at a Christmas party at Ronni Gibson's place last year. Tell him I won't take more than a few minutes of his time."

The receptionist left. Jill wandered around the room, admiring the designs, but her thoughts elsewhere—to her accomplishments. She'd gotten past a workman and the contractor without being questioned. She was counting on her loose connection with mutual friends to get information out of Mr. D'Amato. She wasn't anywhere near as nervous as she'd been. Success did that to a person.

"Ms. Townsend," the receptionist said, having opened

the door to the inner sanctum. "Mr. D'Amato will see you."

For a moment, Jill wished she'd worn something more kind of New York instead of suburban. Black. She should've worn black. She remembered Rafael D'Amato as a slender, dark-haired, dark-eyed man with perfect posture and elegant, chiseled features. Late forties, maybe? Not six feet tall, but close. A slight Italian accent. And sexy. Very, very sexy. The woman he'd brought to the party had been younger by probably twenty years, with a supermodel face and body. Men like Rafael could get away with dating someone like that.

"Mrs. Townsend," he said now, walking around his huge mahogany desk. "How good to see you again." He clasped her hand. His was warm and strong and sure. He didn't let go. "I read about your husband's death. I am so sorry."

That stunned her into silence.

"He looked like the picture of health at the party, which was only a few weeks before, wasn't it?"

She nodded. She hated sympathy, especially the direct sympathy he offered, his hands encompassing hers, his eyes focused on her face.

He released her. "Please, have a seat."

She tried to get her bearings, to recapture the confidence she'd felt when she'd come into his reception area. "Thank you so much for seeing me."

"You caught me between appointments." He sat behind his desk, his domain. The view behind him was spectacular, Manhattan in all its glory. "How may I assist you?"

She went for broke, figuring she wouldn't get a lie past him. He'd known Wade, knew of his death. "I found a set of keys in Wade's desk. They are for a sixth-floor loft in Ronni Gibson's building, and I'm trying to figure out why he possessed those keys. I'm told you're the architect of record on the remodel. I don't know how to ask other than to just ask. Did Wade, um, own that space?" It cost her a lot to ask the question, which obviously meant her husband had kept secrets from her, but she tried to ask it in an I'm-just-curious tone of voice.

Rafael leaned back in his chair. "Not to my knowledge."

"Who does?"

"I'm not at liberty to say."

"Is it Ilene Stillings?"

Silence hummed. His expression changed—or was it a trick of the light framing him in the window, giving him the advantage of seeing who sat before him clearly while keeping himself in somewhat of a shadowy silhouette.

After a moment he said, "I can't help you, Mrs. Townsend."

Dismissed. She thanked him for his time and rushed out the office, then the building, embarrassed and confused. Wade hadn't owned the place— No. That wasn't a sure thing. He didn't own it now, but he might have owned it before.

No. She pressed her fingers to her throbbing temples.

She would have known, after the fact, as part of settling his estate, wouldn't she? Bills would've come in. Her accountant would've questioned them, or at least Jill would've noticed in the monthly summary of income and expenses he sent her.

Did Ilene Stillings own it? What was the connection between her and Wade?

She pulled the key ring from her pocket and stared at the phone number written on the tag under the woman's name. Jill took out her cell phone and moved close to the building, turning her back on the noise. She dialed the number, held her breath—

"Ilene Stillings Designs," came the cheerful greeting.

Jill ended the call. One more piece of the puzzle. What kind of designs? Had she had *designs* on her husband? Had she succeeded?

She saw a Starbucks across the street and headed there, ordering an iced mocha and begging for a phone book from the busy counter person. While she waited for her drink she located an address for Ilene Stillings Designs. She glanced at her watch. If she wanted to head home before the commute traffic began, she needed to get moving.

Or maybe she should get a hotel room for the night and start again tomorrow, give herself some downtime first. Except she didn't have a change of clothes or her makeup or other essentials. Now or never. Well…now or another day, anyway.

She flagged a cab, tossed her untouched drink in a

trash bin before she entered, and tried to plan what she would ask the woman.

Did you have carnal knowledge of my husband?

Maybe she should leave it alone. Would having her fears confirmed help her in some way? Knowledge was supposed to be power, but maybe not in this case. Maybe knowledge would just hurt.

And yet, she knew she needed an answer rather than wondering for the rest of her life.

Better to know and deal with it.

See, Shanna? I am doing something.

CHAPTER 4

Ilene Stillings' office was located in a ten-story building under massive reconstruction in Midtown. Jill realized it was the new furniture mart she'd read about a few months ago, a structure expected to house more than a hundred tenants in a designer's paradise, complete with several floors of showrooms.

She tracked down the design studio among the maze of offices on the top floor. She ignored her rapid pulse, concluding that at least it wasn't pounding to the same degree as during the other situations. She also admitted to herself that she only wanted answers now, no matter what they were, no matter how humiliating or hurtful.

The reception area was small, the furnishings as contemporary as Rafael D'Amato's office but softened by fresh flower arrangements, arty but feminine, and more brightly colored and patterned upholstery. No receptionist held court at the sleek desk-and-counter configuration. Jill could see into an area containing a large conference table with an open office door beyond.

"Hello?" she called out, peering into the space.

"I'll be right there," came the quick response.

Jill stepped back into the reception area, crushing her purse in her fists, the bag bouncing off her thighs. She dragged the strap up her arm and settled it on her shoulder, tucking the purse close to her side. She paced a few steps. Anticipation built.

Come on, come on, come on.

A woman came through the doorway, a voluptuous, forty-something redhead wearing a deep-blue suit, the skirt a few inches above her knees, and tasteful gold jewelry, including a pendant that nestled in her cleavage. Flamboyant, Jill thought, but not tacky. The receptionist?

The woman extended her hand. "Hi. I'm Ilene Stillings. How may I help you?"

Not the receptionist. Jill's mouth went dry as they shook hands. The woman couldn't be more different from Jill, like a gypsy and a kindergarten teacher.

"I'm Jill Townsend," she said, pulling her hand free. "Mrs. Wade Townsend."

"Good to meet you."

Nothing. No glimmer of recognition—or maybe she just was a very good actress.

Ilene waited, her smile fading, as Jill tried to decide what to say next.

"Are you in need of a designer?" Ilene prompted.

"No, I—" Jill linked her fingers. "I got your name in a roundabout way in connection with a property in TriBeCa." She recited the address. Still no recognition. "I was wondering if you own the unit?"

"No, I don't. Why?"

"I'm trying to track down the owner. Your name came up in association with it."

"Came up in what way?"

Fortunately she didn't wait for Jill to answer, but went on.

"Maybe I should clarify something," Ilene said. "I'm familiar with the location, as I worked for another tenant in that building, but not on the sixth floor. If you could give me more detail, perhaps I could help?"

Why would this stranger offer assistance? Jill wondered. Did she feel guilty about something? Did she know Wade, after all? Jill didn't want to picture him with this woman who made Jill feel like tapioca pudding to her bananas flambé.

"I'm sorry to have taken up your time," Jill said, turning away, feeling paranoid and not liking that. She needed to go home, to regroup, to decide what to do next.

She got caught in the commute traffic after all, the train to Darien jammed. It seemed like she was the only one without any means of ignoring her fellow riders. Everyone either had their eyes focused on a laptop or were totally engrossed in—what were those little things called? Blueberries? No, BlackBerries. No one just sat and people watched. Those who weren't typing or entering information wore headsets or were reading.

Jill had no distraction, nothing to do but think.

What had she learned? That Wade wasn't the owner

on the loft. That Ilene didn't know him—or so she said. So, why did he have the keys with Ilene's name on the tag?

A property purchase was a matter of public record, right? She could track down the owner, see where that might lead.

Suddenly exhausted she closed her eyes, letting the movement of the train lull her. She missed Barbara. Since divorcing Alan, Barb had stopped being Jill's best friend, and Jill still ached with the loss of her, gone three thousand miles away. She could've talked to Barb about this situation. She would've told Jill she was crazy to think Wade would ever cheat on her. *Crazy*, she would've emphasized.

Or she might have said that the signs were all there—his distraction for months before he died, and his diminished desire.

Jill needed to reestablish some old friendships, get out and socialize again. It hadn't mattered while Tori will still home, but now it did. She had to move forward. It would make her daughters happy, too. She wanted her daughters to be proud of her.

At home she poured herself a glass of Merlot and fixed a salad, then sat by the pool for an hour, her eyes drifting shut. Tired. She was so tired.

She dragged herself up to her bedroom after almost falling asleep on a pool lounge. She washed her face, brushed her teeth, turned down the covers in precise, neat folds. Her gaze shifted to her dresser and their wedding picture. She stared at it from a distance then moved slowly toward it and picked it up.

She'd been so young, twenty-two, and Wade almost thirty. They'd had a big, fancy wedding to please his parents. He'd paid for it. Her parents couldn't have afforded such an extravaganza. It had made them uncomfortable, knowing they should be assuming the expenses, but Wade promised no one else would ever know that her designer dress with the twelve-foot train, and everything else, had been provided by the groom.

Jill had loved him almost from the moment they met. She'd trusted him, believed in him, adored him. She thought she knew and understood him. To be questioning that belief now cut deep. She didn't want her illusions shattered. If she had died first, he wouldn't have found out anything shocking about her afterward, not even in her journals, since the only potentially scandalous items would've involved him. They would've been good memories for him.

Jill slipped the framed photograph in bed with her, resting it against Wade's pillow. She hadn't yet slept anywhere but on *her* side, not even toward the middle.

She grabbed her diary then drummed her pen against the page. Finally she drew a line through the second item. She'd found the doors. She started her list for the next day:

Saturday, August 25
1. Get a bird—they're even less work than a cat, but I can talk to it.

2. Find out who owns the loft.
3. Get laid.

The crude phrase stared back at her, but there was no denying her need. Ridiculous, but there it was in black and white. The truth. She continued writing:

> What's going on? I'm looking at A. like he's my last donut before starting a diet. And then the contractor at the loft, Bobby Link, gave me the eye and seemed like he was ready to ask me out after knowing me for 30 seconds! If he'd actually invited me, what would I have done? Even Rafael D'Amato intrigued me—until he clammed up. Am I so desperate that—

The phone rang.

"I'm coming over," Alan said, then hung up.

She was left sputtering for a moment. Then she threw back the covers and glanced at the clock. Almost 11:00 p.m. What couldn't wait until morning?

She'd already washed her face, but it wasn't as if he hadn't seen her without makeup before. Vanity had her swiping a little gloss over her lips and running a brush through her hair. She slipped a robe over her short nightgown and belted it. Barefoot, she padded downstairs just as Alan knocked on the door to the back patio.

"You okay?" he asked as he stepped inside, his gaze intense, a worry crease between his brows.

Well, my husband may have cheated on me, and he certainly kept secrets from me.... Oh, sure. Fine and dandy. "Why?" she asked.

"I had a message from Rafael D'Amato."

"You did?" So Alan did know something. Could he answer her questions?

"How did you find out, Jill?"

"What do you know?"

"I asked first."

She grabbed her purse from the kitchen counter, pulled out the set of keys and dangled them in front of him. He took them, read the tags then closed his fist around them.

"I'm sorry."

"You need to be specific, Alan."

"Have you been thinking this was a...love nest, or something?"

Yes! Dammit, yes. "I haven't known what to think."

"Ease your mind. It wasn't."

Her knees started to give way. Alan caught her by the arms and guided her to sit at a chair in the breakfast nook. Her throat swelled and burned. Her vision blurred.

He crouched in front of her. "I can't believe you didn't come to me. Ask me. Why didn't you tell me before you went rushing off to the city?"

Wait a minute. *He* was angry? "Hold on. I had good reasons, Alan. First of all, I didn't want you to know that he'd cheated, if that happened to be true. Second, maybe I didn't want to know that *you* knew and had kept it from me. I didn't want *anyone* to know he wasn't the true and honest man I'd always believed."

"The deed to the loft is in my name. But it's Wade's gift to you."

"I don't—" She shook her head. How could it be a gift from Wade? Alan had to be lying, covering up, as a best friend might.

"He knew how hard it was going to be for you when Tori went off to college. He knew you would be floundering. I guess you had also talked about having a place in the city, too, where you could pursue some of your own interests?"

"I said that?"

"So he said."

"Maybe. But I wasn't serious. I was just anticipating the emptiness ahead." She'd been talking out loud, trying to figure out how to live her life without children.

"He was a problem solver, Jill. He took you at your word and did something about your problem. Anyway, Wade had planned it so that the construction on the loft would be done when Tori left for college, but there was a slight delay in the metal work. If you'd waited a week, I would've taken you to see it myself."

She realized they were still holding hands. Gently she pulled hers free. "How is that you own it?"

"He wanted to surprise you, and he couldn't if he bought it himself, since you would have to co-sign. So he gave me the money for the down payment, asked me to be the legal owner and then transfer it to him and you as soon as he could give you the gift."

Jill was torn between astonished pleasure at the gift and irritation at Alan. "You should've told me. He died. There was no reason for the secrecy. None."

Alan stood. His expression turned fierce, as it had yesterday when he'd told her he needed to do something, that he missed Wade, too. Was it only yesterday that she'd found the keys?

"He was my best friend. My best friend. I was honoring his last wish, although he hadn't known that at the time he asked. We'd settled everything just a week before he died. How could I not honor his intentions? Keep his surprise?"

That took the wind out of her. Of course he was right. "But what if I don't want it?"

"Then I can keep it or sell it."

"Why would you keep it?"

"I've been toying with the idea of having a place in the city myself."

"You have?" He'd never said anything about that. She supposed the city would have more action for a single man.

"Yeah. For a while now. I don't really have much of a life here anymore."

The thought of him moving away— Another huge life change for her.

She stood, then didn't know what to do next.

"What are you thinking?" he asked.

"I'm relieved." Biggest understatement of the world.

"Yeah. I did ask him how he knew you would be happy

about it, and he said you'd seen a picture in a magazine once, which you apparently pointed out to him. You said it was your dream, to live in a place like that."

"That was years ago. The girls were tiny."

"He gave the picture to D'Amato to recreate."

She recalled Wade's desk drawer stuffed with cards and mementos. "How is it I've discovered his sentimental side only after he's gone? Why didn't he show me before?"

"Because that wasn't who Wade was."

Alan was right about that, but why had he hidden it?

She knew the answer to that— Wade was the most macho, action-driven, accomplishment-oriented man she'd known. He hadn't gotten that way by showing a soft side to anyone, although it wouldn't have hurt if he'd shown it more often to *her*.

Alan cupped her shoulder, drawing her attention. "Here's what I propose. Why don't you move into the loft as a test run. If you like it, you can buy me out. If not, I'll do a test run myself."

"What about decorating it?"

"Wade left that job unplanned so that you would have something to do right when Tori left. Someone had recommended a designer named Ilene Stillings to him. I think her name was Gibbons?"

"She lives in that building. She must be the one who had worked with Ilene."

"You talked to Ilene?"

"Yeah." She got them both glasses of water and sat at

the bar. She told him the events of the day. "Ilene probably thinks I'm crazy."

"You're not obligated to use her services."

"I liked her, though."

"Your decision."

"But if I decorate it in my style and you end up living there…" She let the sentence drift into a question.

"We'll consult on it. I can't imagine not liking what you do."

"It's got a very industrial look, lots of brick and steel."

"So, you wouldn't be able to feminize it too much." He grinned.

"Oh, you'd be surprised." She was the one surprised, however, when she realized she'd already been decorating it in her head. The vision wasn't crystal clear, but she definitely had ideas. "Are you sure you don't want to just take it over now?"

Alan moved to put his glass in the sink then came up to where she'd sat. "I honored Wade's last wish, and I expect you'll want to, as well. He did this for you, Jill."

His expression did more than hint that he expected her to follow through. He stood so close she could have rested her hands on his chest or framed his face or kissed him. She lifted her gaze from his mouth. "Have you seen it, the loft?"

"Once a month or so since the work started."

"I still can't believe you kept this a secret from me."

"It got easier as time went by." He crossed his arms. She finally noticed what he was wearing—date clothes. A Tommy Bahama shirt, this one with yellow hibiscus all over it, and khakis. "You had a date tonight."

"Just dinner."

"Must've been a late one. Or a very long conversation after." She sounded snippy. Jealous.

He raised his brows at her tone of voice. "It was a first date. There's usually lots to talk about on a first date."

"You seem to have a lot of those."

"What can I say? I wasn't as picky a few years ago as I am now. Been out there on the market for too long."

"So, one date is all you need to decide now. You're that jaded?"

"It's as good a word as any. People are fascinated by what I write and are curious about how much money I make."

"So you question the motives of the women you meet now?"

"I've always questioned them." He cut off further discussion by heading to the door. "We'll talk in the morning about your decision."

"You know what my decision is. Hey. I can loan you a towel, if you want to swim before you head home."

He hesitated, his hand on the doorknob. "Yeah. That'd be great."

She slipped into the laundry room, where she kept a stack of pool towels, and returned with one. "Thank you for coming over. For not letting me suffer through another sleepless night. I was sick about the whole thing."

He nodded. She didn't know whether his nod meant

you're welcome or that he would have been worried, too, or that he knew she wouldn't be sleeping. For a moment, just a moment, it looked as if he would hug her. He angled toward her, one arm lifted just slightly. Then he left.

Her body reacted as if he'd touched her.

Jill left the kitchen, jogged up the stairs and into her bedroom. Stupid, stupid, stupid, she muttered in her head. Don't risk the best relationship you have getting caught up in some fantasy just because your body is coming back to life.

She shoved her diary aside, then she yanked off her robe and tossed it toward the foot of the bed. It slithered to the rug below. She turned off the lamp and climbed into bed, pulling the sheets to her chin.

Almost against her will she got out of bed and moved to the window, which overlooked the pool. She could see a shadow in the pool, moving fluidly. She wasn't aware of time but simply stood and watched. Waited. He finally climbed out of the pool. She saw the silhouette of him, his sleek body. He grabbed the towel and rubbed his hair then his arms, his chest, his abdomen, his legs. He looked up, toward her bedroom, toward her. She didn't move. He couldn't see her, wouldn't know for sure that she watched.

He wrapped the towel around his waist and left the pool area. She watched until he disappeared into the trees that separated their properties. Only then did she pick up her pen and her diary to amend her current list.

3. Get laid SOON.

She stared at the added word then started to laugh—at herself, at her predicament, at her total and absolute relief that she'd been right about Wade. Still smiling she crossed off the word SOON.

Tonight she would sleep well.

CHAPTER 5

Tuesday, August 28
1. Get a ~~dog~~ ~~cat~~ ~~bird~~ goldfish.
2. Get laid. Yeah, like that's gonna happen anytime soon.
3. Invite Ilene Stillings to lunch. Confess.

"I don't mess with married men," Ilene Stillings said several days later, stabbing her fork into a chunk of tomato. Her gold bangle bracelets jingled, the noise just barely rising above the lunchtime din in the deli. "Ever."

Jill had invited her to lunch, swallowed her own pride and told Ilene the whole story. It was a lot easier to humble herself over a corned beef on rye than across someone's desk.

"It's not a moral thing," Ilene added.

"It isn't?"

"It's self-defense. I've seen the results of a vengeful wife." She shuddered. "Hell, *I* was a vengeful wife."

"Your husband cheated?"

"My *ex*-husband. I blamed the woman, of course, because it was easier on my ego."

"What'd you do?"

"Stalked her. Harassed her."

"Ilene!"

She shrugged. "What can I say? I was devastated. It wasn't until she got a restraining order that I woke up to what I was doing, especially the excuses I was making for my jerk of a husband. What an idiot I was. Now, the first bit of crap a guy gives me, he's gone."

That sounded harsh to Jill. No one was perfect. People deserved second chances—or least the benefit of the doubt.

"I can see you don't agree," Ilene said, setting her knife and fork on her empty plate.

"I haven't been burned like you have. I think it's too bad that it made you cynical."

"Hon, if you can't drum up some honest cynicism, or at least a healthy dose of skepticism, you aren't gonna make it in the big, bad city."

"I can be skeptical."

Ilene laughed. "I'm sorry. I'm not making fun of you, but you are refreshingly naïve. I think it's a very good thing that you've come to me for help. We'll get your loft decorated and your outlook adjusted. And we'll have fun doing both."

Ilene was offering friendship—as someone who'd never known Wade, who didn't see Jill as a wife or mother but a woman embarking on a new life. At forty-two, Ilene was only three years younger than Jill, had lived in New York all her life, and had been single for ten years. She mixed and mingled in various corporate and social circles, always looking to drum up new clients.

Jill reached across the table and laid a hand on Ilene's. "Thank you."

"Nothin' like introducing a virgin to the pleasures of the…city," she finished with a wink.

Jill laughed. "Do you do that often?"

"Virgins are few and far between." Her eyes shimmered.

Jill saw why Ilene was successful. "I meant do you take people under your wing often?"

"The simple answer to that is no. Most of my jobs are for people who've been around for a long time. They want the project done fast and perfect." She shrugged. "Some don't want their friends to know they brought in a designer but want people to think they were talented enough to pull the look together on their own."

Ilene was lonely, too, Jill realized. Beneath all that fiery red hair, bright clothes and quick smile, she was looking for the same things as Jill—friendship, fun, and a place in the world. Maybe some women felt threatened by Ilene's looks and personality, consequently not striking up a friendship with her. Jill was grateful they'd met.

"Hey, ladies." A uniformed cop holding a tray with a huge sandwich and a mound of slaw frowned down at them. "You done? Some of us only got a few minutes to eat."

Ilene stood, then angled close to the barrel-chested, fiftyish man. Her smile turned flirty. "Always happy to accommodate one of New York's finest, officer." She used her napkin to shine his badge.

Jill had never seen a man turn to mush before.

"Stay safe now," Ilene said.

The man's gaze never wavered as she strode out of the deli, her short, tight skirt showing off her great legs and swaying rear. Jill swallowed a laugh and followed her.

"That was—"

"Fun, huh?" Ilene interrupted without losing a step.

"Yes."

"Made his day, too, I think."

"I *know* it did." Jill hurried to keep up. Ilene's stride was longer and her pace twice as fast. "Where are we going?"

"To your loft. We're taking the subway."

"Let's just take a cab. My treat." The subway made her nervous. All those people. Someone always making announcements that seemed critical yet were indecipherable.

"Hon, if you're gonna live here, you're gonna become city smart. Come on. Keep up. First rule—keep moving. Don't stop or you risk a twenty-person pileup and their full wrath."

How Ilene could move that fast in three-inch heels mystified Jill, who wore a sensible low heel and who was already feeling her calves burn from the pace. Even having been back at the gym for a week, she was huffing and puffing.

"I'm not sure I'm going to live here," she said to Ilene's back. "I haven't decided anything."

The woman turned around and smiled, her brows raised, but said nothing.

They reached the subway. Heat and nose-wrinkling odors assaulted Jill. Ilene didn't take the time to explain anything. She handed Jill a Metro Card, said, "Stay close," then expected Jill to follow orders. By the time they arrived at the station closest to Jill's loft, she'd caught her breath again. They walked the final four blocks, Ilene teaching Jill the ropes of navigating the city much like a drill sergeant might.

"You need to look like a native. We'll go shopping, update your wardrobe. You have to plan out where you're going so you don't need to stop and look at a map. If a panhandler comes up, tell 'em to go away. Walk like you have to be somewhere *right now*. If it looks like rain, grab a cab right away, because after the rain starts, you won't find an empty one." They entered the lobby. "How is it you know so little about the city when you've lived so close? Didn't you come to shop? Go to the theater? Kick up your heels?"

The elevator doors opened when Jill pushed the up button. "Sometimes I met Wade for dinner, but I took the train then a cab, and I went to his office, usually. He didn't like the theater much."

"You didn't come in to see plays with a girlfriend?"

Jill's body tensed with the implied recrimination. "No."

"Why not?"

"Because I just didn't, okay?" It had been a source of conflict between her and Wade. But he'd rarely done anything social that wasn't business related, a certifiable Type-A personality.

The elevator stopped at the sixth floor. Neither of them made a move to get off, then the doors started to shut and Jill slammed her arm against the edge to stop it from closing.

"I apologize for my big mouth," Ilene said as she passed in front of Jill. "I wasn't being judgmental, just surprised."

"You touched a nerve," Jill said quietly.

"Sorry."

"It's okay." She slipped the key in the lock.

After a moment, Ilene said, "You didn't even come in to *shop?*" Shock coated her words.

Jill stopped, ready to fire back. Then she started to laugh instead—and couldn't stop. Ilene joined her, although with brows raised in curiosity. Maybe Ilene was wondering if she'd made a big mistake hooking up with such a hopeless suburbanite who never came into the city to *shop*, which must break the sister-solidarity rules or something.

"You haven't gone around the bend on me, have you?" Ilene asked as Jill wiped tears from her face.

She shook her head. "We're from different worlds. Until lately I hadn't really thought about how I've been so taken care of. Wade bought my clothes, by the way. I have no taste. I was just living my life."

They moved down the short entry into the main living area. "Don't take this the wrong way, hon, but that's closer to existing, not living. You look ten years older than you should, even in your Ralph Lauren. Your Wade must've been very conservative."

Jill eyed her cotton pants and jacket. "My clothes are kind of classic."

Ilene looked ready to say something but then took in the room. "Wow." Sunlight streamed through the tall windows, reflecting off the metal stairs and catwalk, spotlighting a bright square of light on the hardwood floor.

"Fabulous! Incredible! A-*ma*-zing!" Ilene rubbed her hands together. "This is going to be fun."

She climbed the stairs. Jill followed then found herself in an open bedroom space, with a decent-size bathroom, closet and storage room, that covered the entire area above the kitchen, entry and powder room below. The room connected via the metal-grid catwalk to a space close to the window, the bridge angling across and above the living room.

"Oh, my God, this is great!" Ilene exclaimed. "You can have a little office here. Do you need an office? Otherwise, I'm not sure.... A reading space, maybe. A couple of comfy chairs with a table and lamp."

"An office would be good," Jill said, getting caught up in Ilene's enthusiasm. It would be her own space, decorated the way she wanted, but also an office for Alan, in case he ended up living there instead of her. She didn't know how much time she would spend in the city and had thought in the past few days that she might offer to timeshare the space with Alan. She doubted she would want to live there every month. It wasn't home.

"First, we need to get you a bed so you can stay overnight. And kitchenware and some temporary furniture." Ilene went down the stairs, Jill still at her heels. From her briefcase she pulled out a tape measure, digital camera and pad of paper. "Let's get going."

They spent two hours measuring, planning and visualizing.

"Let's go back to my office. I'll take you through some showrooms—"

"Ilene. Stop. Please. Slow down." Jill's head was spinning. "I can't—I really can't do this all in a day."

Ilene smiled. "Of course you can't. I'm sorry. I just got…caught up. Why don't you get a hotel room for the night. We can start again in the morning."

"I need to go home," Jill said, her voice barely reaching her own ears. "Give me a couple of days. Put some plans together. I'll come back on Monday. No, Tuesday. After Labor Day." Five days. That would give her five days to recuperate from this monumental day. It wasn't just a change of place, but a change of life. She needed to take baby steps.

Ilene patted her shoulder. "Sure thing. Should I order you a bed?"

"Just a box spring and mattress for now. Queen size should fit okay in that space, don't you think?"

"You could do a king, if you wanted."

Jill shook her head. In hotel beds Wade had always seemed too far away from her in a king. Alone, it would feel like being adrift in the ocean. "So, how do I get to Grand Central via the subway?"

"Why don't you stay and have dinner with me first? You can go after the crowds thin out."

She just wanted to be home. "I'll be all right."

Jill repeated those words again and again during the ride home, convincing herself. At least she'd brought a book along this time and could hide behind it during the trip, although she never turned a page.

When she walked into her quiet house, she decided she should think again about getting a dog—someone to greet her, to get excited that she'd come home. Someone to love her unconditionally.

The phone rang. She scooped it up as she dropped her purse and keys on the kitchen counter.

"Hi, Mom."

"Tori! Sweetie, how are you?" Her younger daughter had been far too elusive since Jill had left her in her dorm room.

"I'm fine. It's okay. It's kind of a lot to get used to."

"Give it time."

"I *know*."

The exasperation in her voice had Jill taking mental steps back. *Stop hovering. Stop mothering.* "What do you like best?"

"The English professor is kinda cool. But all the teachers think no one else must be giving homework, 'cause there's a ton every day. A ton."

Are you keeping up? Don't fall behind this early. "How's your roommate?" she asked instead.

"Okay. She's got a boyfriend who's a junior here. He's got a house off campus. She's not around a lot."

She sounded lonely. Jill wanted to assure her that everything would smooth out, but knew she couldn't tell her daughter that, not unless Tori was ready to believe it. "I went into the city today," Jill said.

"Alone?"

The shock in Tori's voice had impact. Jill knew she wasn't the most adventurous person on the planet, but it was kind of pathetic that her daughter was aware of it, too. Not much a role model, was she?

"Yes, alone." She should tell Tori and Shanna that she was thinking about moving there part-time, but until she made her final decision, she didn't want to upset them, especially Tori as she adjusted to college life.

"What'd you do?"

"Had lunch with a woman I met recently. She wants to take me clothes shopping. She thinks I dress too old. What do you think?"

"Well…yeah."

Jill frowned. "Why didn't you ever say anything?"

"You didn't ask."

What a cop-out answer, Jill thought, irritated. But it also showed how tentative her relationship with her daughter was.

"So, do you have any suggestions?" she asked Tori.

"Find a good hairstylist, too."

She ran a hand down her hair. "It *has* gotten pretty long."

"And boring. You're not dead yet, you know."

The silence that dropped between them screamed. Jill struggled for something to say.

"Listen, I gotta go," Tori said in a rush. "'Bye."

"'Bye, sweetie," she said to the dial tone.

You're not dead yet.

Jill hung up, her gaze drifting to the calendar hanging on the kitchen wall. Except for a note in Tori's handwriting saying *College!!!* the calendar was empty. No social events. No manicure or pedicure. Not even a doctor or dentist appointment. No fund-raising luncheon. No committee meeting.

Blank. Nothing. Nada.

You're not dead yet.

She might as well be. Her social life had been inextricably tied to Wade and the girls. Had she done anything purely for herself? Not that she hadn't enjoyed a lot—most—of the projects she'd gotten involved with, but they'd all happened because of her contacts and responsibilities as wife and mother. She'd earned a bachelor's degree in art history, yet she'd rarely visited the city museums and never gone to galleries. She and Wade should've been on the invitation lists to attend new gallery showings. She should have cultivated that scene, if not for herself, for Wade's work contacts. And she loved music. She could've been on the symphony board.

Okay, so you weren't. Who says you can't now? Your life has changed. It's up to you to find your own path. Get busy.

She wandered upstairs to her bedroom and opened her closet. It was a sea of color, not New York black. Everything was perfect for her life—her previous life.

She pulled out a binder—her inventory of her closet. She rotated clothes seasonally, kept track of what she wore to which occasions so that she didn't duplicate items at important events. Her shoe rack held Mocs and Kate Spade and Jimmy Choo. An array of colorful, sparkling Yves Saint Laurent and Oscar de la Renta gowns were reminders of country-club and corporate events. She'd rarely gotten more than two wearings out of each dress, one at the club and one for Wade's work. Fendi handbags, other designer names she couldn't pronounce. Wade had bought the best.

You look ten years older than you should. Ilene's words dug at her. Ilene did look much younger than Jill, for all the three-year difference. Could her choice of clothes make that much difference?

Jill shut the closet door. Did she care if she didn't look as young as she could? She wasn't like Ilene, would never be like her, that open and...sexy.

And in need of a friend, Jill decided. Ilene probably intimidated most women, those who might be competing with her. Jill only wanted to be her friend. At least they each brought something important to the relationship.

Jill had laughed a lot today, and it had felt good, like a fog lifting. She had no intention of going back to a laughter-free life.

No way. No how.

CHAPTER 6

Tuesday, October 2
1. Get a ~~dog cat bird goldfish~~ life.
2. Get laid. Sometime before the twelfth of never, please.
3. Find a quilt for my big, lonely bed.
4. Tell girls about my crazy idea to live in the city, part-time. At some point.

On a cool Tuesday evening more than a month later, Jill passed Ilene a glass of Chardonnay then set a deli platter and napkins on the middle cushion of Jill's just-delivered sofa. The antipasto aroused the senses—sharp provolone, sweet roasted red peppers, briny olives, tangy marinated artichoke hearts and garlicky Genoa salami. Jill loved being able to make dinner out of a quick stop at the deli, one of her newly discovered joys of living in the city.

She grabbed her own wineglass and joined Ilene on the couch, tucking her feet into the cushions. It was the most comfortable piece of furniture Jill had ever owned—plush cushions covered with a red-orange chenille fabric. She could cozy into it forever.

Ilene picked out a succulent olive and popped it in her mouth. "You need to think about throwing a party. An open house."

"Who would I invite?"

"Um, gee, I don't know. Your butcher, maybe? The bagboy at the market?" She looked at Jill over the rim of her glass. "Just a wild guess, hon, but maybe friends and family?"

"My daughters aren't close enough to come, plus I haven't even told them yet. My parents passed away years ago. I keep a safe-and-sane distance between me and my in-laws." Friends? "There's Alan. Maybe a few people from Wade's company. A couple of neighbors in Darien."

"The other tenants in your building, as a goodwill gesture," Ilene added. "The contractor and the architect. Me."

"You just want to meet Bobby and Rafael for the business contacts. This party is more for you than for me."

"Not true." She smiled sweetly. "It's an equal opportunity party. Anyway, the place probably won't be ready for another month, so there's plenty of time to plan it. And fret about it."

Jill ignored the friendly sarcasm. How quickly Ilene had come to know her. Jill sipped her wine and stared out the window. Summer had turned itself upside down overnight, revealing a crisp, satisfying autumn. She'd fallen into a habit of alternating her time in the city and at home, spending a few days in a row in each place. She'd enjoyed planning the décor with Ilene, as well as the companionship, but her days still seemed to drag.

"Thanks for not giving me hell about how long everything is taking," Ilene said, wrapping a piece of roasted pepper in a slice of provolone.

"You never misled me."

"Most people don't have the patience it takes to wait for special orders. I spend more time as a psychologist or something, calming people down."

"Poor baby."

Ilene laughed. "Yeah, life is hard."

Jill finished her wine and set the glass on the floor. She should get up and turn on the only lamp in the living room but she felt too relaxed to move. She closed her eyes and rested her head against the sofa back. "An open house. I suppose I could manage that. Let me think about it."

"Which means a list, I suppose."

"Several lists."

"Hon, you think way too much. Try jumping without a net once in a while. The fall is thrilling."

"Not to me." She opened her eyes, then blurted out an announcement she'd kept close to her for a couple of days. "I'm joining a grief support group. My first meeting is tomorrow night."

Ilene frowned. "What for?"

It had been on her mind for a long time. Most of her

grief books suggested it, not too soon, they all said, but after some time had passed. Alan had also offered up the idea. She'd resisted, because she was doing fine, she told herself. It was her daughters…

"I need to talk about the girls and how to handle them. Help them."

"You can talk to me. You *have* talked to me."

"And you've been great. But you haven't been in my shoes. I have questions you can't answer."

"O-*kay*." The word came out like a dart throw.

"Please don't be upset. It doesn't mean I'm going to stop talking to you."

Ilene didn't say anything for about a minute. "Speaking of shoes…"

Crisis averted. Jill wriggled into the sofa again. "Were we?"

"When are we going clothes shopping? You're still in your dowds. You should get spiffed up before you go to your new group. Never know. You might meet an interesting widower."

Get laid. Her daily-transferred diary entry flashed in her mind. "I'm not going to the support group to meet men."

Ilene patted Jill's knee. "Sure you are."

"I am not."

"Every single woman is on the lookout, and you figure a widower is a good match, 'cause he'll know how you feel."

Another denial was on Jill's tongue, then she clamped her mouth shut. "Maybe," she said finally. "There's a certain appeal in that. But it hasn't been a year. I can't. You know I can't." Oh, but she was lonely. She'd even been avoiding Alan because she was afraid she might try to seduce him. She wanted to feel a man's arms around her again, to be enfolded in an unyielding embrace. Alan's broad chest and his own need as Wade's best friend to help her in some way were far too enticing.

"Saying you *can't* until a year is up is almost like saying you *have to* when it is," Ilene commented.

"It's not the same thing at all."

"Sure it is." Ilene refilled their wineglasses. "There are no rules. You have to do what's right for you. But back to the shopping."

Jill welcomed the change of subject. "I've lost ten pounds." Ten grueling pounds over six weeks of almost daily torture either at the gym or to workout DVDs in front of the television. And she walked in the city as much as possible. She'd also stopped eating French bread slathered with peanut butter instead of fixing a proper meal. "I'd like to lose another ten before I shell out money for new clothes."

"Before your open house, then."

"That'll work." Jill looked around her loft. Pieces of art she'd been collecting leaned against deep-sage-painted walls. Her dining room table and chairs weren't expected to arrive for another month, but she'd purchased brushed nickel-and-ebony bar stools to pull up next to the black granite kitchen island.

The industrial look was growing on her. It was so different from the country style of her Connecticut house, as if she had a dual personality. Even her dinnerware was simple—square white plates with charcoal-gray accent pieces and sleek stainless silverware. She'd bought a wok and made herself healthy stir-fry meals.

And yet as she grew healthier physically, her emotional health deteriorated. She still had no real purpose in life. She was busy, but accomplishing little. She could make a half-day project out of grocery shopping.

"How are the girls?" Ilene asked.

"Quiet."

"Both of them?"

"Yeah. I expect it of Tori. We've got a long way to go in the communication department. But even Shanna's gone silent. It's not like her. Well, no, that's not true. She's been less talkative since Wade's death. I told you how she didn't even come home for the summer, but at least she called. Now I have to be the one to make the contact, and I usually get her voice mail. I'm looking forward to Christmas when I can look in her eyes."

"You think she'll come home?"

It hadn't occurred to Jill that Shanna wouldn't. "She'd better."

"Why don't you go see her?"

"I've told her I wanted to. I went twice during the summer, but now she says she's too busy to entertain me. You know, it's her senior year. I remember it myself. Except I also was engaged to Wade and had a part-time, on-campus job. She only has school."

"Still no boyfriend?"

"Not that I know of. Anyway, I'd go down just to have dinner with her, but I can't surprise her. She wouldn't take that well. When I think back to being in college myself, I understand. You just want to be independent, not to be treated like a child, especially by your parents."

"Your parents were kind of free spirits, though. I don't figure they babied you."

"My mother hovered, but she didn't demand things of me. She was more interested in how I felt. She'd put her hands on my cheeks and make me look into her eyes, then she'd say, 'Tell me how you really feel, Jilly.'"

"Poor baby," Ilene said.

Jill laughed at the dig. Yeah, everyone should have so little demanded of them. "I hated it at the time, but now I know it was just out of love."

"Speaking of doing something out of love…"

Ilene's tone of voice put Jill on alert. "I have a feeling I'm not going to like this."

"I signed us up for speed dating."

Jill went rigid. "You what?" Her voice rang an octave higher.

"We both need a little jump start. And I think you should invest in one new outfit for it. Thursday night, eight o'clock."

"Have a good time." Jill swigged the remainder of her wine and stood. She turned on the lamp then took her glass to the kitchen.

"I already paid for us," Ilene called out.

"I buy my meat in the market, preinspected and packaged up nice and neat." She didn't want or need surprises.

Ilene came up beside her. "What are you afraid of?"

"It's too soon. And that's too anonymous."

"You'd rather it be personal? Come on, Jill. It'll be something different to do. It'll give us a few laughs. And maybe it'll lead to something else. You told me your life is monotonous. Really, what's the worst that can happen?"

No one will be interested, and I'll be humiliated. "I'm not ready for a *regular* date. How can you think I'd want to put myself in the position of trying to shine for ten strangers."

"As many as fifteen."

"Fifteen?" Jill repeated, choking on the word.

"You spend six minutes with each of them."

"That could seem like an hour. Times fifteen."

"Or a minute. Be optimistic."

"Have you done this before?"

"Twice."

"And?"

"I made a few matches. Went out on some dates. One I dated for months. It was fun."

"I think your definition of fun is different from mine."

"Tell me what's fun to you, then."

Nothing came to mind. Nothing. "I don't know. I just know speed dating wouldn't be fun."

"Please." Ilene dragged out the word. "Pretty please,

with a cherry on top. I'll never ask you for something ever again."

Jill smiled. "Yes, you will."

"Okay, so that was a lie. Come on. What have you got to lose? You'll have anonymity. It'll be like getting all the blind dates in the world out of your way."

Jill hadn't thought about it in those terms. It would be practice in small talk, a rusty skill. "Oh, all right," she said before she could change her mind—then immediately panicked. "On second thought—"

"First answer accepted. You are committed."

"*You* should be committed."

Ilene grinned. "We can go for drinks afterward and skewer them all."

"Because we're such great catches ourselves."

"Speak for yourself, hon." She struck a pose. "I am one phenomenal woman."

After Jill climbed into bed later that night she stared at the ceiling. How many twists and turns her life had taken in the past couple of months. Some were exciting, some took all the courage and nerve she could muster.

Wanting something familiar, she picked up her phone and dialed Alan.

"I hope I didn't disturb you," she said after he answered.

"Just shut down the computer for the night. What's up?"

She could hear him settling in, relaxing. It was in his voice, which seemed to get softer and deeper.

"I was thinking about what I would've been doing last year at this time," she said.

"What was that?"

"Fixing healthy, hearty meals every night. And I was on the phone for hours begging for donations for Tori's basketball-team rummage sale."

"And now?"

"I'm eating antipasto for dinner. And the phone rarely rings. No one needs me for anything."

"Having a pity party, are you?"

Was she? "I'm lonely."

"Eight million people live in New York City. Mingle."

His tone of voice wasn't harsh or impatient, yet she took it that way. He was her oldest, most trusted friend. She expected honesty from him—and sympathy. "Well, I'm going to my first grief-support meeting tomorrow. Does that make you happy?"

"The point is, does it make *you* happy?"

"You know how much I love baring my soul to strangers," she said.

"About as much as I do, but I think it's worth a shot. You don't have to go back, you know. And that wasn't really what I meant by mingling."

"I know. Use my education. Become a docent or something."

"Couldn't hurt. What's got you down tonight, Jill?"

Life. And death. She'd learned how to suppress her grief in public, but tomorrow night she would be required to open up. It was a scary thought. She didn't want to regress.

"I'll be okay," she said. "I just wanted to hear a friendly voice."

"Guess I wasn't too friendly, was I? I apologize. I was having my own pity party when you called."

"What's up?"

"I leave in the morning for the book tour, and this book's not cooperating—or rather the characters. I can't get a handle on them. I'm deleting more than I'm saving."

"You say that about every book."

After a moment he said, "Yeah, I guess I do, don't I?"

"Every book." Knowing he wasn't having fun, either, somehow perked her up. "I feel better now, thanks."

"I feel worse. Thanks a lot."

She laughed.

"Let me know how your meeting goes tomorrow, okay?" he said.

"I will."

"And mingle."

"Maybe."

After she hung up it occurred to her she hadn't told him about the speed dating. Why not? Fifteen blind dates could certainly be considered mingling.

And wasn't it just the stuff that every middle-aged woman dreamed of?

CHAPTER 7

Wednesday, October 3
1. Get a life.
2. Get laid.
3. Find a quilt for my big, lonely bed.
4. Tell girls about my crazy idea to live in the city, part-time.
5. Make bribery brownies to take to first support group meeting.
6. Come up with one-liners for speed dating. Ugh.

The grief support group met in the basement of The Church of Personal Identity, which was little more than a storefront tucked between a video rental store and a poster shop two blocks from Jill's loft. She tried to go without expectations, although she'd laughed at the name of the church when she'd spotted the notice on a crowded announcement board at the market. On the same board for the same location were invitations to join groups called "Love Yourself First" and "Peacemaking for Exes."

Jill entered the small building and found the office.

"May I help you?" asked a woman about Jill's age. She didn't look at all bizarre in her black jeans and sweater, her long, graying hair braided into a thick rope that grazed her waist. Jill had been worried from the touchy-feely name of the church that it would prove to be a place where old hippies gathered and meditated. So far she hadn't heard any chanting.

"I'm looking for the grief support group," she said, her nerves settling a little. She was here. She would be among people who shared similar experiences.

"Hi, and welcome. I'm Marcia, the director and cheerleader." She shook imaginary pom-poms. "You go out this door and turn right. The second door on the right leads downstairs. They meet there." She cocked her head. "May I ask how you heard about us…them?"

Jill dug the notice out of her pocket and held it up. "I'm hoping I won't be the only one."

"Oh, no. They'll be there. They don't miss." Marcia looked as if she would add something then just smiled slightly.

"Thank you." Jill turned away.

"A word of advice?" the woman said in a rush just as Jill reached the door.

She turned. "Yes?"

"Don't take it personally."

"I beg your pardon?"

Marcia came around the desk. "The group is kind of…tight-knit, I guess it's safe to say."

"They've been together a long time?"

"The newest came two years ago. Otherwise, five to ten years."

Jill rethought her decision to attend. If they didn't heal enough to move on, maybe this was the wrong group for her.

"Oh, I do apologize," Marcia said. "I can see you're having second thoughts, and I didn't mean to do that, only to prepare you. You have to be determined to break through with them."

Jill relaxed. She'd fretted for nothing. They were a long-established group with close ties, that was all. Help was on the way. Surely they would eventually welcome her. "Thanks for the heads-up."

"The facilitator's name is Mrs. Q. She's tall, around sixty and African-American."

"Thanks again." Jill opened her tote bag and grabbed one of the decadent caramel-and-marshmallow-topped brownies she'd made—her icebreakers. She handed a plastic-wrapped treat to Marcia with a grateful smile.

Jill descended the stairs into a dark, chilly room. The scent of overcooked coffee masked the underlying mustiness that plagued most old basements where no hint of sunshine reached the subterranean depths. Not that it would have been sunny, anyway, since it was 7:00 p.m., but even during the day it would be dank and dingy.

She spotted three women and a man seated in a circle of five chairs, their heads almost touching. She slowed her steps, unsure whether to interrupt if they were praying.

Then she heard more than one voice speaking and some laughter—until someone noticed her and jerked upright. The room went silent. All eyes focused on her.

"Hi, I'm Jill," she said, coming up to them. "I'd like to join your group."

After a few long, increasingly uncomfortable seconds, a woman nodded. "I'm Mrs. Q. This here's Birdie, Iris and Jacob."

A hot-pink cane was propped against the thigh of the eighty-something Birdie. Her hair was dyed a pale pink and her tiny body clothed in a jogging suit that matched her cane. Iris was younger by maybe ten years, and was as slender and elegant as the flower she was named for. Jacob's shocking-white hair, wire-rimmed glasses and sweater vest gave him a professorial look. She figured he was in his midsixties.

The women acknowledged Jill with the barest eye contact before looking toward the center of their circle again.

Jacob hopped up. "I'll get you a chair."

Jill wondered why she couldn't use the empty chair already in place. "I brought brownies," she said, holding up the bag. "Anyone hungry?"

"I am," Jacob said. "I'll get napkins."

Mrs. Q. said with a pointed look at Jacob, "He's diabetic. So's Iris. And I'm on a diet."

"Perhaps Birdie would like one."

"It's impolite to eat in front of others when they can't," Birdie said, her gaze flickering toward the bag.

"I'm sorry," Jill said, sitting in the chair Jacob provided. "I didn't think—"

Mrs. Q. crossed her arms. "Better to get the lay of the land first, I always say."

Don't take it personally. Marcia's advice rang in Jill's ears. So they weren't a sociable bunch. She should cut them some slack, given that they all were grieving.

"Did anyone talk to Wendi today?" Mrs. Q. asked, glancing worriedly at the stairs. "It's the anniversary, you know."

"I called her twice," Iris answered. "She didn't answer."

A group gasp punctuated looks of horror.

"I'll go check on her," Iris said jumping to her feet and heading to the staircase. "I should've already. I knew I should—"

A pixie of a woman came downstairs. Everyone except Birdie raced to meet her, seeming to envelope her inside their protective custody.

Jill assumed the woman was the worried-about Wendi. Maybe thirty years old, Jill thought. Tentative, fidgety, even furtive. Her long blond hair curtained her face. She looked at the floor, not the people as they crowded around her. She also looked ready to bolt, yet at the same time about to fall into their open arms. As a synchronized group they returned to the circle and took their seats. Wendi perched on the edge of her chair, her toes turned in, shoulders hunched.

Jill waited for someone to introduce them, decided no one was going to, and extended her hand. "I'm Jill."

Wendi's gaze darted around the room. "I'm Wendi," she whispered, squeezing Jill's fingertips.

"Wendi should talk first," Iris stated in the tone of a drill sergeant.

"Only if she wants to," Mrs. Q. said, her voice kind and motherly.

Jill was stunned by the instant envy she felt for Wendi. If only someone would talk to her like that, with comfort and understanding.

You don't allow anyone to talk to you like that. You shun sympathy.

I know.

So, quit being jealous. Speak up. Let people know how you feel.

"Maybe I could go first," Jill said, softly insistent. "Then maybe Wendi will be ready."

Everyone ignored her. Mrs. Q. patted Wendi's clenched hands. Iris crossed her arms. Birdie seemed mesmerized by a stain on the worn carpet and traced her sneaker toe around and around the edge of the inkblot-shaped mark. Jacob filled a pipe with a strongly scented tobacco, tamped it down then clenched the stem between his teeth, sucking on the unlit pipe.

Jill started to laugh, which drew all their gazes. She tried to stop but couldn't. She'd waited all this time to get some help, and her help was worse off than she was!

Birdie found the laughter contagious and joined in, giggling. Jacob smiled. Iris's eyes narrowed. Wendi looked even more confused. And Mrs. Q. straightened to an imposing height, even seated.

"What's so funny?" she asked.

"Me." Jill drew a settling breath and looked at each of them. "I was scared to come here. Scared to open up to strangers." A little white lie, a little flattery, might be just what was needed for them to accept her. And maybe, just maybe, this was the "find something to do" that Shanna had meant.

"You all have made me feel right at home," she lied, smiling.

Jacob pointed his pipe toward her. "I think we should let her talk."

Jill didn't wait for Mrs. Q. to agree but plunged in. "My husband died on New Year's day. I think I'm dealing with my own grief pretty well, considering, but my daughters aren't. Shanna is twenty-one and a senior in college. Tori is eighteen and just started college. Neither of them live close and both of them are so angry. I hear Shanna retreating inside herself more every week, and Tori lashes out. I would appreciate any help, any advice you can give me."

She sat back and waited.

Jacob spoke up first. "I've never been married."

"My only child died sixty years ago," Birdie murmured with a sad sigh.

"I never had children," Iris said harshly. "Couldn't."

"Me, either," Wendi added breathlessly. "Well, I don't know if I could or couldn't. But I haven't had any. My husband died a month after our wedding."

Jill leaned toward her. "How long ago was that?"

"Five years today." Her eyes glistened. She buried her face in a tissue.

Mrs. Q. gave Jill a see-what-you've-done? look as she patted the young woman's shoulder. "My man died ten years ago. My kids were twenty-four and twenty-eight."

Jill was stuck on the fact that Wendi had been part of this group for five years and was still an emotional wreck.

"I'm so sorry, Wendi." After Wendi nodded, Jill went on. "Perhaps others who've been to the group have shared insight you could pass on to me. Something, anything to give me hope that my daughters will come out of this okay."

"No one can guarantee that," Mrs. Q. said.

"I'm looking for hope, not guarantees. And some advice on what to do to help them."

"You can't help them if they don't want help," Iris said. "The person who wants the change has to make the change."

Jill decided that Iris was speaking from a different kind of experience, but saw the woman's point. "You're right. But they're so young and haven't gone through anything like this."

"Just love them," Wendi said.

Jill sat back, discouraged. *I do love them! What else can I do?* Biting back an exasperated sigh she changed the subject to another worry. "When did you all start dating?"

"I've buried two husbands and three boyfriends," Birdie said. "I don't like being alone. As soon as someone who meets my standards come along, I grab him. Life's too short to worry about other people's opinions."

Jill smiled. The oldest was the wisest. "What are your standards?"

"Male and breathing."

Everyone chuckled.

"For me, too," Jacob said with a wink.

The grins widened. Jill was so glad to see they had senses of humor. "My friend signed me up for speed dating," she admitted.

Birdie and Jacob were the most interested in hearing about the terrifying event scheduled for the next night. Mrs. Q. kept her arms crossed and her expression noncommittal. Iris was the toughest of them all and yet had expressed the greatest concern about Wendi, who worried Jill the most.

What had she gotten herself into? It was apparent that they weren't going to be of much help to her. Was she there to be of help to them? What an egotistical thing to think....

It was almost 8:30 p.m. when the meeting ended. Jill passed two of the brownies to Birdie, who secreted them in her pockets, a conspiratorial smile her thanks. Jill wanted to give some to Wendi, as well, but Iris and Mrs. Q. hovered like bodyguards on each side of her.

"Would anyone like to go somewhere for coffee?" Jill asked.

A chorus of muffled, "No, thanks," reached her. When they exited the building, the five turned toward the west. Jill was headed east.

"See you next week?" she said, walking backward. Maybe she hadn't gotten much out of the group but she knew she would give it a little more time—for her daughter's sake.

"We'll be there," Mrs. Q. answered, as if used to people saying they would be back but not showing up.

When Jill arrived home, she put the kettle on for tea. While she waited for the water to boil, she looked out her big windows to the buildings across from her and the sidewalk below. People moved at a fast clip, their hands stuffed in coat pockets, knit caps on their heads, leaning as if buffeted by a strong wind, but mostly just in a hurry. Everyone was always in a hurry.

She'd gotten caught up in the frenzy herself, and on the days she went home to Darien would find herself at a loss for things to do. Now that Alan had gone on a three-week, multicity book tour, it would be dull for her at home, too. She'd gotten used to talking about how the loft was progressing, and she missed the everyday comfort of his presence, and his wit and his…history.

Ilene had become a remarkable friend in a short time, but nothing replaced history.

The teakettle whistled. She poured the hot water over a blueberry tea bag she'd found in a little shop last week. It had reminded her of a trip to Maine she and Wade had made a few years ago. Wade had never vacationed well, hadn't learned how to relax. No, that wasn't true. Physical challenges were relaxing to him, so sailing solo headlong into fierce winds relaxed him as much as reading a book relaxed her. He couldn't just go for a walk on the shore. He had to heave rocks and shells into the surf as far as he could, each time trying for more distance.

Memories of Wade were painfully fresh after the meeting, mixed with some guilt that she wasn't mourning as deeply as she had been a mere month ago. She'd been too busy to let her grief have the hold it used to have on her. She couldn't remember the last time she'd cried in the shower, her personal wailing wall.

It was that one-year expectation that was throwing her. She could see that some of the people tonight had thought less of her for even thinking about dating yet. She hadn't told them she'd been coerced into going.

Jill nestled in the corner of the sofa, her hands wrapped around the mug for warmth. Steam rose, the blueberry scent soothing. Her fingertips brushed against her rings. She froze, then she held up her hand and stared at the two-carat brilliant diamond guarded on each side by bands, a plain wedding band and a three-diamond ring commemorating their twentieth anniversary.

After a minute she scooped up the portable phone and dialed.

"This better be good," Ilene answered, drowsy and gruff.

"I can't go tomorrow night."

"The hell you can't."

Jill heard the rustling of bed linens and click of a lamp switch. "It's my rings," she said softly. "My wedding rings."

A long silence ensued.

"It hasn't been a year, Ilene." She remembered the contractor, Bobby Link, touching her rings and coming to the conclusion she was taken. "Any man seeing me wearing them would know I was still pining for my husband. Or figure I was married."

"Transfer them to your right hand. Lots of women do that."

"You're not really seeing my point."

"Yes, I am, hon. You're looking for an excuse not to go."

"You know I won't date anyone I meet."

"It's experience, Jill. You're not cheating. You're living. Judging by everything you've told me about Wade, he would be glad you were doing this."

Would he? Maybe he would be glad she was finding a place in her new world, but…speed dating? He'd probably think it too, oh, too middle class or something. He may have defied his parents' wishes by marrying so far beneath him, but he'd still lived a privileged life. He would probably expect she would date within her old circle, which would mean returning to the country club for more than using the gym early in the morning.

"Are you there?" Ilene asked. "I need my beauty sleep, you know."

"I need to think about this some more," Jill replied. "I'll talk to you tomorrow."

"At least keep your appointment with my hairdresser."

"Maybe," she said, then hung up as Ilene was sputtering.

Jill's tea had gone cold by the time she'd written a pro-and-con list in her diary about speed dating, needing to sort it all out.

Pro
Practice for real dating in the future.
Anonymous.
Gets Ilene off my back.

Con
Rings.
Would have to tell the support group I didn't follow through. Quitter.
What if no one wants to date me?

Aha. Jill closed the diary with a snap. The biggest truth of all.

The phone rang. "I'm still deciding," she said without saying hello, knowing it would be Ilene armed with another argument, one that would have to be exceptional to cancel out the root of Jill's fear, that of rejection.

"I assume you made a list or two." Not Ilene, but a welcomed voice, deep and layered with humor.

"Alan!" She looked at the clock. "It's midnight."

"Yeah, sorry. I realized it after it rang. It's nine here in California."

"How's the tour going?"

"It's only been a day. But it's tiring. And energizing." She laughed at the contradiction.

"You know it's time to switch genres when your fans start showing up in costume," he said.

"As?"

"John-Michael."

"Ah, the creepy vampire. Do your fans have fangs?"

"Yeah. Some of them don't even look fake. So, what's the big decision you're making and who did you think would be calling?"

"Ilene." It occurred to her that Ilene and Alan would make a good match, both of them self-confident, easy talkers and practiced daters. "She wants me to go speed dating tomorrow night."

"You're balking because?"

"Let me ask you this. If you met a widow who still wore her wedding rings, what would you think?"

"That she wasn't ready to date."

"How about if she'd moved them to her right hand?"

"That she wasn't ready to date."

"If she wore them on a chain around her neck?"

"That she wasn't—"

"I'm sensing a trend here," she interrupted.

"Women give off signals when they want to be asked out."

"What kinds of signals?"

"They're not the same for every woman. And it's not something I can define. I just know it when I see it."

"Have you been turned down?"

"Of course."

"How many times?"

"Once."

She grinned. The man was a dating machine. *Once* was an amazing number.

"I'm irresistible," he said.

"Obviously. Alan?"

"What?"

"Should I take off my rings and go?"

"I can't answer that. But you also don't have to *leave* them off, you know."

"So you think I should give it a shot?"

"I think you're scared. And I think the way to overcome fear is to face it. Okay, I've got to get going. I'm having drinks with the publicist in a few minutes. Oh, hey. How'd the support group go?"

"You don't have enough time for me to tell you."

"That sounds ominous. Okay, let me know how the dating goes."

"You assume I'm going to do it."

"I dare you."

As answers went, it was a good one. She grabbed her diary again and started a new list—opening gambits to grab a man's attention.

So, what's your sign? She laughed at herself. She didn't want to ever resort to clichés.

I guess you have to like quickies to do this. Or maybe, *Do you like to skinny-dip?* Not clichéd at all, she thought, smiling.

She crossed out each ridiculous line with a flourish. There was always the mundane, "So. What do you do?"

You can do better than that.

She tapped her pen against the page, stopped, pondered, then she wrote, *Do you think this will be the longest or the shortest six minutes of your life?*

CHAPTER 8

Thursday, October 4
1. Get a dog. This time I'm serious.
2. Get laid. This time I'm not serious.
3. Stop dragging feet about telling Shanna and Tori about the loft.
4. Find that incredible age-defying outfit. This time I'm laughing.
5. 2:00 makeover with Ilene's stylist.
6. 8:00—SpeedingTicket at the Maniac Bar and Lounge. Never forgive Ilene.

Jill had intended to go to Barneys, needing something familiar to hold on to in her new unfamiliar world. She'd made an appointment with the personal shopper Wade had set her up with before and had almost reached her subway station when she spotted the little shop. The window display stopped her in her tracks. She moved closer and studied the outfit on the headless mannequin.

Could she wear something like that or would she come

across as a middle-aged woman trying to recapture her long-gone youth?

I dare you.

She didn't know why she was hearing Alan's voice in her head, but it was enough to prod her into the shop.

The saleswoman wasn't too young or too hip or too Goth, and Jill pointed to the outfit in the window. "Would I look ridiculous in that?" she asked.

"I think you would look fabulous in that. If you don't, we'll find you something else, I'm sure." She pulled items off racks and carried them to a dressing room. "I'm Angelique, by the way. These are my designs."

Jill took off the Armani suit she'd chosen to impress the Barneys shopper and slipped on a white silk blouse with a softly ruffled collar that faded into a deep V, the same soft ruffles at the cuffs. The skirt was black, tailored to mid-thigh then flaring slightly, stopping at just above her knees.

"How does it look?" Angelique called from outside the booth.

Jill pushed aside the curtain and stepped out.

"Ah. Perfect, yes?" the woman asked.

"Yes." Amazingly perfect.

"Here. I have just the right accessories."

Jill stepped into pointy black patent heels that added three inches to her five-foot-five frame. Angelique fastened a skinny leather belt low on Jill's hips, then finished the outfit with gold chains and bangle bracelets. She hadn't felt so daring since college.

After seeing herself in the mirror, she called Barneys to cancel her appointment, then spent two hours with her new personal shopper and designer, Angelique.

Armed with a new attitude, she didn't even have to be talked into blond highlights by Ilene's hairdresser, who also taught her how to use a flatiron to make her hair fall straight around her face from a side part. Then a makeup artist gave her smoky eyes and a lighter, glossier, pinker lipstick and blush.

She oozed confidence that night when she spotted Ilene at the far side of the jammed Maniac Bar and Lounge, the meeting site of SpeedingTicket, a well-established speed-dating service, in business a whole trust-inspiring two years.

Jill had seen Ilene work a room, but she'd never seen her dressed for date action. She wore a plunging black sweater with a flattering red circle skirt and leopard-look heels. Her red hair shimmered in the overhead lights, and her jewelry jingled enticingly, drawing gazes, as did her curvaceous body.

Jill moved toward her, but Ilene disappeared through a doorway while flirting with a much younger man, his spiked hair almost as red as hers—two brilliant flames walking side by side.

Nerves began to crack Jill's composure. She tried to ignore the sensations bombarding her that narrowed her sight to a pinpoint and dulled voices to a steady murmur. She kept her head up and shoulders back as she walked through the doorway. She spotted three sets of long tables. A smaller check-in table blocked her from catching up with Ilene. Jill signed in, was handed a packet, wished good luck and told to go mingle until a bell rang.

She made a beeline for Ilene, who, still talking to the young man, glanced her direction, turned away, then spun toward her again. Ilene's expression told Jill everything. She'd passed muster.

Ilene excused herself and rushed toward Jill, then grabbed her by the shoulders.

"Holy crap, girlfriend. Look at you. Hon, you look thirty."

"I do not," Jill said but smiling at the flattery.

"Okay. Thirty-five. Ten years younger. Turn around."

"I picked out everything myself," she said to Ilene. "Well, mostly." She wondered if Wade would roll over in his grave at her choices.

The bell rang, bringing conversation to a halt. An enthusiastic young woman announced the rules of the game. They'd been divided into three groups ahead of time, based on initial match properties. Halfway through the evening they would break for drinks. They could mix and mingle at that point and then again afterward with people, including those from different tables who they weren't previously paired with. They were to mark yes or no on their forms, which would be turned in at the end, then they could follow up at home on the computer and find out who'd matched. Both participants had to indicate a yes to become a match.

Jill sat where she was told. She smiled across the table at the man dressed in black jeans and a gray sweater. Although he was mostly bald, she didn't think he was forty. He barely returned her smile. The bell rang.

Her memorized opening line decided to play hide-and-seek in her brain. Her throat closed. Finally she said hi.

"How's it goin'?" he asked.

"Good. Um. So. What do you do?" *Brilliant, Jill. Just brilliant.*

"I'm in advertising."

"Oh? For an agency?"

"I change out billboards."

Jill blinked and swallowed hard.

"How about you?" he asked.

She'd thought up an answer for that question ahead of time. "I just moved into the city. I'm still in the process of getting settled. What do you like to do on weekends?"

"Usual stuff. Hang out with the guys. Watch the games. You like football?"

"Not particularly."

"I'm divorced," he said.

Her empty ring finger felt like ice. "I'm widowed."

"So you understand."

"I understand what?"

"The pain."

Not exactly an upbeat opening. "Yes, it's all very painful," she said, then let him talk about his ex-wife and how she'd poisoned his children against him. The bitterness in his voice told a bigger story. She felt sad for him, more than for herself. At least she had good memories of Wade.

She jumped up when the bell rang and moved to the next chair, checking the *no* box next to his number. Why was it that the women had to do the moving, anyway? she wondered.

This candidate gave her a subtle once-over and seemed to approve. He was closer to her age, sported a neat, businessman's haircut, and was dressed in a perfectly tailored suit.

They shook hands. "Sorry. I had to rush from the office," he said with a charming smile. "I know I'm overdressed."

"You look nice," she said.

"Is this as absurd to you as it is to me?"

Ah. A soul mate. "Incredibly. Have you done this before?"

"A few times. I don't date people I work with, and I work at least sixty hours a week."

"This is my first time," she admitted. The buzz of conversation disappeared. She no longer heard nervous laughter or scattered words. She was totally focused on the man across from her.

He touched a finger to the indentation on her ringless one. "You haven't had your rings off for long."

She tucked her hands in her lap. "No. I'm a widow."

"How long?"

"A little over ten months."

He withdrew, maybe not physically, but mentally. She saw the interest disappear from his eyes.

"I see."

Jill smiled slightly at him, hoping to put him at ease. "I take it the interview is over."

"I'm looking for someone with potential," he said, not unkindly. "Your grief is too fresh. Been there, done that, as they say. Twice."

She nodded. "I understand."

"Not yet you don't, but you will."

"So," she said, looking around, hearing the noise again. "How do we pass the next few minutes?"

He clicked his pen open and drew something on the back of his match card. "Wanna play hangman?"

She laughed. "Sure."

They played until the bell rang. He finished filling in the boxes, which said, "Good luck." She wished she could hug him for his kindness. She also felt edgy now. Emotional.

"I know you," her newest match said even before she sat down.

Bobby Link, she realized, stunned at seeing the contractor with the super-short blond hair and incredible shoulders.

"Don't tell me," he said, leaning back and studying her. "I'll remember."

"I wouldn't have expected *you* to have any trouble finding dates," Jill said with a smile, her ego caught between hoping she'd left enough of an impression that he remembered her—and hoping he didn't recall her at all. She'd been hesitant and jumpy around him that day—a month and a half ago already, she realized. After all, he'd met her when she was trying to find out whether Wade had a love nest.

"So, we do have a connection." He frowned thoughtfully. "Have I done work for you?"

Technically not, since Alan had taken care of the construction details before she got involved. "Sort of," she said coyly.

His laughter was appreciative and sexy. "We slept together?"

"No!"

His eyes sparkled. "Kidding. I would've remembered that. Obviously you know what I do for a living. How about you?"

She gave her canned answer. "I just moved into the city. I'm still in the process of getting settled."

"Just moved in." He drummed his fingers on the table, eyeing her up and down again. "Been single long?"

"Not quite a year. You?"

"Four years. Do you have children?"

"Two. At college. You?"

"Two. In high school. They live with their mother most of the time." He cocked his head. "This is driving me crazy. I don't usually forget a face. Especially one like yours."

Flattery will get you everywhere, she thought, pleased and terrified at the same time. "Thank you."

"I'm embarrassed that you remember and I don't." He looked at his watch. "Not a lot of time left. Tell me where we met."

She shook her head, smiling. He excited her, and she wasn't ready to be excited. She knew how to get in touch with him if or when she was ready.

"That's cruel, Number 13652. If I remember later, will I know how to get in touch with you?"

"Possibly." Which was the truth. He might put where they met together with the job he'd done.

He rested his hand on hers. Reaction skittered through her body. *Get laid*. The words had been on her to-do list for a long time—

"Are you going to check me as a match?" he asked, flashing that woman-killer smile she remembered from their first meeting.

Was she? Would she just let the speed-dating process do the work? Had they been destined to meet? She was definitely tempted. "I don't know," she said honestly.

"Do you hold some kind of grudge against me?"

"No." She pulled her hand free and set it in her lap.

"So, I didn't do you wrong at some point?"

She smiled. "No."

"You've made this a challenge."

"No. *You've* made this a challenge."

"Meaning, I should remember you, and you're a little ticked that I don't."

"On the contrary, I enjoyed meeting you *and* seeing you again."

"But not enough to give me the information to find you again."

Why *was* she teasing him? If someone were doing the

same thing to her, she would've been more than a little ticked. "Frankly, I'm not sure this was a good move, Bobby. Maybe I'm not ready yet. I apologize for being elusive."

The end-of-round bell rang. "I'll figure it out," he said, standing as she did, offering his hand. He drew her hand to his lips for a soft, quick brush of farewell.

Her long-denied libido staged an uprising. She stammered. He grinned, slowly, sexily.

"You know how to reach me," he said.

She nodded, was jarred out of her sexual haze to move toward the next station....

She couldn't do this anymore. She wasn't ready to flirt, to be admired openly, to tease.

She didn't stop at the next chair but kept walking until she made it out of the back room and into the main lounge area. She heard Ilene call her name, but she didn't want to talk to her, or anyone. On top of the grief-support meeting the night before, she'd had too many challenges at once.

She wanted to go home. To Connecticut. She wanted to sink into the couch in Alan's office with a cup of coffee and just chitchat, like they used to. But even that relationship was different now.

She hailed a cab. On the ride home she pulled a gold chain over her head and unfastened the clasp. Her rings, which she'd nestled out of sight between her breasts, fell into her hand. She slid them on, then let out a long, shaky breath.

Somehow she managed to get to the loft before she fell apart. She ran upstairs, threw herself face down on her bed and cried—for Wade, for Shanna, for Tori, but mostly for herself. She missed him, and her daughters, and her familiar life. She missed having a partner, and that irreplaceable intimacy that came from years together. Nothing had been comfortable since he'd died.

The phone rang. She ignored it. She heard Ilene leaving a frantic message. She would probably show up later, worried and maybe even irritated at Jill for running out. Ilene didn't understand Jill's need to take things slowly, that anything new exhausted her, but that she'd been working hard to change, to take risks. Not even the most fabulous new outfit in the world could hurry things along.

She knew she had to carve out a new life for herself. She hadn't fooled herself about that.

But she needed to use a pocket knife, not a chain saw to do it.

CHAPTER 9

Wednesday, November 7
1. Get a cat. I know I'm repeating myself, but I can't make up my mind.
2. Get laid. This is never going to happen.
3. No more delays—tell Shanna and Tori about the loft. Ask about Thanksgiving. Keep your cool.
4. Finalize open house plans—check master list, redo sublists.
5. Bite the bullet and invite Wade's parents to open house.
6. Support group. Decide whether to keep going.

In the month since Jill began planning her open house, all of her furniture arrived behind schedule. The last of it, her dining room table and chairs, had just been delivered, only three days before the open house. She dragged her fingertips along the heavy glass top of the square table that would seat eight people. It needed a unique piece of art, maybe just a simple ikebana. Much of her art and accessories was Asian-inspired and blended well with the industrial look.

She looked around the finally finished loft and smiled. Everything fit. Everything made a statement. It wasn't a space that invited clutter, but demanded a simple existence, one without a lot of accumulated possessions. The industrial gray, silver and black background was accented with punches of red-orange and sage, colors she never would have put together before. She'd learned to trust her instincts, had vetoed several of Ilene's ideas, and loved the final result.

What would Alan think? She would know soon enough. He'd promised to come to the open house.

She'd seen him twice in the past two months, and then only briefly. Plus she'd been avoiding him, finding it easier just to talk on the phone.

Jill headed up to her bedroom. The same simplicity greeted her, although with a more feminine slant. Her bedspread was silk-screened, a piece of art in itself, with orchids printed here and there on a shimmery cream-colored fabric. Round paper lamps hung above each side of the bed, softening the hard edges of the room.

She picked up her diary, contemplating the list she'd written that morning. Time to call her daughters. She couldn't invite Wade's parents to the open house without telling Shanna and Tori first about the loft.

She dialed Shanna's number, expecting to get her voice mail. Unlike Tori, Shanna actually returned her calls. Shanna answered right away.

"Hi, sweetie." Jill's pulse picked up speed. "I'm surprised to catch you."

"Just finishing up a paper that's due in fifteen minutes. I can't really talk."

"Then I'll get down to business. Are you coming home for Thanksgiving?"

"I can't, Mom."

Can't or won't? Jill couldn't ask the question. She knew it was a long trip for just a few days, but Shanna had come home for the previous Thanksgivings.

"If that's all, Mom, I really need to go."

"I have a loft in TriBeCa," she blurted.

"What?"

"Your dad bought it before… Last year. He'd hoped we could spend more time in the city after both you girls were gone. So, I've been decorating it. It's all done. I'd hoped you would come home for Thanksgiving so you could see it." Jill didn't bother to detail Alan's involvement and the fact she may not live there at all. The bare-bones information would have to do.

"I can't."

"But you'll be home for Christmas."

"Yes."

Relief swept through Jill like a tidal wave, knocking her tension loose from its moorings. Shanna would be home for Christmas. Jill could see for herself how her daughter was doing.

"Mom, I have to say, I can't picture you living in the city."

"I'm enjoying it." Did she sound too defensive?

"Well, good. I guess."

"You told me to find something to do." That definitely sounded defensive. Jill didn't know why she was being so prickly. Disappointment, probably, that she still had to wait to see her daughter. And maybe Jill was just sick and tired of tiptoeing around both the girls, trying not to make waves. Maybe keeping the peace had been a mistake.

"You're right, I did say that. I'm happy for you, Mom, if it makes you happy."

"It's hard without your dad, Shanna. Really hard. But I'm moving forward."

"Good." The quietly spoken word was layered with emotion. "Listen, Mom, I've really got to go."

Jill closed her eyes, frustrated. "Okay. 'Bye, sweetie. I love you."

"Love you, too."

Jill set down the phone and shoved herself off the bed. She pushed her hands through her hair.

She'd almost connected with Shanna again. There was that quick show of emotion then, bam, no time to pursue it.

Jill probably shouldn't call Tori now while her nerves were stretched taut....

Well, really, what did it matter? She wouldn't get to talk to her, anyway. Tori never answered her phone, her caller ID alerting her to who was on the other end. Tori's self-imposed separation hurt.

But Jill needed to cross the long-listed item off her list, more for her peace of mind than any other reason.

She dialed Tori, got her voice mail. "Hi, honey. I've got something important to tell you, so please call me. I'll have my cell phone on. 'Bye."

Her cell phone rang before she'd even made it downstairs. Tori's name appeared in the screen.

"Hi," Jill said with as much enthusiasm as she could.

"What's up?"

Down to business. Jill tried not to sigh. "Are you coming home for Thanksgiving?"

"I need to stay and catch up on homework, Mom."

"You can do homework at home. I'd be happy to drive up and get you."

"I'll be home a few weeks later for the break," Tori said, leaving no room for debate.

"Well, about that. I'd like to have Christmas in the city this year."

"What city?"

"New York. I've got a loft in TriBeCa."

"You rented a loft for the holidays?"

"No, I own it." She gave Tori the same explanation as Shanna.

"Shanna's not going to like it. She'll want to be home for Christmas."

"And you?"

"I wouldn't mind spending time in the city."

Hallelujah! Jill swallowed hard against her relief and excitement. "Then we'll plan on that."

"Mom?"

"What?"

"How come you didn't say anything about this before?"

"I wanted to surprise you with it all done."

A long pause ensued as Tori seemed to consider her words. "Yeah, okay. I gotta go now."

"I love you," Jill said.

"Me, too," Tori mumbled on the way to hanging up.

Jill should be happy. Both girls would be home for Christmas. So why did she feel like crying?

Because their lives were so disconnected now? Yes.

Because they wouldn't let her in anymore? That, too.

Because she felt abandoned?

She looked at her bedside clock and realized she didn't have time to call Wade's parents before leaving for her support-group meeting. By rote she wound a scarf around her neck and pulled on her jacket. She walked the relatively short distance to the Church of Personal Identity. Marcia spotted her before she went downstairs.

"How's it going?" she asked.

"This is my fifth meeting. Last time they finally called me by name," Jill answered, smiling slightly.

"Hey! Progress. I don't think anyone else has gotten that far, not since Jacob."

"Jacob is an anomaly. They accepted him because he was a man."

"Well, you're either stubborn or desperate," Marcia said with a pat on the shoulder.

Stubborn, Jill thought as she headed to the basement.

Plus she really didn't have enough to do. She wanted to make a breakthrough. She also wanted to get Wendi alone and try to talk her into getting professional help. Five years was more than long enough to grieve so deeply, especially for so young a woman.

Tonight she was about to shake up the world of the Five Musketeers, as she'd begun calling them.

"What are you smiling about?" Iris demanded as Jill sat down and looked at each of them.

"I have a surprise for all of you." She reached into her purse.

"Brownies?" Birdie asked hopefully, peering into the bag.

"Not at the moment, but if you can wait until the weekend, then yes." She knew that none of them ever left town, in fact rarely made plans of any kind, so waiting until the last minute wasn't a problem. She passed an envelope to each of them. "I'm having an open house on Saturday to celebrate my loft being finished. I'd love it if you all came. You're each welcome to bring a guest, too."

Jacob ripped open his envelope. Birdie peeled the flap carefully. Mrs. Q. looked curiously at Jill first then used a key to slit the envelope. Iris held it, glared at it, then finally tapped the envelope on the side, tore off an end, blew into it, then tipped the heavyweight card into her hand. Wendi clenched hers, not opening it at all.

Silence hummed as they read their invitations then looked at each other.

All for one and one for all. Jill saw them question each

other with their eyes. She was fascinated by how readable they were without saying anything.

Do *you* want to go? Mrs. Q. asked with a sweeping glance.

Do we *have* to go? Iris countered, scrunching her nose.

It might be *fun*, Jacob said by raising his eyebrows and smiling.

There'll be *food*, Birdie added, fidgeting in her chair.

I'm *scared*, Wendi conveyed wordlessly, without knowing exactly what she was afraid of, since she hadn't opened her invitation.

Jill let them off the hook. "You don't have to give me an answer. I want you to feel free to just show up, if you decide at the last minute."

They relaxed en masse. The meeting resumed, idle conversations, no delving into emotions, therefore avoiding potential mine fields.

"I'm a little down today," Jill said, plunging into a rare moment of silence. She didn't wait for someone to ask why, because she knew no one would. "I found out that neither of my daughters is coming home for Thanksgiving. They said they'll be home for Christmas break, which is only a few weeks later," Jill added. *Only*. It seemed like years. She never thought she would be this emotionally distant from her daughters.

Birdie patted Jill's thigh. "I've been invited to Louie's daughter's house for Thanksgiving." Louie was Birdie's current amour. He'd just moved into the assisted-living building where Birdie resided.

The discussion turned to Thanksgiving plans. Jill sighed. She might as well give up. Stubbornness was only leaving her frustrated. How long would it take to storm their defenses? Did she want to anymore? And to think she'd been worried about revealing her personal problems.

After everyone left, she sat in her chair for a few minutes, not wanting to watch them all walk away. She'd stopped inviting them to coffee after their session, tired of the rejection. Instead she'd arranged for Ilene to meet her at Starbucks down the street.

The group wasn't in sight as she made her way. She adjusted her knit scarf, pulling it over her chin, preventing the chilly wind from swirling around her neck. She glanced inside store windows as she walked. Since she usually walked the other direction toward home, the stores were new to her.

She could see into Starbucks as she approached but didn't spot Ilene's red hair. However, she did see her entire support group standing in line to order drinks.

Jill skidded to a stop. So…all these weeks when she'd tried to make friends, asked them to coffee, even, and they were going on their own. Together. Without her.

"It's not worth it," she muttered, taking a few steps back, getting out of sight. Tears burned her eyes, made worse by the cold wind.

"What's not worth it?" Ilene asked from beside her.

Jill swallowed. "Them." She angled her head toward the lighted store.

"Who?"

"The Five Musketeers." She pointed. "I've told you about them. You can pick them out. Mrs. Q., Iris, Jacob, Birdie and Wendi. Come on." She spun around and stalked away. "We can go to my place."

Ilene caught up with her. "Or we can walk in there. A little guilt might be good for their souls."

"But not mine."

"Hey, slow down, hon," Ilene said after a minute.

Jill stopped. She stared at the sidewalk, trying to form a sentence that wasn't filled with bitterness or hurt. "I am tired of being the outsider," she said finally. "It's like being in high school again, dealing with cliques."

"You're in *my* clique."

Jill clamped a hand on Ilene's arm. "I'm sorry. I didn't mean to hurt you. I'm just— Crap." She waved a hand toward Starbucks. "I've worked so hard to become part of them."

"Why?"

Jill frowned. Why, indeed? "I don't know. I guess I just want to belong."

"So, it's not *them* exactly, but overall. You exaggerated. For dramatic effect, I assume."

Jill laughed, the sound shaky. Ilene put an arm around her shoulders and got them walking again.

"Neither of my daughters is coming home for Thanksgiving."

"Ah. The real root of this outburst."

"I miss them so much."

"Then I have good news. Your life is about to change, girlfriend."

"The last time you decided to help me change my life resulted in a horrible night of speed dating."

"Talking with three men then running out does not constitute a 'night.' If you'd stuck it out, you might have been having as much fun as I am."

"Bragging is a very unattractive quality, Ms. Stillings."

"What can I say? Four dates with four different men. I like those odds."

Fortunately none of those men was Bobby Link. Ilene had checked the yes box for Bobby, but he apparently hadn't felt the same connection, because she hadn't gotten a match from him. Jill didn't know how she would've reacted if they'd dated.

She and Ilene were settled on the sofa in the loft before Ilene shared how they were going to change Jill's life.

"Internet dating," Ilene announced. She rested her feet on the black-enameled coffee table. "PairUp dot com."

"No." One word. Simple. Straightforward. Definite.

"Why not?"

"It's worse than speed dating. At least there you see the person. I've read plenty of articles on Internet dating. It's not for me." She spun her wedding rings around her finger. "Given what happened with the other thing, I know I'm not ready."

"That was a month ago. And you're the one moping about not belonging. You've even stuck with a support group that isn't supportive."

"If something is meant to be, it'll happen."

"Bull. You have to be proactive. You think some great guy is just going to find you in the produce section of the market or something? And since you don't do much else besides shop ..."

Direct hit. "I work out."

"When you're in Connecticut."

"I've caught up with all the current plays and movies. I've been to museums and galleries. I've gotten to know the city, just like you said I should. The subway doesn't faze me a bit anymore. Plus there's been the decorating to do and planning the open house."

"And next week when those projects are done? What then? Come on, admit it. You wouldn't mind an evening out with an attentive man."

Jill caught herself twisting her sweater hem. She clasped her hands. "Maybe."

"Aha! Okay, go fire up your computer. Let's see what's out there."

Jill put a hand on Ilene's arm, stopping her from rising. "Why is this so important to you? It's not like my biological clock is ticking or anything. There's no time issue facing me."

"In the dating world, hon, you're already hitting the snooze button."

Jill groaned at the image. "I think I should get a job." There, she'd said what had been on her mind for the past couple of weeks. She hadn't even told Alan she'd been thinking about it.

"Here?" Ilene asked.

"Yes."

"Meaning you've decided to stay in the city?"

"I was thinking maybe I could get something part-time. For the holidays."

"I've got connections at Macy's, if you'd like to be an elf."

"Unless Jimmy Choo has redesigned the shoes, no thanks."

"I wish." Ilene frowned thoughtfully. "I would offer you something in my office, but my business slows down then. Plus we both know you have no taste."

Jill gave her a little shove with her foot. "Looking for a job will probably give my ego a workout." Not to mention the plunge into the strange sea of the PairUp.com dating pool. "Hey, do they call PairUp P-U, for short?"

"You stinker, you."

"Okay," Jill said to Ilene. "Let's do it."

By the time Ilene left a couple of hours later, Jill had established a profile online with PairUp.com and had filed fourteen possibilities into her saved-profiles file. Not that she'd contacted any of them—heck, she hadn't even put her own profile into the public arena yet—but it was a first step.

Some of the men were obviously too good to be true, to which Ilene said, "If it looks like a dog, and it barks like a dog…" After all, why would a rich, successful, good-looking, sensitive guy who liked to hold hands, take long walks on the beach and travel with that "special someone" be having trouble finding a date in a city where single men ruled the dating scene? Why would a guy who claimed he was just looking for someone to add to his already-great life have to go into cyberspace to find her? A man like that could find "her" in so many places.

But now you're there, too. That honest little voice in her head took pleasure in reminding her of her hypocrisy. She'd developed a strong streak of cynicism, without good reason. It wasn't as if horrible things were happening to her constantly. Most of it was in her head then made its way into her consciousness when she was particularly lonely.

So. Time to stop whining. Time to take action.

Next point…what kind of job could she do? How could her degree in art history, earned twenty-three years ago, help? She could work in a museum, maybe. Or a gallery.

And what would you put on the job application?

Desperate.

Okay, seriously—what could she do? Ilene would say that Jill had lived in a gilded cage, which was true, but she had to have *some* marketable skills after all these years. The Sunday classifieds would teem with possibilities, and it was six weeks until Christmas, so her timing should be perfect for holiday work. Right after the open house, then, she would get serious about finding a job.

In the meantime she would work up the nerve to post her profile publicly on the PairUp site and see what happened.

"Would that be tomorrow, Scarlett?" that pushy, obnoxious new voice in her head singsonged?

"After the open house," she answered, as if making a solemn vow.

CHAPTER 10

Saturday, November 10—Open House!!
1. Get a stuffed cat. They don't shed, but you can curl up with them in bed.
2. Get laid. Why am I keeping this on my list?
3. Have ego stomped on—make PairUp profile public.
4. Lesson in humility—find a job.

As the owner and her assistant of A Rose is a Rose Catering set out the desserts, Jill took a final look at her master list for the open house. Food: check. Bar: check. Flowers: check. Music: check. Nerves: double check.

She glanced at her guest list, an eclectic mix she normally wouldn't put together at the same party, but since it was an open house, people would come and go, not staying long, not having to mingle much. She'd invited people from Wade's office, the architect Rafael D'Amato, her support group plus Marcia, a few friends from Connecticut, and every tenant in her building. There was Alan, of course. Ilene. And Bobby Link.

The decision to add Bobby came after a long deliberation in which she'd made a pro-and-con list. The *pro* item that turned the tide was her desire to see his expression when he connected the dots between meeting her in the elevator in August and meeting her at the speed-dating event a month ago. The most critical *con* was the question of whether he would think she was signaling her readiness to date. She couldn't answer that, since she'd even been dodging the P-U dating site by using the open house as an excuse. However, as Ilene had pointed out, tomorrow that excuse would cease to exist.

Few people had RSVP'd, but that seemed to be a common rudeness these days. She'd hired a teenager from the second floor to man the lobby door, guest list in hand, so that she wouldn't have to run back and forth to the video monitor.

Wade's parents had politely declined her invitation during a stilted telephone conversation. If his mother was surprised about the loft, Jill would never know it. Nor would she know if the woman approved, disapproved or even cared one iota about Jill moving into the city. Her mother-in-law was a champion of nonreaction.

Let it go.

Yes, she could let it go. It only mattered that her in-laws stayed close with Shanna and Tori.

"Hel-lo?" The welcomed female voice snapped Jill out of her thoughts. Ilene, who had her own key, strolled in, a tall, dark and handsome, leather-jacketed man in tow.

"I figured you wouldn't mind my being prompt instead

of fashionably late," she said, enveloping Jill in a hug. "Everything looks swell."

Jill smiled at the word. "Thanks to you."

"A labor of love."

"And money."

"Yeah. Good thing for me you hired me before we became such good friends. Oh, this is Hans," Ilene said, patting his chest.

Jill tried to place him. His name didn't sound familiar. Had he been a speed dater? Ilene had already ended things with the first four men she'd matched. There were two to go.

"We met last night in the produce section." Ilene's eyes shimmered at the irony.

"I was checking out the melons," Hans said, a slightly lecherous grin on his face. "To see if they were ripe."

Eeuw. Ick. Jill waved toward the kitchen island and dining room table. "There's plenty of food and drink. Feel free to help yourself. There's some cantaloupe you might be interested in."

Hans glanced questioningly at Ilene.

"I'll be right behind you," she said, shooing him with a graceful red-painted-nails hand, the color matching her deep-V-neck sweater. Her skirt was short, black and leather. She wore a wide black belt and boots.

"You're looking quite daring," Jill commented.

"What, this old thing? I could say the same of you. Where'd you find that?"

"At Angelique's." She was thrilled with the outfit—a

slightly off-the-shoulder, beige cashmere sweater with camel-colored suede skirt and below-the-waist concha belt. The matching suede pumps would be killing her feet by the end of the three-hour party, but it was worth it for the overall effect. She felt young and city-hip. "So, I guess I don't have to do the Internet dating thing, after all," she said to Ilene. "I really can find a man in the produce department. How old is he?"

"Thirty. Don't look at me like that. If there were more men my age available, I'd date 'em. You could take a page from my book, you know, hon. Take some chances."

"Maybe I will."

Ilene gripped Jill's arm. "Does that mean you're going to put your face out there in cyberspace?"

The doorbell rang. Jill could avoid answering Ilene's question if she wanted to. She headed toward the door. "It's on my list."

Ilene laughed, then went to join her date, who was flirting with the caterer, Rose Merman, a tall, quiet, competent woman in her early thirties.

Jill opened the door to a group of familiar faces—her support group. All of them. Happiness rushed through her. "Welcome! I'm so glad you're here. Please, come in."

As usual, they moved as a synchronized group. Jill pointed out the powder room, which was just off the entry, then Birdie broke ranks and headed to the buffet, her speed with her cane remarkable. Jill wondered, not for the first time, if the woman couldn't afford to feed herself. She was so tiny and food always seemed so important. Something else Jill should add to her list: find out if Birdie needed more to eat.

Mrs. Q. trailed Birdie, never seeming to look at the surroundings. Iris looked, her brows drawn together, especially when she glanced up at the catwalk. Wendi shuffled behind her.

Jacob passed Jill a baseball bat festooned with a red ribbon. "Housewarming gift. Keep it by your bed."

"How thoughtful," Jill said, scared and appreciative at the same time.

"Your home is stunning, my dear," he said as he eyed the office overhead. "You know, I didn't realize you were rich." He hurried to catch up with the others.

Rich? She didn't think of herself that way. She was comfortable. She didn't have to work if she didn't want to. Wade had provided income and a trust fund that allowed them to live in a beautiful home in an upscale area. It was a far cry from how she'd grown up, living in rentals, getting her clothes from Goodwill, babysitting for spending money, going to college on grants, scholarships and loans. She'd had nothing to compare it with, and had been happy. Her parents had been good people, kind and caring, but not interested in possessions.

Jill had gotten used to the life she lived with Wade—and took it for granted, she realized. She was accustomed to having a gardener, pool service, and a housecleaner when she wanted one. But they'd never had their own jet or a vacation home or new cars every year. It *had* occurred to her lately that she should check with her accountant to see if she could afford to buy the loft, except that surely Wade had known they could.

The Five Musketeers sat in Jill's dining room chairs, which she'd placed by the big windows overlooking the street. The shifting of furniture left the dining room table more easily accessed, as well as giving her extra seating beyond her sofa and the two upholstered chairs in front of the fireplace.

Seeing Ilene totally focused on Hans, Jill was about to join the group when the doorbell rang—her neighbors from across the hall, Sean and Cherise.

After their arrival, a steady stream of guests came and went. She tried to jot down names and brief descriptions of the other tenants, who formed their own groups according to floors. The third-floor tenants were the most sociable with each other because, Jill learned, they'd all made the effort to get to know one another.

"It's working," Ilene said at some point well into the third hour.

Jill nodded. Once the party had gotten underway, she'd been fine, the role a comfortable one. She'd put on big parties, intimate teas and rowdy birthday parties all of her adult life. "It's the lists."

"Is it?"

"Organization is the key to success."

Ilene shuddered. "Too much organization can drive you to drink. I noticed your support group have planted themselves."

"I don't think they get out of the house too often." The

Musketeers hadn't moved from their chairs except to get more food and drink. And Iris seemed to always be studying Jill. "How're things going with Hans?"

"Man can't hold his liquor for anything."

Can't keep his hands to himself, either, Jill thought, watching him pat the caterer's butt and get his hand slapped.

Ilene sighed. "I guess I should haul him out of here. I'll go apologize to that horrified woman."

"Please don't leave the party. I want you to meet Alan." Where was he, anyway? "Just tell Melon Man to either behave or leave. You don't have to go with him, do you? Better yet, send him to the store for more cantaloupe."

"Now that's just mean."

The doorbell rang. Jill saw Ilene head toward Hans and was sorry she had to move out of sight before Ilene issued the ultimatum.

Who hadn't showed up yet? Some of the tenants. Her Connecticut friends. Alan. Anyone from GlobalJet. The architect. Bobby. She pulled open the door.

"Hi, Jill."

"Cheryl!" The sixtyish woman had been Wade's administrative assistant for twenty years, having risen in the ranks with each of his promotions. "Oh, I'm so glad to see you."

They hugged. Jill felt her shake. Or was it herself? Probably both. She hadn't seen Cheryl since a week after the funeral. They'd always liked and respected each other, but Cheryl had retired when a new CEO was appointed, bringing his own assistant to the job.

"I'm happy the invitation caught up with you," Jill said. "The last I knew you were living in Florida."

"I am. We are. Jill, this is my husband, John."

"You got married!"

"I finally had the time." Cheryl smiled.

"Well, come in. I'm afraid there's no one else here you'll recognize."

"I—we can't." She set a beribboned package in Jill's hands. "I just wanted to see you and give you this. We're on our way to a wedding. It's why we're here this weekend. Open it later, when you're alone."

More than a little curious, Jill pressed the package to her chest. "Are you sure you don't want to come in for a minute and see what I've done with the place?"

"I'll take a rain check. I promise I'll call the next time we're in town."

"I'll hold you to it."

"Wade would be very happy to know you went ahead with this," Cheryl whispered as they hugged goodbye.

"You knew?"

"He was so excited."

Excited? Jill tried to picture it. "Cheryl, did he seem different to you toward the end? Quieter?"

She stared silently back at Jill for several long seconds. "I'll call you. I promise. It'll be between Christmas and New Year's."

"Okay." What else could she say?

She watched the couple head down the hall, hand in hand. As they reached the elevator, it opened, and Rafael D'Amato and Bobby Link got out. Jill took a quick step back but was pretty sure they'd spotted her. She didn't shut the door, just gripped it. Would Bobby recognize her?

"Good afternoon, Mrs. Townsend," Rafael said, not extending his hand until she did.

"Mr. D'Amato."

"Rafael, please."

"Please call me Jill. I'm glad you could come." She avoided looking at the man behind him, didn't make eye contact for even a second—even though she'd specifically invited him so that she could to watch him recognize her. "I hope you like the final result of your design," she told Rafael, gesturing for him to come into the loft.

"Good afternoon, Mrs. Townsend," Bobby said with an entirely different tone of voice as he reached for her hand, sandwiching it between both of his. He leaned toward her, his voice soft and husky. "Ms. One-name of speed-dating fame."

"Hi."

"That's all you have to say?"

It wasn't what she wanted to *say* that mattered, Jill thought, but what she wanted to *do*—strip him, toss him on her bed and have her way with him. She wanted to rub his short hair and know how it felt, soft or prickly, stiff or silky?

"After you left the Maniac," he said, "I remembered

where'd I'd seen you before, but I didn't have any idea you lived here. I thought you were a Realtor." He touched her wedding rings as she clutched Cheryl's package. "You weren't wearing these that night."

She shook her head.

He met her gaze.

Don't ask me any more questions.

"We'll talk later," he said, then moved past her.

She followed him stiffly, set Cheryl's package on top of her cookbooks in the kitchen then mingled. Since Rafael and Bobby had each other to talk to, she decided to ignore them for a few minutes until she got her eager and responsive libido under control. She wandered over to talk to the Musketeers. So much for people coming and going.

"Everybody all right?" she asked. "Have you had enough to eat and drink?"

"Everything has been delicious," Jacob said, toasting her with a glass of whatever he was drinking.

"Yes, it has," Mrs. Q. said. "You have a nice view here."

"I can't take credit for it. Wade chose the place."

"You decorated it?" Mrs. Q. asked.

"Yes. With the help of the woman over there, the one wearing the red sweater."

"It's quite tasteful."

The compliments were such a surprise that Jill didn't want to walk away. Was this the breakthrough? Iris was still standoffish, but the others seemed to be warming. "Thank you, Mrs. Q. I appreciate your saying so."

The doorbell rang again. She almost floated across the room and down the short hall.

"Alan!" She threw herself into his arms.

"Watch the flowers," he said, angling back and holding them out to her.

"I'm sorry," she said, taking an awkward step back, a little embarrassed.

She buried her face in the bouquet of purple calla lilies. "I'm just so happy to see you."

"Don't apologize." He smiled that wonderful Alan-smile of his.

"Did you get my e-mail about staying over tonight?"

"Yeah. I can't. But thanks. Maybe another time."

She hid her disappointment. She really wanted to show him the city on Sunday morning, when the tone was so different from the rest of the week. "Come see the place. I'm sorry you won't know anyone but me. No one from Darien came."

The only guests left were the Musketeers, Ilene and Hans, Rafael, and Bobby. She started to make introductions when someone screamed, "Alan Haggerty! It's Alan Haggerty!"

Wendi flew out of her chair and ran to Alan. She grabbed his arms. "Ohmygod. Ohmygod. Ohmygod. I love your books. I just love your books. I've read them all a hundred times."

Alan seemed immune to fan adoration. He smiled and said thank you as he smoothly extricated himself from her grip. The rest of the Musketeers had finally gathered their wits and encircled Wendi, who began to recite the plot of Alan's last book.

"And when John-Michael bit into her neck? Ohmygod. I thought I was going to die! I, like, melted on the couch. And then when Babylonia wrapped her neck with the chain mail? He was so hurt, you know? I cried and cried and cried."

Jill needed to socialize with Rafael and Bobby. She mimed that she was stepping away. Alan seemed to be okay with it. The party would end soon anyway, and everyone would leave. He wouldn't be Wendi's captive for long. Wendi—who would've guessed there was a personality under her waif's appearance?

Jill asked the caterer if she would mind putting the lilies in a vase, then she joined Ilene, who held court with Rafael and Bobby, Hans having passed out on the sofa.

"I was just giving this one—" she tapped Bobby's chest "—a hard time about not remembering me from the Maniac last month. I'm devastated." Her pout was flirty, but Bobby didn't seemed swayed by it. His expression remained friendly, nothing more.

"You also tried the speed dating?" Rafael asked Jill.

She didn't want to give a detailed retelling of that embarrassing story, so she just said yes, hoping that neither Bobby nor Ilene would embellish on it.

"What did you think of it?"

"I'm not in a hurry to do it again."

"And you?" he asked Bobby.

"It was interesting."

"Did you make a date with someone?" Rafael asked Bobby.

"Yes, although the one who interested me the most didn't make a match with me, so that didn't happen."

Jill smiled benignly.

Rafael turned to her. "That man who just arrived. He is someone famous, I gather, but I don't know of him."

"Alan writes horror novels. We've been neighbors for fifteen years. Our children grew up together. So, what do you think, Rafael? Are you pleased with the results of your design?"

"It's exactly right. And your décor suits it perfectly."

"Feel free to recommend my designer," Jill said, looking at Ilene. "She's a gem."

"Do you have some cards with you?" he asked Ilene, who slipped her arm through his and walked him to the island, where her cards were stacked, along with the caterer's.

Jill smiled. *The woman is shameless.*

"If she thinks to make a conquest of D'Amato, she's crazy," Bobby said. "He likes them much more refined. More like you, actually." He didn't give her a chance to respond to the surprising statement. "I've gotta go."

"Already?"

"I'm not much for small talk. Walk me out?"

When they reached the door, he pulled her into the hall with him.

"So," he said, studying her.

"So?" Her nerves were hopping all over the place.

"Your rings go on and come off according to your mood?"

"I had them off for that night only." Her defensive tone was meant to hide her guilt at her indecisiveness.

"You're sort of ready to date?"

"I'm very confused."

He covered her rings with his hand and moved in closer. She felt the heat of him through her clothes. He bent. She waited. His lips brushed her cheek. She held her breath. He lifted his head, waited for her to make eye contact.

"You're ready," he said. "I'll be in touch, Jill."

She watched him walk away. He shoved his hands in his pockets as the elevator door closed. He didn't wave, didn't smile, didn't even nod. She stood rooted in place. Was it Bobby who was revving her up or would any ol' normal, attractive, attentive, sexy man do?

Her front door opened and Rafael came out. If he wondered why she was standing in her hallway all alone, he didn't ask. She smiled at him.

"Thank you for inviting me," he said. "I should also apologize for not being more forthcoming when you came to see me."

Was it her imagination or had his Italian accent just gotten much more noticeable? "I understand you needed to protect the surprise," she said, caught in his unwavering, dark-brown stare. What was going on? Her body must still be on overload or something from Bobby. Everything tingled.

"I wanted to tell you," he said.

"Really, Rafael. I understand. I respect you for not saying anything."

He took her hand in his. "May I call you sometime?"

Good grief. Had she gone from having no dates to possibly having two? Amazement warred with curiosity and, well, lust, if she was being honest. The attention from both men excited her, Bobby's in a more base way than Rafael's, but just as intensely.

"May I?" he repeated.

"Yes." Was there another answer?

"Thank you." He kissed both her cheeks then walked away.

This time she went inside her loft rather than watch him leave, not wanting him to see how he affected her. She bumped into Ilene.

"Your friend needs rescuing from the Musketeers," she said.

Jill glanced at her watch. It was a little past three, anyway. She looked toward the kitchen as she went to shoo her group out the door. The caterers were almost done cleaning up. She made a quick detour to ask Rose to package some food separately for Birdie, then continued on.

"Thank you all for coming," she said, her hand on the back of Alan's chair. "I appreciate it more than I can tell you."

She saw Wendi's newly displayed excitement transform into distress, but they all stood, clutching their coats, which none of them had given up, and shuffled toward the front door. As unobtrusively as possible, Jill grabbed the doggie bag for Birdie and passed it to her. Birdie's sweet smile said everything.

"Why'd you do that?" Jacob asked as the others exited.

"She doesn't seem to get enough to eat," Jill said. "I'm worried she can't afford much."

Jacob chuckled, then he laughed. "That woman could buy and sell all of us combined."

"What?"

"She's a multimillionaire." He laughed again, shaking his head.

"But she lives in that run-down facility—"

"She's also the world's biggest penny pincher. See you on Wednesday, Jill."

See you on Wednesday, Jill. The words were music to her ears. At least one person expected her to show up.

Hugging her pleasure, she turned around, only to come face-to-face with Alan.

"You owe me," he said, although not with any heat.

"I know I do. I've never seen Wendi look up from the floor for longer than a couple of seconds at a time before, or heard her speak more than a few words."

"I was kidding. It's not a chore to listen to a fan. She's interesting. A little weird, but interesting. Your Musketeers are quite a group."

"Aren't they? I'm still trying to break through with them."

He touched her hair, startling her. "You look…different."

As with Rafael and Bobby, she reacted to his touch.

How could she come back to life so suddenly? So…desperately. "Um, is that good or bad?"

"Different."

She batted his shoulder. "Brat."

Ilene caught up with them. "I'm going to need some help getting my date into a cab. Maybe a big, strong man like you wouldn't mind," she added with a flutter of her eyelashes and a toss of her head.

"Oh, brother," Jill said, thinking to catch Alan's eye and laugh with him, but finding him checking out Ilene, slowly, thoroughly. She watched them wake Hans up enough to maneuver him between them, his arms resting on their shoulders. Jill ran ahead to open the door then punched the down button for the elevator.

"Be right back," Alan said with a wink after they made it inside the elevator.

"Great party, hon," Ilene said. "Call me tomorrow."

The doors closed.

By the time Alan returned, the caterers had left, and Jill was moving her dining room chairs back into place. Silently he helped.

Did you line up a date? she wanted to ask but didn't, knowing her tone would be snippy. She had no right to be snippy. "Did you get anything to eat?" she asked instead.

"Yeah. While you were saying goodbye to your court."

Who sounded snippy now? She set down a chair and slid it under the table. "My court?"

"D'Amato and Link."

"Why do you call them that?"

He turned away to get another chair without answering.

"Why, Alan?"

"Are you dating them?"

"No." *Not yet, anyway.* "Did you ask out Ilene?"

"Not my type."

She ignored the relief—or whatever it was—that flooded her. "Didn't look like it to me. Looked like you liked what you saw."

"Hell, Jill. She's got a great body, and she puts it out there to be seen. I'd have to be dead not to look."

"And admire."

He paused as they crossed paths. "What's your problem?"

"I don't want you to admire her." There. Direct, honest, to the point.

"Checking out her body is not the same as admiring her. She's too…flagrant. Anyway, why do you care?"

"What if you dated her and things went bad? Then I'd be stuck between my two best friends, taking sides and making sure you never met up again."

He scrutinized her. "I won't be dating her," he said finally, then resumed carrying the chair to the table. "Unlike you with Link and D'Amato."

"No one's asked me out." She grabbed the last chair.

He took it from her and put it away, the movement abrupt. "They will. And soon. Are you ready for that?"

"Ready in what way?"

"It hasn't been a year, Jill." His voice went rough with emotion.

"Like I don't know that?" she almost shouted, her worries tumbling out. "And I miss him. I miss him every hour of every day. I'm trying to live. I don't even have my daughters anymore. It's either move forward or become… I don't know, like Wendi. I refuse to become like Wendi."

She stalked away, anger and hurt and guilt piling up on her. She couldn't look at him. "And I'm scared."

"Of what?"

She told him what she hadn't told anyone, hadn't even written it in her diary. "Of drying up." She pressed her shaking fingers to her lips as if to block the words, but they kept coming. "Of losing everything that defines me as a woman, physically and sexually and maternally. I'm worried about the future."

She faced him. "So, I'm a little excited that a couple of good-looking, successful men are interested in me. What's wrong with that? My daughters don't need me, and I have to acknowledge that and let them be independent while I'm scared to death for both of them. They don't need me. No one needs me anymore. No one. I deserve—"

She stopped as her throat closed and her eyes burned. "Dammit."

"Jill …" He took a step toward her.

"Just…give me a minute." She raced up her stairs.

CHAPTER 11

By the time Jill headed back downstairs, the sky had transformed from twilight to dark, although only twenty minutes had elapsed. She'd changed into jeans and a sweater, washed her face and applied fresh makeup and perfume, calming herself with the mindless tasks. She'd heard Alan moving around, the refrigerator door open and close a couple of times, the clink of glass hitting glass, then silence.

Had he gone?

No. He stood looking at the night through the big windows, his hands tucked into the back pockets of his black slacks. He'd taken off his sweater, revealing a gray silk T-shirt. She moved to stand beside him.

"I apologize," he said.

"Me, too."

He slipped an arm around her shoulder and squeezed, then let her go. She wanted to turn into his arms and find comfort. She hadn't been held for such a long time, not for longer than three seconds at a time, anyway, which seemed to be the measure allowed for a nonintimate hug.

"I poured wine and set out snacks," he said. "I figure you didn't eat much while the party was going on."

"Thanks. You're right."

She didn't tell him her stomach was still too tied up in knots to allow for food. He'd put everything on the table between the upholstered chairs in front of the fireplace, which he'd also lit, the gas logs not needing anything more than the flip of a switch to light. Instant atmosphere and no ashes to dump.

"It's a great view," he said, gesturing with his wineglass. "And I like what you've done with the place."

"Thanks. I really enjoyed pulling it all together."

"Are you going to stay? Keep it?"

"I don't know yet. Is it okay not to know yet?"

"Sure."

She reached for a prosciutto-wrapped asparagus then set it down again. "Would you live here or sell it?"

"Don't know."

She considered telling him her idea of sharing it with him, then decided against it. She should present him with an actuality, not a possibility.

"So, what's next, Jill?"

"I'm thinking about getting a job."

He gave her a speculative look. "That would seem to indicate you plan to stay."

"No. I thought I'd look for holiday work, something to help me make my decision about my next step, but not locking myself into anything."

"Are you having money problems. I can—"

"Absolutely not. I'm bored, that's all."

"Okay. What do you want to do?" he asked.

"The question is, what am I qualified to do?"

"Your degree is in art history, right? Why did you major in that? What were your goals?"

"Originally I'd planned to work in museums, eventually as a curator."

"What stopped you?"

"Marriage and family. My—*our* decision for me to be a stay-at-home mom, which I loved. And I don't mean to seem ungrateful to Wade that he took such good care of me, but in the end I've been left unprepared for finding a job."

"I don't know, Jill. I doubt you're as unprepared as you think."

"What do you mean?"

"Tell me what you think your skills are," he said.

"My skills," she mused. "I never had a cook, so I always did the cooking myself, even for fancy parties."

"Okay. And your husband was a CEO. You'd be an executive's chef."

She smiled.

"What else?" he asked.

"I was an extraordinary classroom volunteer."

He thought for a moment. "Education consultant."

"I ran charity rummage sales."

"Director of charitable fund-raising."

Oh, he was good. "I managed the snack stand at soccer matches and basketball games."

"Manager of inventory and retail sales."

"I plan great parties."

"Well, aside from the obvious, how about public relations consultant? And you've been a personal assistant to an executive."

"A very personal assistant," Jill added. "And I can decorate a mean birthday cake."

He frowned, cocked his head, frowned some more. "I can't think of anything for that."

"I can," she said, almost breathless. "I really can. Why couldn't I work in a bakery as a cake decorator?"

"Minimum wage, Jill? Really?"

"Maybe not minimum. At the assembly-line places that might be true, but at a specialty shop? You know, where the cakes are artistic creations?" The idea took root. "And probably looking for Christmas help."

"Probably."

They didn't talk for a while. "I need to go home and get the photos of the cakes I've done. I've got an album." Thank goodness she'd taken pictures of every cake. "My resume would be short."

"Think of it as concise."

She smiled. "Okay."

"You know, we've been joking about job possibilities, but I have to say, Jill, you've got a degree from a highly respected institution. That's going to help open doors."

"If or when I look for full-time, permanent work, I hope my degree will help. For now I want to fill my time with something fun. Is there something wrong with that?"

"Not at all."

She didn't want him to leave. She wanted him to stay so that they could talk more in the morning, after she'd thought about things for a while, and written down some ideas in her diary. "Are you sure you won't spend the night? We could take the train home together. I'll fix you eggs benedict," she sing-songed.

"Bribery will get you everywhere."

"You'll stay?"

"Yeah."

She tried not to show her surprise. He'd seemed so definite earlier about not staying. What had changed his mind?

Suddenly she was starved. She popped some olives in her mouth then debated about what else to eat from the assortment on the plate.

"Why don't I take you out for dinner?" he said. "You can show me the neighborhood."

"You're on country hours. People don't eat dinner around here for hours yet."

"So we'll beat the rush. Come on. Be daring."

They wandered the streets for a while, found a restaurant she hadn't eaten at before then lingered until they felt guilty taking up space with people waiting to be seated. She told him about the girls not coming home for Thanksgiving. He said his sons were staying put, too. They both lived in California, Matt a grad student at UC Berkeley and Jason a video-game designer in the Silicon Valley. Even as close as they lived to each other, they apparently didn't get together much.

"But we're all meeting in Vail for Christmas," Alan said as they took the elevator up to the loft. "Funny how they can free up time for the old man if he pays for a ski trip. Anyway, I decided to head down to Florida to see my folks for Thanksgiving. I'll probably go on Tuesday and come back on Saturday."

"Have you checked to see if they're going to be home?" They'd reached her door. She unlocked it.

"Amazingly, yes. They're headed to Hawaii for Christmas, though. For three weeks."

"No dust settles on them."

"We should all be so active at seventy-five."

Jill and Alan stopped when they reached the living room. "Well," she said, suddenly at a loss. They'd never spent so much time together. She could've gone on talking for hours, but decided against it. "Ten o'clock. I think I'll go to bed. I'm exhausted."

"Okay."

"I'll get your bedding, if you want to open the sleeper sofa." She headed upstairs. "I know you don't have a change of clothes for tomorrow. Do you need to wash something? I can put a small load in the washer tonight, then dry it in the morning."

"You don't need to take care of me."

Why not? It was what she did. What she was good at.

Slightly annoyed at the rejection, she carried an armload of linens downstairs. He'd moved the coffee table aside and opened the sofa. She dumped everything in the middle of it. He didn't want help? Okay, then.

"The television is inside the armoire," she said. "Good night."

She heard him laugh quietly as she stalked upstairs. "What's so funny?"

"You."

At the top of the stairs she leaned over the railing, saw him tug the fitted bottom sheet onto the mattress. "Yeah, I'm a barrel of laughs."

He looked up, seeking her, then smiled. "You never used to get annoyed."

"Yes, I did. I just didn't show it."

"Well, that's interesting. Can I see the upstairs?"

Was he stalling ending the evening? Or was she reading more into it than the fact he might own the place…well, actually did own the place, and he just wanted to see it?

"Sure." She glanced around the room, wondering what he would think. He must've taken the stairs two at a time, because he was there so fast she didn't have time to grab her party clothes from atop the bed to stuff in the closet.

"It looks like you, Jill."

His hands were tucked in his back pockets—when had she started noticing that was how he stood?

"Nothing like the Connecticut house," she said.

"Nope. And yet, you."

"Is it something you could live with?"

"All except the girly bedspread." He pointed toward the bathroom. "Can I take a look?"

She nodded, but didn't follow him.

"Great room," he called out. "Spacious. Terrific shower. Whirlpool tub. Have you used it?"

"A few times. I thought you chose all the fixtures and appliances, though."

"Yeah. I did a good job, didn't I?"

She laughed and agreed.

He came out of the bathroom. "Storage room through that door, right?"

"Yes. It could be made into a second bedroom, if necessary, although not a large one."

He opened the door, flipped on the light and stepped inside. "Not much in here."

"I decided not to bring a whole lot until I decide whether I'm staying."

He walked past her then headed onto the bridge leading to the office. She didn't follow because the area was small and she would be too close to him for comfort. Everything already felt too…intimate.

Too late she realized she'd left a stack of profiles of potential Internet dates next to her computer. She saw him glance at the top page, but he said nothing. Embarrassment wrapped her in heat. She wanted to crawl in bed and pull the covers over her head.

"On the hunt, are you?" he asked as he came up to her.

"I knew you couldn't resist."

"Teasing you? Nope."

But his eyes said something different. His eyes questioned, showed concern, worry.

"I haven't put myself out there yet, Alan. I'm just sort of exploring the whole idea."

He laid a hand on the side of her head. "Just be careful."

"I will."

He didn't move. She needed for him to move, to stop touching her, so she decided to irritate him. "Are you sure I can't throw your clothes in the washer? I mean, I know you can turn your underwear inside out, but …" She waited for him to snap back.

He did take his hand away, which helped, then he whispered, "I don't wear any," and left.

That image was burned into her mind as she climbed into bed fifteen minutes later. He had the television on, the volume low. If he didn't wear underwear he would be naked in bed. She closed her eyes but it didn't stop the image of him climbing out of her swimming pool months ago—the broad shoulders, kind of hairy chest and very nice rear end.

She could go downstairs and slip into bed beside him. Maybe he would take her into his arms. Maybe he would reject her. He liked her, she knew that, but he was her friend, had been Wade's best friend. It put a barrier between them, one she didn't want to tear down. She valued her friendship with him too much to risk putting him on the spot.

But she definitely needed to find a man like him.

CHAPTER 12

Sunday, November 11
1. Get some goldfish crackers.
2. Get laid. There's hope!
3. ~~Have ego stomped on — make P-U profile public~~.
4. Create an employment plan.
5. Portfolio of cake designs.
6. ~~Write~~ Fabricate a resume.

"I'm making hollandaise sauce," Jill said to Ilene the next morning, the phone notched between her ear and shoulder as she stirred.

"Eggs benedict! I'll be there in fifteen minutes."

"Um. I have company."

"Why you sly minx. Spill."

"Alan spent the night." She turned the heat off under the sauce so that she could move into the living room and listen for sounds from upstairs. "He's in the shower now."

"Well?"

"Well, what?"

"How was it?"

"I didn't sleep with him." She probably should've put some heat behind the words, act surprised that Ilene had suggested such a thing. "He's my friend, Ilene. Friends don't sleep together."

"That's so totally naïve."

The shower stopped. Jill moved back into the kitchen. "Did you get Melon Man home okay?"

"Ah. The subject is closed, hmm? Okay. As for Hans, I had to give the cab driver an extra twenty to help me get the jerk into his apartment."

"Your experience doesn't make me want to run out there and find a man, you know. Heck, they even end up costing you."

"Not me. I took a twenty out of his wallet."

Jill grinned. "Of course you did."

"We're gonna make you street-smart yet, hon."

"Probably so. You're an education in itself."

"Thank you very much. Are you sure I can't join you for breakfast? I mean, if you don't want him ..."

You're not his type. Jill couldn't say the words aloud, couldn't hurt her friend that way. "We're headed back to Connecticut shortly."

"That wasn't in your plan, was it? Are you staying long?"

"A couple of days probably. I'll call you when I get back. Do you think Rafael might refer you to his clients?"

"I'm sure he has friends in the business he already recommends, but who knows? He sure had his eye on you. Don't deny it," she added. "You had to have seen it."

"He asked if he could call me."

"I figured. And you spent a long time in the hall with Bobby."

"I did, didn't I?" Jill waited, wondering how Ilene felt, knowing she'd flirted with both men—well, three, really, counting Alan—and not interesting any of them. It seemed ridiculous to Jill that any man would prefer her over Ilene.

"Looks like going public with P-U is going to stay on your list a while longer."

Hopefully forever. "It hasn't happened yet. They have to call. I have to say yes."

"They will and you will. It'll be fine. Well, I think I'll go get myself some groceries so I can feed myself."

"Bypass the produce section."

Ilene laughed, and they said goodbye. Jill heated the water for the poached eggs. She'd already toasted the English muffins. They were being kept warm in the oven, along with the Canadian bacon. As soon as Alan came down she would fix the eggs.

She sipped her coffee, waiting, admiring the gift that Cheryl had brought the night before—a beautifully framed page from a magazine of the loft she'd admired years ago and Wade had torn out and kept, then had built for her. In his handwriting in the lower right corner he'd written, "Wishes come true." Smiling, she ran her finger along the words then propped it against her cookbooks. She needed to find the perfect place to hang it. In her bedroom, probably. Someplace personal.

Jill glanced around the room, making sure everything was ready for breakfast. The dining room table was set.

A platter of grapes, strawberries and cantaloupe left over from the open house made a colorful centerpiece on the table. Alan had slipped out earlier to get the Sunday *Times*, but she hadn't glanced at it yet, although the classified section sang a siren song, tempting her with the help-wanted ads. Now that she'd made up her mind, she wanted to act.

Jill heard him turn on her blow-dryer. It had been strange waking up and having him there in a place she'd come to associate with starting over. He was part of her past, yet he was firmly in her present.

The phone rang. She glanced at the clock. Barely nine. Since she'd already talked to Ilene, and the girls would call her cell phone, she guessed it might be Bobby. She didn't want to talk to him. Not yet. But if she let it go to the answering machine, Alan would hear it, since it sat on her bedside table.

She snatched up the receiver after the third ring, just in time to avoid the machine automatically answering.

"Hello?"

"Good morning, Ms. One-name."

Shoot. "Hi, Bobby."

"Did you get a good night's rest?" he asked.

"I did, thanks."

Silence hovered for a few seconds. "Aren't you going to ask if I slept well?"

"I figure you're about to tell me."

He chuckled. "I barely slept. Kept having dreams of a certain gorgeous, mysterious woman."

The blow-dryer stopped, limiting Jill's options for a response.

"How about spending the day with me?" he asked into her silence. "Picnic in the park. Sound good?"

"I'm headed home for a few days."

"Go tomorrow instead."

His voice enticed. Promised. I'll make it worth your while, it seemed to say. "I can't. I'm riding with a friend."

"The writer?"

"Yes."

"I see."

"No, you don't." Alan was making his way down the stairs. She wasn't sure what to say next that he could overhear and Bobby would accept without further question.

"Can I call you later in the week?" Bobby asked.

"That would be great."

"Would it, Jill?"

"What do you mean?"

"It's not a complicated question."

Alan raised his brows as he drew near. He knew, had figured out she was talking to a man.

"I mean what I say," she said into the phone.

"Okay. Have a good trip."

"Thanks. 'Bye."

"Which member of your court was that?" Alan asked.

She turned away. The water for the eggs was boiling. She added a teaspoon of vinegar. Acrid steam rose, making her eyes tear up. She'd already cracked three eggs into three separate bowls and now slid them into the water. She'd always loved that part of the process, watching the eggs cook in the water.

"That was Bobby," she said.

"I thought so. D'Amato wouldn't call this early in the morning."

"You've got it all figured out, don't you?"

"Wish I did. Want some help?"

The quick change of subject relieved some of her tension. "Everything's under control. Go ahead and pour yourself a cup of coffee."

A few minutes later they sat down to eat, then kept to safe topics. After cleaning up the kitchen they had time to read some of the paper, each claiming a corner of the sofa, commenting on what they read. Jill enjoyed herself. She'd missed this kind of—

Actually, she'd never had this kind of Sunday morning. Wade had a standing tee time for early Sunday mornings, or handball when the weather didn't cooperate for golf. Or he'd gone somewhere to ski. Or hike. Sunday hadn't been a family day, much less a lounge-around-with-the-*Times*-and-have-brunch day.

He'd spent time with the family on weeknights and some Saturdays. Jill and the girls were so used to his routine that she hadn't thought about his selfishness in planning most of the weekend hours away from them.

He'd played hard. Lived hard. Loved hard, too. Maybe he'd somehow known he would die young and had needed to fill his time on earth to overflowing. Jill had been proud of how she hadn't held him back from accomplishing his dreams, including climbing Mt. McKinley, then the more challenging Mt. Everest.

And his daughters had loved him, no matter how much—or little—time he'd spent with them, quality time, which the experts claim is important. Except... Shanna was never particularly close to him. Tori had openly adored him, copying his athletic interests, silently seeking his approval, which hadn't resulted in his spending more time with her. Her grief now was all the more devastating to watch. She was so much like Wade in her drive to succeed.

But Tori needed to find balance in her life better than he had. So did Shanna. Her all-work, no-play life could come back to haunt her.

"You're quiet," Alan said, setting aside the newspaper.

"Thinking about the girls."

"Still upset that they won't be home for Thanksgiving?"

"I've accepted it. I'm just worried. Shanna seems to be sinking into the same abyss as Tori. She doesn't call, and when I do connect with her, I can't ask her any questions. Even 'How are you?' is enough for her to clam up."

"What do you talk about?"

She heard a hint of something in his voice, as if she were to blame. "What are you saying? That I push too hard?"

"I'm not privy to your conversations."

"That's not an answer, Alan. I try not to mother them.

I know they need space, and now that I've told them about the loft, we talk about that a little. Mostly they're both just wanting me to keep myself busy and off their case. At least Tori wants to spend some time here over Christmas, which makes having this place a good idea already. I think she'll love being in the city. She can't see enough plays to make her happy."

"Has she tried out for campus productions?"

"If she has, she hasn't said so. I hope she has. She needs something to focus on. It sure helped me, having the loft to decorate and the city to explore."

"I can see that." He glanced at his watch. "We should probably head to the station."

Jill spent enough time in both homes that she didn't have to transport much when she traveled back and forth. She grabbed her tote bag to carry the help-wanted ads and her purse while Alan pulled his sweater over his head.

Now that she knew he didn't wear underwear she worked at keeping her gaze above his waist, but for the split second it took for him to pull the sweater past his eyes, she looked. She'd decided to stop criticizing herself for her interest, acknowledging that her needs that had sparked back to life a few months ago were now behaving more like Mount St. Helens, unpredictable and ready to erupt at any time.

The phone rang as they were leaving.

"That would be D'Amato," Alan said, holding the door open so that Jill could run back and answer the phone.

"I'll pick up messages from home later."

"Chicken," he taunted.

She made clucking sounds of agreement, keeping things light.

Her across-the-hall neighbor opened his door then and said good-morning. He was one half of a power couple in their early thirties, he a lawyer, she a stockbroker. He eyed Alan speculatively, then they all moved toward the elevator.

"I suppose you have Thanksgiving plans," her neighbor said, punching the down button.

"Nothing firm." She figured she and Ilene would do something, but they hadn't talked about it.

"Cherise and I have invited a small group. We'd love to have you. You're welcome to bring a guest." His gaze shifted briefly to Alan and back.

"How nice, thank you, Sean. I appreciate the invitation. Can I get back to you in a couple of days?"

"No problem."

"Oh, and thanks again for the caterer recommendation. I was really happy with the job Rose did."

"She's consistent and reliable. Cherise and I use her quite a bit."

They chitchatted until they left the building and went separate ways.

"There's a source," Alan said as he hailed a cab.

"What?"

"Your neighbors. You've already made contact. Start asking about jobs."

She turned in the direction Sean had gone, but he was already out of sight. "I'll do that."

Jill couldn't get a handle on Alan's mood as they made the trip home. She was aware of him, their arms touching as they sat side by side on the train. He read ads with her. She circled very few possibilities.

When he dropped her off at her house, he seemed like a different person—distant and distracted.

"Are you okay?" she asked as he pulled into her driveway.

"Yeah. Sorry. I was thinking ahead to the scene I'll be working on."

Was that the truth? There'd been a shift in their relationship. He'd seemed annoyed—or something—that she might start dating before the official year of mourning was up. She felt guilty enough without him adding to it, however.

"Thanks for everything," she said.

He nodded. That was all. A nod. As if they were mere acquaintances.

As soon as she went inside she checked her messages at the loft. It hadn't been Rafael who'd called but Mrs. Q. thanking her for the invitation.

Jill hugged herself. Three down, two to go. She would win over Iris and Wendi somehow, some way.

A few minutes later Jill changed into jeans and a sweatshirt, then climbed the stairs to the attic, which she'd commandeered as her own years ago. Part of the large space was storage, but the rest was all hers. Her sewing machine sat on an antique sewing table overlooking the backyard. Memories flooded her—making sundresses for the girls when they were little, and costumes for Halloween and school plays. Tables were set up for cutting fabric, wrapping presents and doing crafts. Bookcases held photo albums. She could put her hand on the exact album she needed. She'd always ordered double prints of each cake, putting one copy in the album showcasing the occasion then the other copy in her cake binder.

She thumbed through it, moseying down memory lane. She'd come a long way from her first simple efforts for the girls' birthdays. Eventually she'd even done two wedding cakes, small ones, but intricately decorated. Every kind of holiday was represented, as well as baby and wedding showers, graduations and congratulations.

Jill closed the album and hugged it to her chest. She was about to go downstairs to use the scanner and computer in the family room, but instead returned to the bookcase with the albums and chose one from the year she and Wade met. He'd been transferred to San Francisco with the airline and had hooked up with an old college buddy who taught at Mills College in Oakland, one of Jill's professors. Wade had arrived at her professor's office for lunch just as Jill was finishing up a midsemester conference.

Love at first sight. The seven-year age difference had meant nothing to either of them. Neither did the fact their backgrounds were so different. He'd been raised in an upper-crust New England family with roots traceable to the Mayflower. Her parents had embraced the counterculture movement. She'd spent her teen years being dragged to protest marches, and dressed in tank tops, torn jeans and sneakers. He'd escorted young women to debutante balls, and wore suits and ties, khakis and polo shirts. His style had never changed. Hers had turned 180 degrees within a month after they married. After three years in San Francisco he'd been transferred to New York City, and she was uprooted from her family to live in a world she'd seen only on television and in movies.

Although she'd had to make a lot of adjustments, she'd been happy. She would've been happier if Wade's parents had made her feel welcome, especially after her parents died five years after her wedding, but it hadn't happened. Nor had Wade's death brought them closer.

Jill slid the photo album back into its place then went in search of a box stacked in the storage side of the room. She dragged it into the main room and hefted it onto a table. Inside were her diaries, one for every year since she was ten.

Every book was different, representing where she was in life that year. She pulled out the one from the year she met Wade. The flower-printed cover made her smile. She perused the rest of the books, filed in chronological order, the covers transitioning from bright colors and designs to sedate ones, from plastic to cloth to leather. The last five were identical—maroon with gold trim.

What would she choose this year? Something hopeful. Something full of life.

She carried the diary and cake-photo album downstairs, then spent the day scanning and designing and printing copies for her portfolio. Her resume was definitely concise. Without paid employment, she was limited to listing her skills and education.

If only someone could see how organized she was, how competent she could be, how reliable. Those were coveted skills in the business world.

What kind of clothes should she choose for job-hunting? It took only a few seconds in her closet to know those outfits wouldn't work. Everything branded her as a suburban homemaker. There was nothing wrong with that, except that wasn't who she was anymore. She'd gotten into a habit of wearing clothes from her Darien closet when she was there, and New York in New York.

But she didn't want to put on her Darien clothes anymore.

She wanted to look like she belonged in the city, no matter where she was. She liked her new hairstyle and her smoky eye makeup. She'd lost fifteen pounds—almost back to her weight before Wade's death. And she'd come to terms with the fact the last five were never going to come off. So be it.

Jill spent the evening reading the diaries of her courtship and early marriage. She smiled at the pro-and-con list she'd written about Wade a month after meeting him. There were no con items. She'd been blindly, ecstatically in love.

Could that happen again?

Did she want it to?

Getting married at this age presented complications that were nonexistent the first time around. There would be a melding of households and finances. Children. There was emotional baggage to deal with. Histories. Hurts.

She started a list in her current diary:

> What he should be:
> Smart
> Fun
> Funny
> Sexy
> Loyal
> Successful
> Available

She stopped to contemplate the list, which had poured out of her, one item after the other without her stopping to think. Was there a reason for the particular order of things? Probably. The only item that surprised her was the last one—available. Anyone reading her list might think she meant available as in single and ready and willing. But she'd meant it as being available to her, to them as a couple, each of them working at what made them happy, but then coming home and being together.

That was what she'd missed the most with Wade. She'd loved him, and she knew he'd loved her. But she'd spent too much time without him.

It would be different with the next man, if there was one. She would insist on it.

CHAPTER 13

Wednesday, November 14
1. Never get a dog. What was I thinking? It couldn't commute with me.
2. Get laid. If I keep ignoring phone messages from potential dates, it's never going to happen.
3. Practice cake decorating skills.
4. Pound the pavement for a job. What idiot said change is good? Change is just plain scary.

Jill stayed in Darien less than twenty-four hours. In the city she bought cake pans to turn upside-down and practice on, researched specialty-cake bakeries and found more than she would've imagined. Over the next few days she made a couple hundred frosting roses from buds to full blooms, even practicing tinting the icing to add color just to the edge of the petals. She piped scalloped edges until her eyes crossed and her hands cramped. She bought powdered sugar in bulk. Her entire kitchen was dusted with the white stuff.

She also screened her phone calls, not wanting Bobby

or Rafael to know she'd returned, needing to focus her time and energy on the job search.

How much time and energy does it take to answer the phone?

She ignored the pointed question her conscience asked and instead checked out her reflection in her bathroom mirror. It was nine o'clock. Time to head out to the first bakery on her list.

It hadn't been easy finding an outfit to wear, something not too casual nor too dressy. She'd settled on a pumpkin-colored T-shirt, black jacket and slacks, and low heels. She'd mapped out the first sequence of five bakeries, having decided to start with the most prestigious and work her way down to the obscure.

Butterflies swirled, not just in her stomach but everywhere inside her. She didn't mind. She'd gone from taking baby steps to a leap. She would find a solid place to land.

By sheer force of will she didn't open her briefcase in the taxi and double-check her portfolio. Everything would be in place. But the lower half of her face turned numb, so she shifted her jaw back and forth, catching the driver frowning in the mirror at her.

"Trying to make myself relax," she said, forcing her mouth into a smile.

He nodded, then didn't look at her again. She had him let her off a half a block from Suzanne's Cakes, then walked the rest of the way, striding into the shop like she was a pro at job-hunting. She went directly up to the counter.

"May I help you?" The young woman behind the counter wore a long-sleeved black T-shirt, jeans and an electric-blue apron with the Suzanne's Cakes logo on it.

"I'd like to speak with the manager, please," Jill said.

"About?"

"A job."

"Wait over there."

Jill walked to the far end of the counter, pulling out one of her presentation packets as she went but also eyeing the display cases. The cakes and other confections were works of art, unlike any she'd seen in person. Not a frosting rose or scalloped edge in sight, but wonders of fondant and spun sugar and painted-on color and form that spoke to everyone's inner child. Artists had created these visions.

"You're looking for work?" a woman Jill's age asked from across the counter. She looked like she'd never eaten a piece of cake in her life.

"Yes. Hi, I'm Jill Townsend." She tried to pass her portfolio over the glass case, but the woman didn't take it.

"Your experience?"

"Nothing commercial," Jill said, still holding the packet. "I have photographs of my work."

The woman smiled, but it wasn't warm. "I'm sure they're just *lovely*—" the word came out layered with sarcasm "—but we hire only journeymen decorators. If you're willing to work your way up the ladder, we have an opening for a dishwasher."

Jill didn't mind working her way up or proving herself,

but she wasn't desperate. "Thank you for your time," Jill said, then left.

She wasn't discouraged, merely irritated at the woman's brusqueness. She hailed a cab and went to the next place. Sugar House had been in business longer than Suzanne's.

"Not hiring," the counter clerk said with cool politeness, then turned to the person who'd come in behind Jill. "May I help you?"

It became the phrase of the day: Not hiring. Because each encounter took so little time, Jill managed to get to fourteen businesses on her list. No one even looked at her portfolio—until the last one.

The Cakery was a newer business but had garnered acclaim for their creativity from day one. The staff dressed like Parisian artists—tight black T-shirts, black pants and cute red berets. The manager was a man in his thirties who talked and moved at top speed.

"Come on back, honey," he said, signaling with his fingers.

Jill was so startled she didn't move for a second. Someone was actually going to interview her?

"Time's money," he said, his lips thinning.

She followed him into the back room, a large space made small by the array of equipment and tables. She saw refrigerators but no ovens.

"We bake off-site," he said when she questioned it.

She wanted to ask his name, but he took her to a table and told her to stand there, grabbed her briefcase and employment packet, then snapped his fingers for her to give him her jacket. He tossed her an apron and hair cap.

He was putting her to work?

Panic mixed with excitement as she watched him grab two ten-inch round undecorated cakes and a bowl of white icing.

"Show me what you can do," he said, then stood back, his arms crossed, his toe tapping.

White cake and white frosting. A small wedding cake? she wondered, her mind working fast to decide. It was all she could envision.

Her hands shook as she grabbed a knife and sliced off a bit to level each layer. She scooped frosting with a spatula and topped one layer, then stacked the other on top of it. She started working on the sides, smoothing the icing in a thin first layer to seal the crumbs. She would top it with another, thicker layer. She was thinking ahead to how she would decorate the top. She was glad she'd practiced the roses, although she would need a different kind of icing, and a bag—

"Stop." The man pointed to her apron and cap, snapping his fingers.

She passed them to him, heat creeping up her neck to her face.

"Honey," he said, not unkindly. "You don't have what it takes."

I do! "May I show you my portfolio?"

"Doesn't matter. You're probably talented. But what we need is speed. It takes a long time to be able to work under this kind of pressure. Look over there. In the time it took for you to get as far as you did, Maria decorated an entire cake."

"I could become that fast, with practice."

"I don't train on the basics. It's not cost effective. Good luck, honey." He piled her belongings in her arms.

Dismissed.

Jill decided she'd had enough rejection for one day. She headed home, punched the up button with more force than necessary, then paced as she waited. She needed a new game plan. Her lack of experience would brand her wherever she went, at least at the better bakeries.

When the doors opened, Bobby came out. He smiled, blocking her path. She only wanted to get into the elevator and up to her loft. Home.

"I just rang your bell," he said, moving closer. The doors shut before she could get on.

"How'd you get in the building?"

"I'm doing a remodel on the third floor."

"So, this is like your jail," she said, trying to smile, trying to shift gears from her lousy day. "You just move from unit to unit, and when you're done with everyone, you'll start over."

He cupped her head with one hand, gently, soothingly. "You're upset."

Her first reaction was to jerk back. Her second was to throw herself in his arms. He wore a flannel shirt that looked soft and welcoming. His shoulders were broad, his chest wide. His arms would wrap all the way around her.

"I'm all right," she said after a moment.

"No, you're not. But I guess it's none of my business."

He moved back a little, giving her breathing room. She finally managed a smile. "Thanks. How have you been?"

He put a hand to his chest. "Lonely."

She laughed at the pathetic way he said the word. She really did like him, and couldn't understand why he had any problems finding dates. "I'm sorry I haven't returned your calls."

He looked as though he was about to question that but said, "How about having dinner with me Saturday night?"

"Yes." It felt good to make a decision and act on it.

He didn't seem surprised by her answer. "I'll pick you up at eight. You can dress up, if you want."

She nodded, mostly because her throat had started to burn. A date. For the first time in twenty-five years she would being going out with a man other than Wade. "I need to go," she said, angling around him and punching the elevator button. The doors opened instantly, and she hurried inside. Her gaze met his. He hitched his head back in a kind of reverse nod, saying "Yo" without saying the word.

As soon as she got into her loft she called Ilene. "No one wants to hire me, and I just said yes to a date with Bobby," she said in a rush.

"Which bothers you the most?"

Jill had to think about that. "The date's scary."

"What're you going to wear?"

"He said to dress up." She filled her teakettle and put it on the stove. "I need something new."

"Something sexy."

"Not too. I don't want to give the wrong impression."

"I think his impression is already pretty clear."

"I won't sleep with him on the first date."

"Okay."

"I won't. I have much more self-control than that."

"Okay."

Ilene's doubtful tone made Jill laugh. She grabbed a mug and a blueberry tea bag.

"Just in case, hon, you should buy yourself some spectacular new lingerie."

"On the contrary, I should wear my oldest, plainest stuff. That way I won't be tempted at all."

"And some condoms," Ilene continued as if Jill hadn't spoken. "And make sure he uses them. No excuses. Obviously you light his fire, but you don't know where he's dipped his wick."

"That's blunt."

"All part of the big-city education of Jill Townsend. You can't tell me you haven't thought about it."

"I've thought about it."

Ilene gave a knowing laugh. "Okay. No excuse for being stupid, then."

Despite the light tone, it was the most serious Ilene had been. "I've given my daughters the same talk," Jill said.

"You mess up and I'll be ticked at you forever."

"I won't mess up. And maybe someday you'll tell me why this is so important to you."

"Maybe I will. Listen, I've got to meet a client. You want to get dinner tomorrow night?"

"Sure. I'll check with you tomorrow about where and when."

A few minutes later Jill curled up on her sofa, both hands wrapped around her mug, the blueberry scent relaxing her. What a day. She needed to rethink her job search. She dragged the contents of her briefcase into her lap. Next to each bakery she'd gone into she wrote the reason why she was turned down. Five said there were no openings, although the one offered her the dishwasher job. Nine said she didn't have enough experience.

Okay. She needed to set her sights a little lower if she wanted to get a job that would give her enough experience to move up the hierarchy of bakeries.

She tapped a finger on the paperwork. Maybe she should create a design of her own, something tangible. People could choose not to open a photo album, but they couldn't ignore an actual product.

She sketched a design for a Christmas cake, spent time refining it, then realized she needed to head to her support group. She'd been too wrapped up in her project to eat, so she grabbed an apple as she headed out her door.

She needed fortification if she was going to confront Wendi tonight. It was time she became a full-fledged member of society.

* * *

"Jill!"

Jill had taken two steps down the basement stairs when she heard Wendi call her name. By the time she reached the bottom, Wendi was there, clutching a large manila envelope and looking animated. And *smiling*. So, her excitement over meeting Alan had carried over.

"Hi, Wendi. How are you?" Jill became aware of Iris moving toward them.

"I'm good." Wendi shoved the envelope at Jill. "I need for you to give this to Alan Haggerty. Please."

"What is it?"

"My book."

"Your…book. One that you wrote?"

"Uh huh. I know he'll want to read it."

A rock and a hard place crushed Jill from both sides. She knew Alan got sent manuscripts frequently through his publisher or agent and read none of them. Occasionally acquaintances would ask him to read their efforts. He turned them down, as well. He'd figured out how to say no without offending anyone. Well, almost. Some people sniped, but he didn't care.

So, what should she do? Squelch Wendi's return to the world by giving her manuscript back to her? Or beg Alan to break a fifteen-year, self-imposed, never-before-broken rule of never reading amateur work?

Jill had come prepared to confront Wendi about getting professional help, yet here she was, looking recovered. Or at least hopeful. She'd even pulled her hair into a ponytail, which had opened up her pretty face.

"I'll give it to him," Jill said. "But he's on deadline, so I'm not sure when he can get around to it."

Wendi hugged her. "Oh, thank you. Thank you so much."

Jill looked past her to Iris, who stood with arms crossed and forehead creased. Wendi's transformation brought light to the gloomy basement. In fact, the dynamics of the entire group had seemed to change since the open house. Except for Iris, everyone was more friendly.

"I'm surprised you're still coming here," Iris said to Jill, as they trailed Wendi back to the group.

"Why wouldn't I?"

"Seems to me you run in circles none of us do. You have a lot of friends. Anyone can see that. Why here? Why us?"

So, it was time for a showdown. Jill had come week after week, giving herself something to do, hoping for help, but having the subject changed whenever she brought up her grief or her daughters'.

Now or never, she decided, then took her seat. "I'll answer that, but in return I'd like for each of you to also answer that question. Will you?"

They all exchanged glances. Jill almost sighed. They were so attached to each other, they couldn't make a simple decision on their own.

Finally, Mrs. Q. said okay.

"All of you?"

Everyone except Iris nodded. Wendi even made eye contact.

"Four out of five will have to do." Jill folded her hands in her lap. "Iris seems to think that since I have a lot of friends, I have no reason to be here. The people I call friends are actually few in number. Regardless of that, what I don't have is any widowed friends. Everyone tries very hard to understand what I am going through, but they haven't lived it. With all of you, I thought I would have a shorthand, since you've been through it. I know we all experience grief individually, but there are commonalities, too. I needed to be with people who understood those."

"Have you found that with us?" Mrs. Q. asked.

"I wish I could say yes. Maybe because I've been widowed the shortest amount of time, I'm in a very different place. Maybe I have more needs than you. How about the rest of you?"

"I come out of habit," Mrs. Q. said. "Been alone for ten years. Here and church is where I feel at home."

"So you only see this as a social outlet?" Jill asked. "Your grief is behind you and you have no need to talk about it?"

The stately woman was quiet for several long seconds. "I grieve the loss of my man every day. I don't talk about it because people think like you do—that after ten years I should be over it. I had my soul mate. There isn't another one like him. Everyone here understands that."

"Not me," said Birdie. "I think there are lots of people

in this world you can love. Maybe there is that one soul mate, but there are plenty of men who come close enough."

"So why do you keep coming?" Jill asked.

"I guess it's habit for me, too, after seven years. It gets me out of the house and gives me a place to be. No one here tells me what I should or shouldn't be doing. Everyone is just my friend."

"You also date."

"That's right. And unlike others here—" she glanced at Iris and Mrs. Q. "—I see no problem with you dating whenever you're ready."

Jill caught the censure in Birdie's tone. "You talk about me?"

"Of course we do," she said with a mischievous grin. "You're fresh blood. We always talk about the newcomers."

"I hear you chase off newcomers."

"Didn't chase you off," Iris said.

"She's not easily intimidated," Jacob commented.

"That's how you see me?" Jill asked, surprised.

"That's the truth."

She would think that over later. "And why are you here, Jacob?"

"I live in the neighborhood."

"It can't be that simple."

He shrugged.

"Do you expect to keep coming forever?" she pushed.

He didn't answer for a while. Tension crept into the room as they all waited.

"I've been thinking about leaving," he said.

The reaction came fast and strong. Cries of "You can't" and "No" and "We won't let you" rang out.

"This is all her fault," Iris said, pointing at Jill.

"Mine? Why?"

"You're always encouraging us to get out there and live."

Silence followed her accusation.

"Do you hear what you're saying, Iris?" Jacob asked kindly.

"Well, I didn't mean it exactly like that. I meant she's pushy!"

"We each have our own timetable, as Birdie says," Jacob said. "I met someone a few months back. I will never forget my Daniel, but Gordon makes life worth living again. I'm only sixty-three. There's a lot of life left in me."

Iris glared at Jill, who ignored her. "I'm happy for you, Jacob."

"Thanks, Jill. And you, sweet Wendi? What keeps you coming?"

"These are my friends."

"I don't even know if you have a job or how you fill your days," Jill said.

"I'm a live-in nanny."

Jill tried to picture her in that role. Maybe with children she was different, more lively, more adventurous. "Have you dated at all?"

"No."

"And you've been widowed for five years?"

"Yes, since I was twenty-five."

"Do you want to date?"

"I've been thinking about it, especially since you started coming and asking questions. But I don't have many opportunities to meet men."

"I did go speed dating," Jill said. None of them had ever asked if she'd gone through with it, and she'd kept quiet, embarrassed that she'd left the way she had. She told them now about the process but not her particular experience, which then led to talk about Internet dating.

"Here's what I learned about that," Birdie announced.

"You?" Mrs. Q. asked in amazement.

"How do you think I find so many men? Been doing it for years. Not a lot to choose from when you're my age, but they're out there. Anyway, here's what I know. First, they're usually shorter than they say. Don't know why, but they lie about it most of the time—unless they're five ten or more. Second, they always find a way to tell you how much money they make, maybe not the exact amount, but how successful they are. It defines them."

Jill started to smile. She hadn't figured out Birdie at all. The woman was a multimillionaire and knew all this stuff about men. Go figure.

"Third, they all say they look and act younger than their age."

"Did you find it true?" Jill ask.

"Not usually. Sometimes, though. Men really don't have a realistic perception of themselves."

Jill laughed, but she was the only one.

"Fourth, they let you know the size of their penis."

Audible gasps came from everyone except Jacob, who chuckled.

"I swear." Birdie crossed her heart. "Whether you sleep with 'em or not, they find out some way to tell you. Sometimes it's a warning, like they're really small or really big. Sometimes it's a brag. Nine out of ten men have let me know, though. So, take that information and file it, Miss Wendi."

"I will," Wendi said seriously.

"Me, too," Jill said with a grin.

"Last…" Birdie frowned. "There's one other thing, but darned if I can remember. When I do, I'll let you know."

"Thank you, Birdie," Jill said, a little shell-shocked. "I'm sure you saved me a lot of stumbling around, trying to sort these guys out."

"Glad I could be of help. You've been very sweet to me."

They invited Jill to go to Starbucks after the meeting. Although flattered and grateful, she declined. "I'm exhausted after job-hunting today," she said. "Next week, though. If we're meeting, that is."

"Why wouldn't we?" Mrs. Q. asked.

"It's the day before Thanksgiving. Is everyone staying in town?"

"I'll be gone," Jacob said. "Heading to Vermont."

"Are you going to come back?" Mrs. Q. asked. "I mean, to here, to us."

"Maybe not every week."

Everyone got quiet. Things were changing. Jill knew

that if this relationship worked out for Jacob, he probably wouldn't be back. But that was how it was supposed to be. He'd healed enough to move on.

Jill gave him a big hug when they all left the church and were about to go their separate ways. "Good luck, Jacob."

"Same to you. You're going to be fine, you know."

"Two steps forward and one back."

"It's the forward ones that matter most, but backwards gives you time to regroup, too, and stay sensible." He regarded her with a thoughtful appraisal, as if he'd suddenly figured her out. "I don't think you ask for help much, so you probably need those backward steps more than most."

He'd figured out her biggest weakness. "I hate asking for help."

"I've learned that friends feel helpless. They'd love to do something for me, but don't know what. Maybe your daughters feel that way, too."

"How can I ask them for help? They need more help than I do."

"Maybe if you ask them, they'll ask you in return. Maybe they see you being so strong and independent, and think they need to be like you. You're the role model, after all." He patted her on the shoulder. "It's just a thought. So long." He caught up with the rest of the group, who'd gone ahead.

Could she do what Jacob said? Could she let her daughters see her weaknesses? Her vulnerabilities? *Had* she been too strong? She hadn't realized there *was* such a thing.

Food for thought.

CHAPTER 14

Saturday, November 17
1. Get a statue of a cat. Get two—one for each house.
2. Get laid. But not tonight. Resist all temptation.
3. Finish Christmas cake sample.
4. Find someone willing to take a chance on me for a job.
5. Date with Bobby.
6. Breathe in. Breathe out.

It was date night. Because Jill was standing at her front window overlooking the street, she saw Bobby get out of a cab at 7:59 p.m. His blond hair glinted under the streetlights, offering a golden contrast to his all-black clothes.

The cab drove off and Bobby looked up. She waved, not knowing if he could see her. Then after a moment, the lobby-entry doorbell chimed. Surprised, she hurried to the video screen by her front door and saw him waiting at the outside entry.

She pushed the speaker button. "Hi. Did you forget your key?"

"Thought you'd rather I give you a few seconds' warning." He killer-smiled into the camera. Her question was answered. He hadn't caught her looking at him.

"That was thoughtful of you, Bobby." And surprising. He hadn't exactly been subtle since she'd met him—about anything. She'd been prepared for him just to show up.

Jill pressed the unlock button, waited until he entered the lobby, then made one final check of herself in her powder-room mirror. It was a good hair day, thank heavens. Her makeup looked a little dramatic, but suited to an evening date. Simple black sheath. A gold-heart pendant hung from three twined strands of freshwater pearls. Tall, sexy high heels. Even her perfume was new. Ilene was right—when you feel sexy, it shows.

Because she was standing near her front door she heard the elevator ping its arrival on her floor. She pressed a hand to her stomach for a moment then opened her door. It was silly to wait for him to knock, since they both knew he was arriving.

He didn't rush, and his smile broadened as he neared. She smiled back, her nerves not settling but not incapacitating her, either.

"You just stepped out of my dreams," he said, then bent to kiss her cheek, his warm breath dusting her ear, sending shivers through her. "Smell good, too."

"So do you." She didn't touch him in return, was afraid she wouldn't let go. She already seemed drawn to him like the proverbial iron to a magnet. In her case, a piece of *rusty* iron.

"What are you smiling at?" he asked, presenting her with a cellophane-wrapped bouquet.

"Myself." She buried her face in the blooms, enjoying the sharp, distinct scent of the gold, red and orange mums. "These are beautiful, thank you. Come in, please. I need to put them in water."

She felt him watching her and decided to just enjoy the attention. She would have plenty of time later to wonder what he saw in her, especially on that first meeting last August when she'd been dressed in her suburban best and stressed about trying to find out Wade's connection to the loft.

Jill went into the kitchen and grabbed a vase. Bobby followed, stopping at the island, where she had set her cake-in-progress. He spun the turntable slowly, studying at it from all sides. She'd made the sample base out of cardboard, the design that of a wrapped Christmas present, complete with fancy bows and edible gold stars. Smaller, iced boxes were piled around the package. While it wasn't exotic, she thought it was a design that people would buy, because it didn't intimidate. Cutting into it wouldn't break anyone's heart like, say, a sugarplum fairy or a bust of Santa Claus.

"What's this for?" he asked.

"It's an experiment," she said. "What do you think?"

"That we haven't even had Thanksgiving yet."

She smiled. "I'm hoping to find a job as a cake decorator at one of the specialty-cake bakeries for the holidays, but I don't have any paid experience. I thought if I made a sample, people might actually interview me."

"You need to work?"

"No, I *want* to work. Not having much luck, though. I don't suppose you have contacts in the industry." A friend? Family member? Someone you dated?

"Nope. Sorry."

"I've got about thirty more places to apply to, at least of the shops where I'd want to work. This time I'm taking my sample with me."

"Sounds practical." He moved by her tall bookshelf next to the entertainment center. "Are these your daughters?"

"Yes." She set the vase of flowers on the dining room table then joined him. "The blonde is Shanna. She's a senior at Wake Forest. The redhead—at the time of the picture, anyway—is Tori, short for Victoria. She's a freshman at Revere College in Boston."

"Cute girls. Shanna looks like you."

"I guess that's a compliment?"

"A major one."

"Then, thank you. You said you have two kids, too?"

He pulled out his wallet. She caught a quick look at his driver's license, did the math and realized he was only thirty-eight. Seven years younger.

She needed to think about how she felt about that….

She smiled, deciding she felt perfectly fine about it.

"There you go again," he said.

"Sorry?"

"You're smiling. What do you know that I don't know?"

She liked that she threw him off his game a little. He'd always had control, always taken the lead. "I'm enjoying myself."

"Good."

She continued to smile until he finally looked at his wallet again and pulled out his children's pictures. "Twins. Michelle and Michael, age fifteen."

"You made a couple of cute ones yourself. You have a good relationship?"

"Most of the time. Unless I'm playing the dad card."

"I know what you mean. Shanna was a dream to raise, but Tori has always been a challenge. Do you and your ex-wife get along?"

"Yes. Now."

"You didn't used to?"

"She wanted the divorce, but then she made things ugly for a couple of years. It's okay now. She's remarried."

"How do you feel about that? About your children having a stepdad?"

"Nothing I can do about it." His tone was curt, as if he'd said the same thing too many times, maybe to convince himself. "So. We've got eight-thirty reservations. We should go."

As he shoved his wallet in his back pocket, Jill laid a hand on his arm. "I'm sorry for ruining the mood."

He shrugged. "You didn't. I'm okay. You have a coat?"

She'd left it on a hook near the front door. The coat was made of soft, curly wool woven into a zebra pattern. She'd debated two days before buying it. She'd loved it the moment she laid eyes on it but had never owned anything that so loudly said, "Look at me." And people would probably look twice, the coat was so unique. She'd never cared about that kind of attention. In the end she bought it because she loved it. Period.

Bobby took it from her. "Did you bag this on safari?"

She turned her back to him, laughing, as he held it for her. He lifted her hair out from the collar, then cupped her shoulders and turned her toward him. He made eye contact and held it as he slid a hand down her arm and wrapped her hand in his. His thumb slid across her fingers.

"No rings," he said.

"No."

"For tonight or forever?"

"I don't know yet," she said honestly. It felt like cheating if she left them on, but she couldn't keep taking them off and on. Maybe she should move them to her right hand, as Ilene suggested.

He didn't say anything, but guided her out of the apartment, his hand resting on her lower back. When they got into a cab a few minutes later, she didn't slide all the way across the seat but stopped in the middle, leaving just enough room for him.

He leaned close. "Did I tell you how good you smell?"

"Yes."

"It's not just the perfume."

What could she say to that? *Thanks, I make it myself?* She started to laugh.

"Another inside joke?" he asked.

"I'm sorry. That's probably really annoying."

"Yeah, kind of."

"I'm not laughing *at* you."

"Then let me laugh *with* you."

"Okay. A rabbi, a priest and a minister—"

He put a hand against her lips. "Ms. One-name, you're toying with me."

"I'm just enjoying myself."

"You say that as if you didn't expect to. And if that's the case, why did you say yes?"

"I did expect to, or else I wouldn't have said yes." She touched his hand, which rested on his thigh. "Tell me about your children."

Jill had a wonderful evening, although it grew increasingly uncomfortable as she anticipated the end of the night. She had no complaints about the upscale Italian restaurant. Bobby was attentive, her smoked-chicken risotto perfect, and the panna cotta with berry sauce a sweet delight. After dinner they walked a few blocks, people watching and letting their food settle. He took her hand and nestled it with his in his jacket pocket.

"Should I take you home now?" he asked. "Or would you like to get a nightcap somewhere? Listen to some live music, maybe? I know a few places. Just tell me what kind of music you like."

He surprised her. He kept his flirtations to a minimum

while still letting her know how attracted he was. It was an art, Jill decided. A well-practiced art, probably, and as automatic for him as breathing.

And now he'd left the decision about the rest of the evening in her hands. Which accelerated her discomfort even further. She didn't know how the evening would end. Planner that she was, she needed to know. The only thing she knew for sure was that she would to stick to her self-imposed rule about not sleeping with anyone on a first date.

"You're taking a long time to make a simple decision," he said, his breath turning to frosty vapors in the chilly air. "Are you worried about something in particular? Because I want you to know that you're in charge here. Nothing happens that you don't want to happen."

"I wasn't worried about that." *Right. Sure you weren't.* Maybe she needed to test herself and her convictions. "Why don't we just go back to my house for a nightcap or coffee or something."

"Sounds good."

"I'm not going to sleep with you," she blurted.

He nodded seriously but his eyes twinkled. "Noted."

His answer should have relaxed her, but instead added to her tension. As did the cab ride back to her loft. He put his arm around her shoulder and drew her close, not saying a word. She closed her eyes, enjoying the contact, the first long-term touching she'd had in so long. So very, very long.

He held her hand as they went up the elevator and

walked to her door. Her apartment seemed unusually quiet after the city noise. She hung up their coats then started up a CD, a compilation of old jazz classics. She turned the volume down low. She would've lit a candle or two except she thought it might give him the wrong impression.

"What can I get you?" she asked. "Coffee? Brandy?"

"I'm fine."

Jill felt the need of a prop, so she poured a glass of water and brought it with her to the sofa. He'd taken a seat at one end, giving her the option of how close to sit. She sat in the middle, keeping a distance of maybe a foot between them. She took a sip of water then set the glass on the coffee table.

"Do you have Thanksgiving plans?" he asked.

"I'm staying here. Some neighbors invited me to dinner. Ilene's coming, too. How about you?"

"Going to my parents' place in Trenton."

"For the whole four days?"

"Just Thanksgiving. One day with all the relatives is enough. Uncle Sid will start a fight with Uncle Joe. Everyone will take sides. There'll be yelling and gestures and eventually Uncle Joe will grab Aunt Eva and take off in a huff. It's as predictable as having to loosen your belt after the meal."

She smile at the image. "Whose side do you take?"

"I like to mess with them a little. I'll take Joe's for a while, then Sid's."

"A bizarre King Solomon. I've never had family parties

like that. I was an only child, and my parents were nomadic. My grandparents died before I was born. Wade was an only child, too. We celebrated holidays with his parents sometimes, but it was always…quiet. And formal."

"I wouldn't like that."

"Sometimes we have to do things because we have to."

"Yeah." He picked up her glass and took a sip.

There was a certain implied intimacy about his drinking from her glass. If she drank from it again, did that say something?

Oh, brother. She was worrying about stuff that didn't matter. Chances are he was just thirsty and the glass was sitting there. She hadn't asked if he wanted water, after all.

They seemed to have run out of things to say. After a whole evening of almost nonstop talking, they'd reached saturation point. He liked sports and action movies. She liked art and romantic comedies. He did things spur of the moment. She planned, made lists, followed through. He was family oriented. She had almost no family.

What was left was physical attraction.

"Maybe I should go," he said, angling toward her.

Go? Already?

"I had a good time, Jill."

"Me, too."

He stood, so she did, as well. She followed him down the hallway. Why did she feel like crying? She felt assaulted from all sides by loneliness, need and fear, but especially loneliness. He was being a gentleman, taking her at her word that she wouldn't sleep with him. She should be grateful for that. Instead she wanted him to just throw her over his shoulder and carry her upstairs, so that she would have no responsibility in the matter.

He lifted his jacket from the coat hook, then turned to her. He frowned. "What's wrong?"

She didn't know what to say. She needed him. Needed to be touched. And held. Cherished. She needed to touch him, too, to get lost in passion. To feel like a woman, desired and special. The absolute vulnerability stunned her.

His gaze fixed on hers, he rehung his jacket, the action seeming like slow motion. And then he kissed her, not with a slow lead-in but an all-out assault. His mouth tasted exotic in its unfamiliarity. His arms tightened around her as his tongue plunged into her mouth, then his hands slid down her back and cupped her rear, lifting her higher and closer. He dragged his mouth along her jaw, touched his tongue to that tender spot below her ear. She wriggled and gasped and dug her fingers into him.

He groaned, then went still. "What now?" he asked, harsh and low.

"Don't go." The spontaneous order startled her. She had a second before he responded when she might have taken back her words, but she let them stand.

"Are you sure?"

She didn't want time to reconsider. "Yes."

He took her hand and headed for her stairway, then

set his hands on her waist and guided her up the steps ahead of him. When they'd almost reached the top, she heard the rasp of her zipper as he pulled it down, then a wash of cool air making her shiver, and then the hot touch of his hand on her exposed flesh. They hadn't even made it to the bed before her dress was on the floor, pooled at her feet.

She had no idea what to do with her hands. Her first inclination was to cover up what her revealing lingerie didn't.

He whistled, long and low and flatteringly. "I would've guessed you were a panty-hose woman, One-name."

"I surprised myself, as well." It was the sexiest lingerie she'd ever owned—a scallop-edged bra, matching French-cut underwear and a lace garter belt, all in black. When she'd looked at herself in the mirror before stepping into her dress, she'd felt almost a physical shift from middle-aged mom to hot mama.

Her anticipation was raw in her shaky breathlessness—and Bobby knew it. His smile was slow and sexy. He peeled his shirt over his head and tossed it aside.

"There's something I've been wanting to do," she said in a rush, his incredible chest filling her vision. She lifted her gaze. "To know."

"Go for it."

She ran her hand over his head, touching his short hair. "It's softer than I expected."

He grabbed her hand, pressed his lips into her palm,

then slid her hand down his chest, over his belt and beyond.

"This isn't," he said.

Everything speeded up. Time stopped... and flew. Demands were met, and new ones created. She didn't know what to expect, what to do, what he liked, so she gave up control, gave in to need.

Only when he relaxed against her later, breathing as hard as she, did she consider the consequences of what she'd done.

CHAPTER 15

Wednesday, November 21
1. Get a dog. I know. I'm fickle. But dogs do love you, no matter what.
2. Get laid better.
3. Skip job-hunting until after Thanksgiving. But practice more. Design a second cake?
4. Return Rafael D'Amato's message.
5. Return Bobby's three messages. Stop being a coward.

Jill tossed her diary aside without finishing her list and dropped back on her mattress. She stared at her ceiling. She'd been doing that a lot in the past few days—since Saturday night.

Get laid better. The to-do item wasn't exactly accurate, since the act itself had been good—better than good—but the aftermath was disastrous, and it was all her fault.

She'd made Bobby leave right after. Her gaze had landed on a photo of Wade on her dresser and her world had collapsed. What had she done? She'd broken her own rule, and for what? A moment of comfort? The physical satisfaction of an orgasm? Well...two, to be exact, one following the other without a break, but who was counting?

She pressed her hands to her face, covering her eyes. Obviously, she was counting. But she'd come aware of him, a man she barely knew, naked and heavy atop her, breathing hard. And it'd been so easy for him. He'd moved off her, settled close, laid a hand on her abdomen and tried to kiss her.

He'd taken one look at her face and stopped. "Second thoughts already?" he asked.

"You need to go."

"Just relax," he said, brushing his lips against her hair.

"No. You really need to go." She needed to be alone.

"Jill, it's normal that you would be a little shy after. I'm your first, right? Since your husband died?"

"Don't analyze me. Please. I really, really need you to go. I'm sorry. I know this is horrible of me. Please, Bobby."

She didn't watch him dress. She grabbed the blanket and pulled it up, squeezing her eyes shut. The mattress dipped as he sat beside her. He brushed her hair with his hand.

"Don't be hard on yourself," he said.

He didn't get it. He didn't understand that she wasn't being hard on herself—she was hating herself. Hating her loss of self-control, hating how she'd given in to lust and slept with a man who meant so little to her. She was not a casual woman. Nor did she hurt people, and this would hurt Bobby.

"I'll call you," he said, then he was gone.

She'd taken the train home that morning, retreating, but that hadn't worked, either. She was in transition, not knowing who she was or what she wanted. She wasn't comfortable in her own skin anymore. Reinvention was complicated.

She'd found solace in a couple of visits with Alan, but they'd talked about her job-hunting. She couldn't tell him about Bobby, about her reaction to sleeping with the man.

And so she'd returned to the city Wednesday morning, no better off than when she went. She would go to her support group that night and then Thanksgiving dinner at her neighbors' place the next day. After the holiday weekend, she would hit the pavement again in search of work, this time armed with her sample. She had a good feeling about it.

She glanced at her answering machine. Four messages she hadn't returned, three from Bobby and one from Rafael.

She needed to talk to Bobby. She'd been rude, not returning his calls. She rubbed her face with her hands, blew out a breath then dialed his cell phone.

"Hi, it's Jill," she said when he answered. "Is this a bad time?"

"Not if you can hold on a second."

"I can hold."

About thirty seconds passed. "You still there?" he asked.

"I'm here."

"I was in a meeting. I had to find an empty office."

"I can call you back."

"I'm the boss. They'll wait. So. Not the best first date of all time, huh?"

Oh, why did he have to be so nice? "It was a really good date, Bobby. I just realized that I'm not ready. I thought I was, but I'm not."

"Ready to date or ready for sex?"

How could they possibly backtrack to dating only? It seemed impossible. "Both, I think. Although the sex was really good."

"Yeah?"

She could hear him smile. "Doubly really good."

He laughed. "I kinda thought that, but I wasn't sure. It was good for me, too."

"I'm sorry I kicked you out. It was rude."

"I should've gone with my gut, Jill. My gut said you weren't ready. Then you looked at me with those big gray eyes…The rest is history."

"Yes. History."

"I don't like the sound of that."

She drew lines with her fingers in the quilt. "I can't continue this. But I'm really glad it was you."

A long silence hung between them. "Okay," he said at last, then ended the call.

She dropped the phone onto the bed. He'd been nicer than she deserved.

***

"It seems strange without Jacob here," Jill said to the four remaining Musketeers that night, eyeing the empty chair where he usually sat. The comment earned her a glare from Iris, who blamed Jill for driving Jacob away, when all she'd done was wish him well.

Maybe that wasn't entirely true. She did tend to harp on, when she got the chance to talk at all, about healing and moving on.

"I can't stand it another minute!" Wendi exclaimed. "Did you give my book to Alan?"

"I left it at his house. He's out of town, plus I told you he's on deadline, so I don't know when he'll get to it." Jill had decided to take the path of least resistance. She could've given it to him before he left to visit his parents, but instead went over after he'd gone and left it on his kitchen counter.

"Did you read it?"

"No." Which wasn't entirely true. She'd read the first chapter and had serious concerns about Wendi's mental health. Jill thought Alan wrote dark and twisted stuff, but Wendi's was a cheerless labyrinth.

Wendi slumped. "Oh."

"It's not my opinion that matters," Jill said kindly. She'd enjoyed watching Wendi blossom and hated seeing her shrivel up again. "I hope you're working on another project."

"I am. A sequel."

Jill started to respond when the basement door

opened. Jacob came down the stairs, followed by a shorter, thinner man who looked as professorial as Jacob.

"Hi, everyone," Jacob said. He seemed to be smiling from head to toe. "We're headed to Vermont, but I wanted Gordon to meet all of you."

Gordon was greeted in about the same way that Jill had been months ago. Birdie smiled sweetly. Iris glowered. Mrs. Q. was polite. Wendi ducked her head. At least this time her hair was pulled back in a ponytail instead of cloaking her face.

Jill sighed. Maybe there wasn't any hope for them, after all. Maybe she shouldn't even be trying. It was pretty egotistical of her to think she could change their lives, that she'd been sent here to do that, to help them go forward. Maybe she was only supposed to get out of it what she'd gotten out of it already—a safe place to air some of her grief, and like Birdie and Mrs. Q., somewhere to go.

Jacob and Gordon didn't stay long, didn't even sit. Citing the long drive ahead, they said they needed to go. But before they left, Gordon looked at each person, his eyes showing a deep kindness. He put his arm around Jacob's shoulders.

"I promise I'll take good care of him," Gordon said.

Tears welled in Jill's eyes at the tenderness between them. She wanted that for herself again. Missed it so much. And being touched. It was excruciating sometimes not being touched.

She went up to Gordon and hugged him. "Thank you," she said. "He's very special."

"Don't I know it."

She moved on to hug Jacob then. "Be happy. You have my number. Maybe the three of us could go to dinner sometime?"

"I'll call, my dear. I will. I admire you very much."

"I don't think he'll be back," Birdie said after the door closed.

"Maybe if it doesn't work out," Mrs. Q. said.

Birdie shook her head. "He's done here."

He's done here. Jill thought about Birdie's statement as she walked home later. It was good to see progress—and success. It made her think of her daughters, who weren't progressing at all. Shanna had at least made a pretense before of dealing with her grief, but that wasn't the case now. Jill feared that the more time that went by, the deeper into darkness Shanna sank. And as for Tori, she may be dealing with her grief differently, but she was in the same precarious position of sinking beyond help.

When Jill got home she called them both, got their voice mail and left upbeat messages wishing them happy Thanksgivings. At Christmas, things would be different. She would have them home. She would find a way to help them before it was too late.

She decided to return Rafael D'Amato's phone call so that she could erase his message and start the next day with a clean slate. He'd called her a week after the open house. It had taken her four days to call him back. She expected to get his voice mail, but he answered.

"Hi, this is Jill Townsend. I'm sorry I took so long to get back to you. I had to go home to Connecticut."

"You are staying in town for the holiday?"

"Yes. Are you?"

"Actually, I'm in Los Angeles. I won't be home for about two weeks. Could we make plans for dinner when I return?"

Jill didn't know how she would feel in two weeks, except that she would handle things differently this time, and she certainly wasn't going to sleep with anyone, not until she could make a reasoned decision. He didn't seem like a man who would push her on the subject, though. Nor was she as physically attracted to him as she'd been to Bobby.

"That would be nice," she said, as if Ilene were standing beside her, prodding her.

"December eighth, then? That's a Saturday."

Plenty of time to change her mind. "It's a date."

"I look forward to getting to know you better," he said, but then told her he needed to hang up, which was fine with her, although she did wonder why there'd been no small talk, no effort to get to know her better, as he'd said.

Anyway, she'd dodged the dating bullet for a little while longer.

"Your neighbors do all right for a couple of youngsters," Ilene commented to Jill the next day at the Thanksgiving gathering. Jill and Ilene were grazing from the appetizer trays and trying not to eat too much before the main course.

Jill had to agree. The couple lived well. Given their jobs as a lawyer and a stockbroker, they could afford it. "I wonder if people called us youngsters when we were thirty-two. That was only thirteen years ago for me, you know. I'm not in my dotage yet."

Ilene grinned. "It *is* all relative, isn't it? Interesting mix of people here."

The "small" group that Sean had said were invited turned out to be twenty-two—his parents and hers, a couple of old friends in town for the weekend, and a few people from work, including two thirty-something single men, the age difference not stopping Ilene from flirting, nor them from flirting back.

Jill hadn't shared details of her date with Bobby, except to say that she wouldn't be seeing him again. Ilene hadn't asked too many questions.

As the party progressed, Jill managed to work into each conversation that she was looking for work. Although she would love to pursue a cake-decorator job, she realized she was being foolish—and way too picky—if she didn't open herself up to possibilities she hadn't considered. There would be a comfort level in decorating cakes that appealed to her, but it didn't mean she couldn't do any number of jobs.

As the buffet was being set out, Jill went up to the caterer. "A lot of people commented on your excellent food and service at my open house, Rose. I think you'll be getting calls."

"We already have, although we're booked solid until

after New Year's." She eyed the tray of sliced turkey, adjusted the serving piece slightly to the left, then moved a couple other items around.

"You wouldn't by chance know of a bakery that might be looking for a cake decorator, would you?" Jill asked.

"For you?"

"I'm looking for holiday work, something to keep me busy. I don't have paid experience, but I won't make anyone cringe, and I'll work hard and show up on time. I can't seem to get my foot in the door anywhere. Not that I blame them. Training takes time, and there are no extra hours this time of year."

"Let me think about it," Rose said. "I need to finish setting things out while they're hot."

Let me think about it. It was the most hopeful response she'd gotten.

The dinner menu was surprisingly traditional, including turkey and stuffing, mashed potatoes and gravy, yams and green beans, although lighter versions of the old standbys. Jill indulged in a slice of pumpkin cheesecake, and decided she needed to find a gym locally, since she wasn't in Darien regularly these days to work out at the country club. Not that she'd minded having a reason to skip the workouts....

A crowd had gathered in front of a big-screen television to watch football. Jill scooted around people jockeying for position and took her empty dessert plate into the kitchen.

"Yum," she said to Rose, who was stacking clean trays and dishes in boxes.

"Thank you." She looked up from her task. "I thought of a possibility for a job for you, by the way. Can we talk when I'm all done here?"

"Absolutely." Hope beat a happy drum inside Jill. "If I'm not here, just knock on my door across the hall."

"You look like you just met Santa Claus," Ilene said when Jill tracked her down. "Or a sugar daddy."

"Better. A lead from the caterer on a job."

"Doing what?"

"I don't know yet." A cheer went up as a touchdown was scored.

"Speaking of scoring," Ilene said with a wink. "Scott and Justin would like to take us out for drinks after the party's over."

"Okay."

"Now, it's just for drinks, so you— Did you just say yes without me having to argue?"

"I can't imagine why you're so surprised."

"I'll go…tell them," Ilene said. "I told them you might be a tough sell."

"Well, if you like, I can get into a debate with you."

"Your saying yes that fast is going to give them confidence, you know."

"What? That I'm easy?" She definitely didn't want that.

"Gotcha. Let's tell them together. Otherwise I feel like a pimp."

Jill laughed. She watched the men's faces as she and Ilene walked across the room together. Jill decided that

Justin had zeroed in on Ilene, which was fine with Jill. Scott was cute, too.

If only her daughters could hear her now. Or see her. She felt pretty good in her new outfit. She'd stopped shopping at department stores in favor of Angelique's and other specialty shops. Last week she'd bought her Thanksgiving outfit—an openwork knit camisole and trumpet skirt in autumn colors, with a chunky necklace and macramé heels with straps that criss-crossed her ankles. She was finally making a statement, her own statement about herself. And she liked what it said.

Rose caught her eye later and motioned her over. "I'm done here. Maybe we could just slip over to your place for a couple of minutes?"

"Absolutely." Jill fished her key out her pocket. "Do you get to have a Thanksgiving dinner with your own family now?"

"I'm having it catered."

Jill hesitated, the key in her lock. "Are you serious?"

Rose smiled. "Yes and no. I made extra of everything we served today. Just have to heat it all up. My husband has gotten used to us eating really late on holidays, if at all. It's not the easiest career in the world this time of year, but I can't imagine doing anything else."

"How long have you been in business?" Jill walked ahead of Rose down the hallway then into the kitchen.

"My mother was a caterer, so I grew up in the business. I started my own six years—what's this?" She stopped in front of the Christmas cake.

"A sample of my own design. I thought I would take it around with me during my job hunt. What do you think? You can be brutally honest."

"I like it." She spun the turntable. "People wouldn't be afraid to cut into it."

"That's exactly what I thought!"

"What else do you have in mind?"

Jill grabbed her photo album and let Rose flip through the pages. Jill was less nervous than she'd expected to be, probably since it wasn't a real job interview.

Rose closed the album. "How would you like to come work for me?"

"You?"

"It'd only be through the holidays. I generally outsource my cake business. Can't seem to keep a designer, so it's easier to order from a bakery. But I think we could work together okay."

"Without experience you're willing to hire me?"

Rose smiled at Jill's obvious shock. "For three reasons. First, this Christmas cake of yours. Second, the other cakes you've done, which show a real creativity. Third, and the reason why the idea came to me in the first place—I've seen you in action. I've seen your lists. I have never in my entire career seen anyone as organized as you, yet you were totally relaxed during the party. You made your open house seem effortless, because you planned well. That's an immeasurable value."

"I—" *I'm flattered. I'm thrilled.* "Yes. Thank you, Rose. Yes."

"Come to my facility on Tuesday and we'll work out the details. You can expect to start work on Wednesday. You'll be busy every weekend from now until New Year's Eve. If that doesn't work for you, tell me now."

Jill couldn't tell her about her daughters coming home for Christmas. She would just have to convince Shanna to come into the city, too, so they could all spend time together. "It works for me."

"Would you be interested in working the parties?"

"Can we start with the cakes and go from there?"

"Sure. Okay, I'll see you on Tuesday, around ten?"

"Ten is great."

"In the meantime, come up with a few more designs for Christmas, as well as Hanukkah and New Year's. Maybe take a stab at something for Valentine's Day. If everything works out, we can talk about you coming back for various holidays. 'Bye, Jill."

"Goodbye. And thank you."

After her front door shut, Jill danced around her kitchen then up her stairs in a joyous, uninhibited moment. "I have a job," she said to Wade's picture. "Would you be proud of me? I'm proud of me. My life is so different without you and the girls." She kissed her fingers then laid them over his mouth, the glass cool and slick. "Thank you for giving me the loft. Thank you for seeing I would need something new to focus on."

It wasn't as if he'd known she would be on her own, but still, it was his planning that had made the difference. She would always be grateful.

CHAPTER 16

Sunday, November 25
1. Fourth floor neighbor's cat just had kittens.
2. ~~Get laid better~~. Be adult about sex.
3. Finish New Year's cake design. Figure out how to make icing fireworks.
4. Steal ideas.

Once the creative juices started flowing in Jill's mind, they refused to shut off. She hardly slept. When she lay down in bed, visions would overwhelm her, pushing and shoving to get out. She would get up, sketch the image, then try to sleep again. Excitement and exhaustion fought for dominance. Excitement usually won. There would be time to sleep in January. She wanted to show Rose a ton of designs at their first meeting on Tuesday.

But this cold Sunday morning, she was taking time to meet Ilene for brunch then wander around town looking at Christmas displays. In years past she'd complained about how early all the stores decorated for the holidays. Not this year. Armed with her digital camera and a small sketch pad, she would record—okay, steal—ideas she could recreate in cake. She felt like a native, dressed all in black—a turtleneck sweater, lined wool pants and low-heeled boots, comfortable for walking.

Her lobby doorbell chimed. She grabbed her zebra coat and headed downstairs to meet Ilene. But when she got there, it wasn't Ilene at the door, but Alan, carrying an overnight bag, his finger on the bell again. And he didn't look happy.

She forced a smile as she opened the door. "How come you didn't use your key?"

"Is this your idea of a joke?" he asked, dragging a large manila envelope out of his bag and shaking it at her.

"A joke?"

"You know I don't read wannabe work."

"I know. I explained it in the note I left you."

"*I'm* supposed to feel some sort of responsibility for bringing Wendi out of her shell? She's *your* project."

"But she connected with you. She's been different ever since she met you."

"Dammit, Jill. I don't want to get involved."

"How involved can you get? You read as much of it as you can stand, write her a little critique, encourage her to join a writers group, then you're done."

"There's a flaw in your master plan."

"What's that?"

"She's good."

Jill's mouth fell open. "She is? Truly?"

"Would I kid about something like that?"

"Wow. Now what?"

"You understand that I'm really pissed about this," he said.

She grinned. "I understand. She'd be competition."

His lips thinned. "Hardly. She's got some work to do, but there's raw talent. I just don't need this right now."

She gestured to a couple of chairs. "Would you like to—"

He strode away from her. "I'm on deadline."

"I know that. I told her that."

He came back, not looking at her but at the floor. "I've never wanted to be a mentor."

"I know that, too."

"You had no right to assume I would do this."

"I'm sorry." She somehow kept herself from smiling.

He stopped pacing. "You're laughing at me."

"No. No, I'm not. I swear." She'd never seen him like this, all worked up and irritated. It fascinated her. "What are you going to do?"

"I want to meet her. Today. I want to go over the manuscript with her and see if she'll make changes. Then when she's done I guess I have to show the manuscript to my agent."

"Seriously?"

"No, I came all this way for my health."

"Okay. Let's go upstairs. I'll call her for you." She glanced at the bag he carried. "Are you spending the night?"

"I expect we'll be working until very late. Is that a

problem?" He finally seemed to focus on her. "You're on your way out. A date?"

"With Ilene."

"Would I be interfering in plans you have if I stay overnight?"

"Not at all."

They were about to step into the elevator when Ilene knocked on the lobby door.

"Just a slight delay," Jill told her when she let her in. "Are you starving?"

"I can wait. Hi, Alan, how are you?"

"He's feeling put upon, poor baby," Jill said before he could answer then explained the situation as they rode the elevator and went inside her loft.

"It's a tragedy," Ilene said, tongue firmly in cheek.

Alan finally laughed. "All right, you two. I got it. I'm being stupid."

"I would've said selfish, but what do I know?" Jill said with a dramatic shrug.

"Yeah, yeah, yeah. I'm gonna put my stuff upstairs while you call Wendi."

"That man is so hot," Ilene whispered to Jill as she tracked down Wendi's number and dialed. "How can you stand having him here and not jump his bones?"

Jill didn't want to think of Alan in those terms—he obviously didn't think of *her* in those terms. She wouldn't risk their friendship that way. Fortunately Wendi picked up the phone before Jill could answer Ilene's question.

"Hi, Wendi, this is Jill Townsend."

"Oh. Hi."

"I'm wondering if you get Sundays off?"

"Yes. The children I care for spend Sundays with their parents. Why?"

"Because Alan is here and he wants to talk to you about your book."

Silence. Nothing but low static.

"Wendi?"

"I'm…here."

"Can you come to my place?"

"I guess."

"Wendi, do you understand what I'm telling you? He likes your manuscript. He wants to help you polish it."

"I…can't…breathe."

"Suck it up, girl, and get yourself over here. You've got the opportunity of a lifetime."

"Okay. Yes, okay. I'm on my way." She hung up without saying goodbye.

Jill smiled. "I know how she feels. When Rose offered me the job, I almost couldn't put a cohesive sentence together."

"You got a job?" Alan asked, coming up to her.

"As a cake designer—" she liked that term, which Rose had used, better than decorator "—for a caterer. I start this week, and it's just for the holidays, so far. I owe you a huge thank-you, Alan. I don't think I would've come up with the idea of looking for that kind of job if you hadn't brainstormed with me."

"That's what friends are for." He raised his brows. "That's some coat."

"You like it?" She turned around, showing her zebra from all angles.

"I hope you're not headed to the zoo today."

She wrinkled her nose at him. "I like it, and that's all that matters."

"You're looking quite citified these days."

"Is that a good thing?"

"On you it is. You look younger…and happier."

"Life's gotten pretty good, Alan. If I can help Shanna and Tori find their way, too, I'll be ecstatic." She glanced at Ilene, who was uncharacteristically quiet. "We should go, I guess."

"Sure."

She showed Alan how to use the lobby-door unlock button and told him the refrigerator was stocked, that he should help himself, as should Wendi.

"To answer your question from earlier," he said, "I left my keys at home. I keep them on a different key ring," he said. "Do you have a spare?"

She tracked down an extra set, then said goodbye.

Going down in the elevator a minute later, Ilene said, "I've never had a friendship with a man. Seeing you two together makes me envy that."

Which was the biggest reason why Jill wouldn't do anything to risk that relationship….

Good heavens but that was beginning to sound like a mantra with her. Still, she knew she wouldn't find it with anyone else. They had fifteen years' investment in what they had. It wouldn't come again. "He's been a rock for me, Ilene. Truly, a rock. I know he's been hurting, too, missing Wade, but he's just been there for me. I know I'm lucky."

Later that night Jill sat at the computer in her second-level office making sketches from the digital photos she'd taken that day. Ideas poured out of her—gingerbread boxes filled with candy, snowmen, Santa's sleigh. She would have to learn new techniques, understand the engineering of construction so that a piece wouldn't fall apart, especially as it was transported. There wouldn't be enough hours in the day to learn it all, no time for a lot of trial and error. But at least now she felt prepared to meet Rose on Tuesday and show her ideas. She would have a portfolio of at least fifteen designs.

Jill listened to Wendi downstairs arguing a point with Alan, who'd kept his cool, for the most part.

"I don't see what you see in my book," she said, frustration in her voice. "You're picking it all apart."

"Because the elements are there, but they're in the wrong order and they're not as focused as they need to be. You're a good, instinctive storyteller, but you have to learn how to rein in. You're repetitive, your turning points are lackluster and your conflict is weak."

"See?" she cried. "It's awful."

"If it was awful, I wouldn't be giving you time that I should be spending on my own book. Do you want to sell this?"

"Yes."

"More than anything in the world?"

"Yes." Her voice got stronger.

"Then listen. And do. And quit telling me you're no good. You insult me with that."

"Okay," she said meekly.

Jill smiled. She'd enjoyed the solitude of her loft, needing a quiet place in the hubbub of the city as she made the transition into her new life, but she was enjoying having Alan and Wendi there, loved listening to them argue a point and get excited about an idea.

She went to bed around midnight, and they were still working. Surprisingly, she fell asleep. She came awake with a start later and realized she'd heard the door shut. Alan must've gone out, probably to put Wendi in a cab. Jill had piled his bedding on the sofa earlier.

She listened to him get ready for bed—the rustle of the bedding, his footsteps as he moved around the room, even the flush of the toilet. Then the lights went out and it was quiet.

It was nice having him there. She felt safe. Not that she'd really felt unsafe, as the building was fairly secure, but a different kind of safe. Emotionally safe. She didn't have to pretend with him. Didn't have to explain. He knew where she came from, how she'd lived, how she'd felt.

Plus he'd acknowledged the changes she made and seemed to approve.

There was no better definition of a friend than that,

she thought, then closed her eyes and went back to sleep, knowing he would be there when she woke up.

In the morning, however, she found only a note.

> Good morning. Needed to get home. I'll be back next Sunday, if that's okay. Wendi has a lot of work ahead of her, but I think she finally understands what she needs to do. I will grudgingly admit to enjoying myself. So—thanks. I didn't know I'd been in a rut. Congrats on the job. I figure you'll come to be known as the Picasso of the cake-design world. I can say I knew you when. Alan.

CHAPTER 17

Saturday, December 8
1. Read an article about how rabbits make good pets. Hmm.
2. Job security—show Valentine ideas to Rose.
3. Date with Rafael. Wear old underwear.

In Rose's office Jill watched her boss flip through the small stack of new design ideas. Her desk was a mess, which made Jill fidget more than having to wait for Rose's reaction to her designs. The sounds from the catering kitchen just outside the office door were like music to Jill. She'd worked there for only a week and a half, yet it felt like years—in a good way. From the moment she'd walked through the doors, she'd fit.

"Are you sure this is structurally feasible?" Rose asked, turning a drawing toward Jill.

"I'm going to try it out at home tomorrow. I'll let you know. I just wanted to know if you like the design."

"I love the design. What will you use for the arrows piercing the heart?"

"Everything will be edible. White chocolate for the shafts and fruit leather that I'll fringe for the feathers."

"Go for it. So…how are you enjoying working here?"

"I've never worked so hard—or happily—in my life."

"I'm glad, since I've blessed the food gods for sending you my way."

Jill warmed from the inside out at the compliment. "May I propose another way I might help?"

"Of course."

"Can I get your office organized? I don't see how you work in all this—"

"Can you start yesterday?"

Jill laughed. "Well, you know the schedule. I've got four cakes to decorate for tonight. How about Monday? I'm sure I'll have to ask questions of you, so it'd mean you might have to come in on your day off."

"If it also means I can actually put my hands on a piece of paper I need, I'm willing to do that." She opened her desk drawer, dug way into it and came up with a key. "I'll show you how to use the alarm code." She dropped the key in Jill's hands. "I want you to know I've only given keys to three employees in all the time I've been in business."

"You need to learn to delegate."

Rose cocked her head. "You know, most people would've thought it was a trust issue, but I think you're right." She stood. "And now to work. Four parties. What was I thinking?"

"That you'd like to stay in business for at least another six years?"

Rose's eyes sparkled. "Good point."

When Jill got home she only had time for a quick shower and primping before Rafael was due to pick her up. He'd called her a few times during his two weeks in Los Angeles. Their conversations weren't long but were comfortable, although he seemed to do the most talking, and mostly about himself and his work. In person it would be better. They were both creative. That would give them something in common to start.

She decided to wear the same outfit she'd worn for the date with Bobby, including the zebra coat, since Rafael hadn't seen it before.

Bobby. She'd run into him in the lobby one day as she was leaving for work. He'd nodded and kept walking. See? her conscience had screamed in her head. See? This is why you don't sleep with someone until you know the relationship is going somewhere. Everyone gets hurt.

She'd felt bad the rest of the day. Guilty. She wished she could talk to Alan about it, to get his opinion, but that would leave it open for him to talk to her about the women he dated, and that was too much information for her. Then she considered telling Ilene, but she and Ilene were polar opposites about the subject of sex and dating. She finally decided to keep the experience to herself. It was only important that she learn from her mistakes.

She wasn't nervous about going out with Rafael because he didn't seem the type to push. She would take this one slowly, let the relationship grow, if it was meant to.

Jill spritzed on a little perfume then went downstairs to await his arrival. She'd just reached the bottom stair when someone knocked on the door. Sean or Cherise, she decided, or someone else from within the building.

"Good evening," Rafael said, then presented her a bouquet of roses, each bloom perfect, the fragrance sweet and strong.

"I…hi. How did you get in?" She knew she sounded rude, but he'd surprised her, showing up without ringing the bell downstairs.

"I still have a key from when I designed your space."

"I see. Um, thank you for the flowers. They smell heavenly."

He kissed both her cheeks as she stood, stiff and awkward.

"You look lovely." He followed her down the hallway. "It's good to see you."

"It's good to see you, too. May I have my key back, please," she blurted, holding out her hand. The date had gotten off to a very bad start. She did not like him having free access to her space. An unwilling comparison to Bobby popped into her head. He'd also had a key but had rung the doorbell. Rafael, with all his sophistication, should've known better.

He hesitated, then retrieved the keys and dropped them in her palm.

Jill smiled. "Thanks." She moved into the kitchen to get a vase. "How's the weather? Does it look like rain?"

"It's cloudy but it doesn't smell like rain." He walked

across the living room to peer out her windows. "You're happy with your loft?"

"Happier every day." As she slid the bouquet into water, she made an unwilling comparison of the heavily scented traditional roses to Alan's distinctive calla lilies and Bobby's brilliant mums....

She joined Rafael at the windows. "And I love my job."

"Cake decorating, you said?"

"Well, really more designing. It's not your mother's cake decorating anymore," she said with a smile.

"Pardon? My mother?"

Oops. He wasn't up on pop-culture references. "I just meant that how cakes are decorated today is far different from twenty years ago, at least professionally. Now it's an art form."

"An art form? Really? I would like to see something you've done."

"It just so happens I have pictures." She made sure to photograph each design and was building a portfolio along with commercial experience for the next time she had to job-hunt.

"These are impressive," he said, as if surprised. "You must have an engineer's mind."

His flattery eased whatever tension had remained after the key incident. They'd jumped the hurdle. "I'm a planner. It helps."

"Yes, I see that. And you have vision."

She smiled. "Thank you."

He glanced at his watch, something thin and gold. "We should get going if we are to be at the restaurant on time."

Jill took her coat from its hook. Rafael didn't make a move to help her into it, which she really didn't mind. It always seemed an awkward moment to her, anyway.

"That is an interesting coat," he said.

She really hadn't realized what a conversation piece it would be.

"It's quite...memorable, isn't it?" he added.

Jill noticed that he'd ducked saying he liked it. "I like to think so."

"It's not real, is it?"

She grinned. Was that why he didn't want to touch it? He had a zebra phobia? "It's wool."

He eyed her speculatively. "This is a new style for you, is it not?"

"What? Zebra?"

He gestured. "The whole look. When we met last year at the Christmas party downstairs you wore an elegant gown. It was lovely. Classic."

"You remember that?"

"It was a deep green, and the color changed when you walked. I notice things like that."

She didn't want to admit that Wade had chosen the gown. "I liked it, too. But I felt a need to update my look now that I'm living in the city."

"Ah."

Ah? What did that mean? "I remember you were with a stunning younger woman, who looked like a model."

"As she was. Shall we?"

Okay. Discussion over. Jill couldn't get a handle on him. He was cool one moment, then warm the next, keeping her off balance. She liked him, and yet… He wasn't fun, like Bobby. Or clever, like Alan.

Stop making comparisons. Enjoy the evening.

Which turned out to be an easy order to obey.

"You are a fan of opera, I imagine?" he asked on the way up her elevator later.

"I've only been once."

"Really? Your husband was the CEO of an international corporation. I would have expected you to be patrons. And of the ballet and a museum or two."

"We weren't."

"I am surprised. It seems to be a necessity in the business world to socialize with similar people."

"Hypocritical or not, I guess."

"What do you mean?"

"I mean you should mix with people you like, shouldn't you? Yes, I see the occasional need for business connections through social connections, but if you don't enjoy opera, why attend the opera?"

"So, you do not enjoy the opera?"

They had reached the door to her loft. "I don't really know. I think, like all things, you enjoy something more after you've studied it, which I haven't."

"The Met is performing 'Carmen' on Wednesday night. I would like it very much if you would attend with me."

It would mean missing her support meeting, but maybe it was time to start weaning herself from that, anyway. More importantly did she want to see him again? "Yes, I'd like to very much," she told him, deciding another date was necessary at this point.

He took her hands in his and smiled warmly. "Would you wear your green gown?"

She was stunned by the request, even a little offended, as if he didn't trust her to wear something appropriate for the evening. She wasn't even sure a long gown was appropriate for other than a premiere. "It's in my closet in Connecticut, and I don't have time to go get it. I won't embarrass you, Rafael."

"I was not worried about that."

She wished he sounded a little more sure of that.

"Would you like to eat before or after the performance?" he asked.

"Before. I'll need to get home and to sleep right after. I get up very early to get to work."

"All right. I'll pick you up at six? We'll eat in the Belmont Room, as I am a guild member and have those privileges."

"Perfect."

They stared at each other. *Are you going to kiss me or not?* she wanted to shout, not even sure she wanted him to, but the build-up was nerve-racking. Finally he did lean close and pressed his lips to hers. He'd just deepened the kiss, his arms encircling her, when the elevator pinged and she jerked back. A moment later the door opened and Alan stood there. Rafael's arms were still around her.

As awkward moments went, it ranked high. For Alan, too, she decided. He didn't take a step forward until the doors started to close, then he stuck out his arm to stop the doors, and exited.

"I'm sorry." He hitched a thumb over his shoulder, angling away slightly. "I'll come back later."

"We're done," she said overly brightly, then felt Rafael stiffen. "That is, we were just saying good-night."

Alan reached them and extended his hand to Rafael. "This isn't what it looks like," Alan said in a hearty tone, one in which he might have added, "old chum" in another time and place.

"Alan's been mentoring a young writer. They meet here on Sunday." Jill looked pointedly at him after emphasizing the word *Sunday*.

"I left a message earlier to tell you I was coming in tonight instead of tomorrow. I guess you were out and haven't heard it yet. Is it a problem?"

"Of course not."

Rafael had yet to speak. Finally he turned to Jill. "I'll see you on Wednesday, then."

"Yes. Thank you for a lovely evening."

He bowed slightly. He never looked back, even after entering the elevator.

"That member of your court was royally pissed to see the castle intruder," Alan remarked as they walked into the loft.

She smiled at the description. He'd nailed it. "Rafael was caught off guard. As was I."

"I did call."

"I'm sure you did." She hung up her coat. "Still you can't blame him for being a little, well, irritated."

"Sure. I would've been upset, too, had someone interrupted me kissing you good-night." He clamped his mouth shut for a second then walked away from her. "I mean, my kissing any woman good-night. Interruptions are not good at times like that."

A slip of the tongue? Jill wondered. Had he thought about kissing her?

"Did you already go out with your other court member? What was his name? Billy? Bucky?"

She shoved him a little. "Bobby. And yes, I did."

"How was it?"

"A one-time experience." She put the kettle on to make tea even though she didn't really want any. "How is Wendi doing with her rewrites?"

He leaned a hip against the island. "She e-mails me her changes. I e-mail back my critique. She gets mad. I get madder. Then she revises. All around, a great working relationship."

"It's already made a huge difference in her personality. I've never seen anyone come out of a shell that quickly. She's like an entirely different person—animated and friendly. She smiles. I can see her leaving the group soon, and Iris is going to be very upset with me about it."

"From what you've told me, Iris is upset about most everything."

"Yes, but this more than most things will hurt her.

She's been Wendi's mother hen." Jill opened a cupboard to get a mug. "Would you like some tea? Wine?"

"Scotch. I'll get it."

He knew his way around the kitchen. She liked having him there with her. Liked it way too much. "Why'd you come in tonight?" Why didn't you have a date tonight? was what she really wanted to ask. He always had a Saturday-night date.

"I felt like it."

She turned and looked at him, curious about his tone of voice, which was defensive. "How's the book coming?"

"I'm ahead of schedule. Been doing nothing but writing, really. I'll be done before I head to Vail to meet the boys. I'll read it through when I get back, then turn it in on time." He took a quick swig of his drink, the ice clinking against the glass. "I think it's my best work so far."

"That's saying something. What's different?" She poured hot water over her tea bag. The steamy blueberry scent relaxed her.

"Several things, but mostly I think it's been mentoring Wendi. It's made me look at my own work differently, sort of revved me up. I've never taken what I do for granted, never done anything by rote, but I've enjoyed the process more this time than in a long time." He lifted his glass to her.

"You're welcome."

"So. Any chance of eggs benedict tomorrow?"

"If you'll go get some Canadian bacon when you get up. I've got everything else."

"Deal. I suppose you'd like to get to bed."

She should be exhausted. She'd been up since five o'clock, had put in a long day at work, having started on Rose's office, after all, after finishing the cakes. Then the date with Rafael, which hadn't drained her, but hadn't excited her, either. "I'm good for a while," she said.

She helped him make up the sleeper sofa, then, like an old married couple, they propped themselves on it and watched the news, then *Saturday Night Live*.

The next thing she knew it was morning. She eased awake, found herself on the sofa bed. Alone. The blankets were tucked around her, her necklace on the end table. She pressed a hand to her neck. He'd unclasped it and she never knew.

Where was he? Gone to get the bacon and newspaper? Had he slept beside her?

She brushed her hand over the other pillow. *How do you feel about that?*

She decided taking the Fifth was the wisest move for now.

She grabbed her shoes and necklace and went upstairs. Might as well shower and dress while he was out, then he could have the shower while she fixed breakfast.

But when she reached the top of the stairs she saw him in her bed, lying on his back, the blankets pulled to just below his waist, that lovely, narrowing line of hair disappearing under the covers.

He doesn't wear underwear.

Her skin heated. Her gaze traveled up his body. She saw that he was watching her, silently, intently.

"Morning," he said, sitting up and stretching, the blankets puddled in his lap, but more skin exposed along his side. "I didn't have the heart to wake you last night."

"Thanks." She gestured toward the bathroom. "Do you want to get in there before I shower?"

He smiled crookedly. "You want me to get out of bed now and walk over there?"

She crossed her arms, smiling back, calling his bluff. "If you need to." She waited.

"I would have no problem doing it, Jill. But I think you would have a problem…seeing it."

"You've seen one, you've seen them all."

"Which shows your inexperience."

"And you base that on …?"

"What I've been told, mostly."

"By women?"

He nodded.

"And they tell you this because?"

"It usually comes in the form of a compliment."

So. Birdie was right. Men do let you know the size of their penis. And, if he could be believed, apparently Alan's was…worth knowing.

Without conscious thought, she dropped her gaze. Oh, yeah. Morning proof of his statement made a ridge behind the blanket. It looked like he was entitled to bragging rights.

Get laid better.

It never would've been Alan Haggerty who helped her draw a line through the item, if she'd left it on her list.

What a way to ruin a friendship.

CHAPTER 18

Wednesday, December 19
1. Saw the neighbor's kittens. Three weeks old. Still time to make a decision.
2. No temptations ahead, thanks to the jerk Rafael.
3. Confront Rafael.
4. Tori arrives!!!

Jill stood back to admire her Christmas tree, which had just been delivered and set up in the stand in front of the big windows overlooking the street. The fresh pine scent assaulted her with memories, all of them good. Boxes of new ornaments sat on the floor, waiting to be hung. The rest of the loft was decorated and looked festive. Tori was coming. She should be there any minute. She'd finagled a ride with someone driving to the city and had called fifteen minutes ago, saying they were close.

Jill turned on a Christmas CD and the fireplace. Soup simmered on the stove, Tori's favorite minestrone. Chicken parmesan baked in the oven, a green salad stayed crisp in the refrigerator, and garlic bread was ready to slide under the broiler. Welcome home, my darling daughter. Welcome home.

The doorbell rang, and she raced to the monitor, could see Tori standing there.

"You're here! Hi!" She pushed the unlock button. "Come on up. I'm on the sixth floor."

"I need help carrying my stuff. Jarod is double parked."

"I'll be right down."

Jill hurried down the hallway. The elevator couldn't come fast enough for her. She raced across the lobby, yanked the door open and threw her arms around Tori.

"Oh, you're so thin," Jill exclaimed, hugging Tori tighter, wishing she was three years old again so that Jill could pull her into her lap.

"So are you." Tori pulled back. "You look…different."

"You like it?"

"Yeah. Wow. Um, we'd better get my stuff from the car."

Jill thanked the young man who'd done the driving, passed him a few bills to help pay for the gas, which lit up his face, then dragged suitcases out of the trunk and hauled them upstairs.

"Did you pack everything you owned?" she asked, struggling.

"We have to empty our dorm rooms at the end of semester, you know. Start all over again in January. I got to store a few things with a friend. My stereo and TV. My bedding. The big stuff."

"I'm so glad you're here, sweetie. I can't tell you how

much I've missed you." Tori looked worn out. Not just tired, but beyond that. Her hair looked like she hadn't had it cut since she left home. It was straggly and limp, and now dyed black. Her eyes looked haunted in her pale, thinner face. "Here we are. Home sweet home."

Jill followed Tori into the loft. She was nervous, waiting for her daughter's reaction.

Tori set down her load as she looked around. Jill purposely hadn't sent photos of the place, wanting both the girls to see it in person for the first time.

"What do you think?"

"It's...awesome. I don't know what I expected, but not this."

"In what way?"

"It's not you." She turned and looked at Jill then. "Well, maybe it is. Now."

"Is that bad?"

"I don't know yet. I have to think about it. Get used to it."

Tori wandered around. She dragged her fingers along the dining room table, then the fireplace mantel. She closed her hand around a tree branch then smelled her hand. A tiny smile appeared.

"My bedroom's upstairs," Jill said. "The couch opens up, though. You'll sleep there."

"You don't even have a guest room?"

"No. Although there's room for one. I'm thinking about fixing it up."

"So you plan to spend a lot of time here?" Tori headed up the stairs.

"Yes." The answer came out of her mouth before she thought about it. She'd made up her mind. Which meant other decisions would need to be made. Big decisions. "I have a job, you know."

"I thought it was just for the holidays."

"Maybe." Jill was making herself indispensable at A Rose is a Rose. And she loved it, every minute of it.

"This is totally awesome, Mom."

She'd done something right? *That* was awesome. Jill heard her poking around, checking out the bathroom, opening the door to the storage, soon-to-be guest room.

"Dinner'll be ready as soon as the garlic bread is done," Jill called up to her. "I thought maybe we could decorate the tree tonight."

Tori came down the stairs. "I'm going out."

Jill froze, the tray of garlic bread in her hand. "You just got here."

"I've got a bunch of friends here. We're meeting at seven."

An hour. They hadn't seen each other for four months, and— "We've got five days here before we go to Darien for Christmas. Can't you at least give me tonight?"

"I have *plans*, Mom."

I had plans, too. Jill's disappointment threatened to spin into anger. She decided not to go to war with her daughter her first night home. It wasn't the way to start off the break. "You'll still have dinner with me?"

"Sure. It smells great. Man, I'm tired of pizza. I never thought I'd say that."

Jill saw Tori's shoulders relax. Backing off was the best thing to do. She wished she didn't have to tiptoe around her own daughter. They should be able to have fun together, especially now that Tori had been on her own for a while, responsible for herself, more adult. Although Jill wasn't sure Tori had done a very good job of taking that responsibility seriously.

"Can we plan to decorate the tree together tomorrow night?" Jill asked after sliding the garlic bread in the oven.

Tori sighed. "You might as well get used to the fact I'm going to be out with my friends a lot, okay? As you said, we'll have time in Darien."

The words were delivered in a defensive tone, one that said there would be no arguing about it. She wouldn't go back to Boston until three weeks after Christmas. There would be time, Jill reminded herself. Time to rebuild their relationship.

"Why don't you invite your friends over here for dinner tomorrow night," Jill said casually. "I'll feed everyone. You can all help me decorate, so it'd be done in a hurry, and you'll still have plenty of time to go out."

"I'll think about it."

I'll think about it. The teenager's motto when it came to planning. Jill dredged up a smile. She dug deep into her memory from when she was eighteen and home after her first semester. She must've felt the same as Tori. Jill had been surprisingly rebellious herself—open-minded, she preferred to think at the time—but the rebel had disappeared when Wade came on the scene, never to be heard from again.

That wasn't entirely true, she realized. She'd rebelled, but only inwardly. And she hadn't regretted anything, then or now.

"How did your finals go?" she asked as she put the finishing touches on dinner.

"Fine." Tori was looking at the photos on display in the entertainment unit. She picked up one of the whole family—Christmas, last year—and touched a finger to one spot, then set it down again.

Jill saw Tori slump. *Do you cry, sweetie? Do you get mad? Or do you just hold it in and let it fester?*

She went to her daughter then and slid an arm around her shoulders, felt her stiffen but didn't let go. "It's hard, this first Christmas without him." Every first had been hard, but Christmas more so, and less than two weeks from now, New Year's Eve, what would've been their twenty-fourth wedding anniversary. Then the next day, the first anniversary of his death. At least they would be together, she and her daughters.

Tori said nothing but she didn't pull away, either. They might have stayed that way for a while, but Tori said, "I think the bread's burning."

Their dinner conversation was strained, but in the end Jill felt all right about how things were going. When Tori took off a little before seven, Jill decided to go to support group rather than be alone for the evening.

"What are you doing here?" Iris asked as soon as Jill came down the stairs.

"I'm glad to see you, too," Jill countered.

"She meant—" Mrs. Q. took charge "—Wendi said that you probably wouldn't be here for several weeks."

Jill had missed last week. She was supposed to have gone to the opera with Rafael, but he'd cancelled at the last minute. He hadn't called since.

"My younger daughter arrived today, and I thought I'd be with her, but she's out partying with friends." The bitterness that coated her words told Jill how comfortable she was with the group. "I'm feeling a little unloved, even though I understand, too. And this is on top of not hearing from a man I went out with. It's like he disappeared off the face of the earth."

Birdie brightened. "*That's* the other thing I learned about dating, Internet or otherwise—that thing I couldn't remember before. If a man doesn't want to keep going in a relationship, he just stops calling."

"You mean he doesn't even say goodbye?" Jill was stunned.

"Not all of 'em, but a lot. You have to get used to it and not take it personally."

"*I* would take it personally," Wendi said, looking festive in Christmas red.

"You learn not to. You know, most of 'em are just serial daters, anyway."

"Yet more reasons why I don't want anything to do with any of them," Iris said, fire in her voice.

"How do you know for sure the guy is gone, not incapacitated or something?" Jill asked.

"You don't," Birdie answered. "In my case, though, a couple of 'em died and I didn't know it for weeks."

The silence that fell over the group of women was loud as they each absorbed what Birdie said, then Jill started to laugh, then the others joined in. Even Iris smiled.

"Birdie, you are a gem," Jill said, reaching across to squeeze her hand. "I want to grow up to be just like you."

Birdie beamed.

"I'm going to confront him," Jill declared after a moment. "I'm not going to let him get away with such rudeness."

"I don't think that's a good idea," Birdie began.

"Oh, yes, it is. I need to. For myself. I need closure."

"Why?" Iris asked. "Birdie has told you it's typical. Why put yourself on the line like that?"

Why, indeed? "Maybe because I didn't get to say goodbye to Wade. That was the hardest thing. I need closure, or else it will linger for a longer time than Rafael deserves."

"Do what you have to, then, but I think there's a big difference between your husband dying and some idiot you dated once not calling," Iris said. "Let's talk about something else."

Implied in her tone was that Jill had been hogging the attention. Apparently Jill was never going to break down barriers with Iris—even though she was right about the whole closure issue.

"Okay, different subject," Jill said, turning to face Iris directly. "Why do you hate me?"

The three other women went still. Iris straightened. She made eye contact and held it. "I don't hate you."

"You do. You've criticized me for moving on, for dating, for making friends with the others in the group. For helping Wendi."

"Wendi is bound to get hurt."

"I don't care," Wendi said vehemently. "I haven't felt anything for so long, that even hurt would be okay, Iris. Truly."

"You're not going to need me—us, soon."

"Yes, I will." Wendi laid a hand on Iris's shoulder. "You'll always be my friends. Maybe I won't come as often…."

"You see? It's already changing."

"For the better," Jill said quietly. "She's living. That's a good thing."

"And you, Jill? Are *you* living?"

"What do you think? I've got a new home in a city I'm enjoying. I've got a great job. I'm dating—well, such as it is. Am I happy? Not in the way I was before, but in a new way. I'm proud of what I've accomplished. And I have Wade to thank. He started it by buying the loft. Maybe you should try living, Iris."

A shocked hush came over the group. Jill knew she should apologize but didn't. The time was ripe for a showdown with Iris. If Jill wasn't allowed to come back, so be it, even though she'd come to depend on them, too.

"I've been part of this group for nine years," Iris began, her voice frigid. "I've seen people, women mostly, come and go. I've noticed that those who had happy marriages are looking for that again, so they put themselves out there, and then they criticize those of us who don't want the same thing."

"I wasn't criticizing."

"Oh, yes, you were. You've been criticizing ever since you walked into this room the first time. Maybe not directly, but it was implied in everything you said and did."

After a moment, Jill nodded. "Maybe you're right."

"No maybe about it."

"I don't want to become like you," Jill said.

There was a long silence, then Iris said, "I'll bet your husband never laid a hand on you in anger. Never yelled at you. Never belittled you in front of your family and friends. I'll bet he adored you and said so." She didn't wait for Jill to answer but kept spilling icy words.

"I was glad when my husband died. Ecstatic. I haven't missed him for one second. Don't you tell me how I should be living my life. I like my life just fine now. It's peaceful."

Jill felt like the lowest of the low. She'd never hurt anyone like that before, had always been careful with her words. Nothing she said now could make up for it, but she had to say something. "I'm so sorry, Iris. You're right. I was putting my values on you. I didn't know. I didn't understand. I'm very, very sorry I hurt you."

Iris didn't respond.

The ridiculous notion that Jill had been sent to this group to help them weighed heavy on her now. She'd learned the biggest lesson of all—not to presume to know someone else's pain.

She stood. "I want to wish you all a Merry Christmas. I'll see you…in the new year."

No one spoke. She left the room. Nothing she could say or do now would help any of them. She would leave them to talk about her so that they could settle back into their routine again, if that was possible.

"You're quiet today," Rose said, coming up beside Jill as she frosted three four-layer snowman cakes, assembly-line style but each with its own twist—three totally flamboyant snowmen that were supposed to look like transvestites. "I figured you'd be wired, with your daughter coming home and all."

My daughter doesn't want to spend time with me, and I hurt Iris last night, unforgivably.

"Just tired," she said to Rose. "I was up late." Not that she hadn't tried to sleep. "Plus I've put off Christmas shopping and now it all seems overwhelming."

"Why don't you take your lunch break early? Go shopping before the noon rush?"

Jill's work ethic screamed no in her head, but the I-hate-crowds angel prodded her toward a different answer. "Thanks. I'll do that. Clear the cobwebs at the same time."

She wasn't sure she could talk herself out of her mood, but she tried to get caught up in the holiday spirit.

Bloomingdale's teemed with people. She headed for the escalator, was just about to step on when she spotted Rafael coming down. He saw her, looked around, apparently for a place to hide, then seemed to resign himself to speaking with her as she moved to the bottom of the down escalator. Since the fates had conspired to put her in front of him, she would do the follow-through.

She put on her best Mona Lisa smile. "Good morning, Rafael."

"Jill." Oh, he'd perfected the cool greeting.

"How have you been?"

"Busy." He held up a Bloomie's bag and looked around. "Shopping. Like you, I imagine."

She kind of liked that she made him uncomfortable. She was about to make him more so. "I'm really surprised you've decided to just ignore me. If you don't want to continue this relationship, why don't you just say so?"

He hesitated, then, "I don't want to continue."

"Why not?"

"I answered the only question I intend to."

He turned. She touched his arm, staying him.

"You know I'm really new to dating. How about doing me a favor and telling me what went wrong?"

He seemed to sigh. "You aren't what you advertised."

Jill pulled back. "Excuse me?"

"I thought you were conservative and unemotional.

You were a corporate wife. That's what I want. That's what I'm looking for. You are too...flashy."

He didn't realize the compliment he'd just given her. What if he'd seen Jill unleashed? What would he have thought then? She'd been much more herself with Bobby.

Jill shook her head. Rafael had judged her in the same way that she had judged Iris—without full disclosure. "I appreciate your telling me," she told him. "In return, just for being honest, I'm going to give you a little advice."

She leaned toward him. "When a relationship isn't working, all you have to do is call and say, 'I really enjoyed meeting you, but I just don't see this going any further.' It's kind and mature, and it shows class. Goodbye. It's been an experience."

Oh, yeah, that felt good. Sort of. It felt good to get answers, to know why he'd given up, and now she knew she wouldn't push a man for answers again, because emotional confrontation for them was too hard. And they apparently had no need of closure.

Well, the jerks, anyway. Maybe someday she would get a chance to tell Iris she was right about that.

CHAPTER 19

Monday, December 24, Christmas Eve!
1. Absolutely no pets for anyone's Christmas stocking.
2. Nothing like having my daughters home to keep temptation under control.
3. Home for Christmas. Hope everything was delivered.
4. Shanna!! I can hardly wait!

On the train trip home to Darien on Christmas Eve, a sleeping Tori bumped steadily against Jill, who had hardly seen her daughter awake during the past five days. She was asleep when Jill left for work in the morning and gone when she got home. Jill would hear her come in about 2:00 a.m. Tori didn't wake up while Jill showered, dressed and ate in the morning, not even when Jill kissed her goodbye. The little bit of time they'd shared had been tense, with Tori bordering on belligerent. Jill had no idea what'd she'd done to warrant such treatment.

But now she would have Tori—and Shanna—all to

herself for three days, away from the influence of friends and the lure of city life. Jill had to go back to New York on Thursday, work until New Year's Eve, then she would be off for a whole week, the party season over. She and her daughters would spend the anniversary of Wade's death together—she would demand that. She hoped both Shanna and Tori would go back with her to the city while she worked, but since Shanna had delayed coming home until yesterday, she probably intended to return to Wake Forest soon, not staying for her whole winter break. She'd been silent on the subject.

Jill had hoped to start new Christmas traditions, but she also understood the girls' need to keep to the familiar this first year.

"Are you sure we should surprise Shanna?" Tori asked as they got in a cab at the Darien station.

"We're only two hours early. Surprises are fun."

"If you say so."

Happiness swirled around Jill as they pulled into the driveway. Her heart felt ready to burst when she fit her key into the lock and opened the front door.

"Shanna!" she called out. "We're home!"

Silence. Jill looked around and noticed that none of the curtains had been opened. The house looked unoccupied.

"Maybe she's asleep," Tori said.

"At four o'clock?" She'd talked to Shanna the night before, right after she'd gotten home, so Jill knew she'd arrived. "I'll check the garage for the car. You can run up and check her bedroom, okay?"

But as Jill headed through the living room toward the back of the house she spotted Shanna stretched out on the sofa. "Never mind, Tori. She's here."

Shanna jerked awake. "Mom! Jeez. You scared me." She glanced at the mantel clock. "What're you doing here? You weren't supposed to be home yet."

"I was done early at work." A happy glow filled Jill. She moved to hug her daughter, who at least didn't look gaunt like Tori. In fact, Shanna seemed to have gained weight. Her face was rounder. "Well, get up so I can hug you. I've missed you."

Shanna shoved aside the afghan and sat up. After a moment she stood. Jill took a step forward then stopped. Her gaze dropped. Blood rushed to her feet.

"You're pregnant."

Shanna nodded.

"Holy crap," Tori said from behind her.

"You're pregnant." A cannonball landed in Jill's stomach, hot and hard. "How can you be pregnant?"

"The usual way?"

Shanna's attempt at humor fell flat. "How far along are you?"

"Almost four months."

Four months. Which meant it'd happened around the time her new semester had begun. "I don't understand. I asked you specifically if you were dating anyone. And you're premed, for heaven's sake! How could you let this happen?"

"Don't yell at me, Mom." Tears welled in her eyes. "I need you."

I need you. The words shook Jill to the core. She scooped her daughter in her arms and held tight as Shanna cried. Jill felt like crying, too. What had happened? Shanna had always been her easy child. She'd never had a boyfriend in high school, had never spoken of a boyfriend, or even dating, since starting college. While Tori had been the drama queen of the family, Shanna was always steady, cool and motivated to achieve. She knew about birth control, about consequences.

"Tori, go put the kettle on for tea, please," Jill instructed her younger daughter.

"Mom's cure-all," Tori muttered but left to do her bidding.

Shanna tucked her face against Jill's neck. Her breath hitched as she tried to stop crying. Jill kissed her forehead and ran her hand down Shanna's hair. "Who's the father, sweetie?"

"I don't want to talk about it."

"We have to talk about it. He has a responsibility, too. Does he know?"

"No. And I'm not telling him."

"You have to."

"No, I don't." She pulled away from Jill, swept her fingers along her cheeks and lifted her head, shaking back her hair, a purely rebellious pose, utterly new for her. "He's not part of my life."

"Well, he's going to be part of your child's life forever." She couldn't believe her serious, reliable daughter could be so irresponsible. It wasn't as if she'd just found out.

She'd had months to think about it, to figure out the right thing to do.

I'm going to be a grandmother. The thought struck Jill like a lightning bolt. "What *do* you have planned?"

"I want to stay in school. My due date is the same as finals week. I was hoping you would come look after the baby until I graduate."

Come? To Winston-Salem? "What about med school? You've already been accepted at Wake Forest."

"I'll apply someplace around here. The baby and I can live with you. You could babysit, right?"

Live full-time in Darien again? Babysit? The shocks kept coming. Jill needed to take a few steps back and think. Organize her thoughts. Plan.

She needed to talk to Alan.

"I need a few minutes alone," she said, scooping up her tote bag then going calmly up the stairs to her bedroom. She felt anything but calm.

She sat on her bed, her mind numb, for several minutes, then she dialed Alan's cell phone, knowing there was only a slim chance of catching him not on the ski slopes, but she would leave a message. She was wrong. He answered, but with a lot of background noise.

"Merry Christmas Eve," he shouted.

"Same to you. Where are you?"

"At the base of Avanti, getting ready to go up the lift. What's up?"

"I have news."

"What'd you say?"

"I have news," she shouted, then realized she didn't want the girls to hear her. "Can you call me back when you're someplace quiet?"

"Give me five minutes."

"Thanks."

Jill pushed herself off the bed, needing to expend... what? Energy? Disappointment? Anger? Why hadn't Shanna confided in her earlier? Why wait until Christmas to spring the news? Jill had offered—begged—to go visit Shanna many, many times. Was this why Shanna had put her off?

Jill should've trusted her instincts and just surprised her daughter. Shanna shouldn't have been dealing with this alone.

And where was the father? Who was the father? Why wasn't Shanna talking about him?

The phone rang. Jill grabbed it, then heard a click.

"Hey," Alan said. "Is this better?"

"I've got it," she said to whichever daughter had picked up an extension.

"Alan?" Tori asked.

"Hey, kiddo. How're things going?"

"Things are pretty interesting around here."

"Yeah? What's going on?"

"I'll let Mom tell you. She told me you're skiing with Jason and Matt. Are they kicking your butt on the slopes?"

"Of course. They got me snowboarding just so they could kick my butt. They're not nice to their old man. Where did I go wrong?"

She laughed. "Tell them hi for me, okay? See ya."

Jill had been pacing, waiting impatiently until she heard the other phone click off.

"She sounds good," Alan said.

"She's fine. It's Shanna."

"What about her?"

"She's pregnant. Four months."

Alan whistled, low. "Well, at least your question has finally been answered."

"What's that?"

"She's not gay."

Jill laughed grudgingly.

"It's not the end of the world," he said more gently. "When's the wedding?"

"There isn't going to be a wedding. In fact, she won't even name the father. Or tell him."

"Like hell she won't."

His support meant the world to her. "How can I force her?"

"The father has a right to know."

"Alan. What if he's married? Or one of her professors?" She voiced her worst fear. "What if she was raped?" What other reason was there for her not using birth control?

"I'll fly back tomorrow. We'll make her talk."

"You are not cutting short your time with your sons, and especially on Christmas Day. No way. Nothing here is going to change between now and Saturday when you're supposed to get back. I'll figure things out. I just needed...a friendly voice."

"Yeah, all right. But I'll call every day, and you call me if you need to talk, or brainstorm, or whatever. I'm here. I'll always be here, okay?"

Her throat ached. She was grateful she wasn't alone. "Thanks. It goes both ways."

"I know. 'Bye."

Jill washed her face and brushed her hair. She rubbed lotion in her hands, which always soothed her, as she decided what to do next. A couple of minutes later, a plan in mind, she went downstairs. Her daughters were sitting at the kitchen counter, drinking tea.

Jill issued her ultimatum. "Okay, here's the plan. It's Christmas Eve. Tonight, together, we will decorate the tree I had delivered here yesterday, which should be in the backyard. Have you seen it?" she asked Shanna.

"I haven't been outside."

Jill pulled the kitchen blinds. The tree sat in the middle of the door, already in a stand. "It's here. So, we'll decorate the tree, then have dinner, then we'll go for a drive and look at the Christmas lights, like we always do. We'll come home and have cocoa and cookies in front of the fireplace, like we always do. We'll talk about Christmases past, and what your favorite moments were, like we always do. And then we'll talk about Dad—because we need to. Tonight will be about us. Family. Memories. There's plenty of time to deal with reality later. Okay?"

"Okay," Shanna said, looking relieved.

Tori looked ready to argue, then nodded instead.

"Okay. Let's go up to the attic and get the decorations." She put an arm around each daughter before they climbed off their stools. "I love you both so much. I've missed you horribly. And I'm going to stop tiptoeing around you. I'm playing the Mom card, whether you like it or not. I love you too much not to."

"Okay," Shanna whispered, leaning into Jill.

Tori resisted but didn't argue.

That's one small step for Mom, Jill thought, one giant leap for Momkind.

She smiled.

When they all escaped to their bedrooms later that night, drained from sharing memories and shedding tears, Jill opened her diary. It was time to come up with a plan. While mentally considering her options, she thumbed through the past four months of diary notations. How she'd changed, she thought, from the hesitant suburbanite to a much more confident city woman. She'd come to love the hustle and bustle of New York, her new friends and her job. And her loft. She especially loved her loft, thank you, Wade.

Her list took form then:

What I know:
1. Shanna needs me—physically, emotionally and financially,
2. I don't want to give up my new life and independence.

That was it—opposing needs. Her future was a blank slate, waiting to be written on, so there was nothing more specific or concrete to add. She moved on to the next thought:

What I need to know:
1. Who is the baby's father?
2. Why won't Shanna share that information?
3. Why hasn't she told him?
4. How much can I give up to help her?

Jill could hardly believe she asked herself that question. Of course she was willing to give up everything for either of her children, even her life.

How do I feel about being a grandmother? she added.

At least that one she could answer. She would love the new role, of that she had no doubt. Four months ago she would've totally devoted her life to helping raise a grandchild so that Shanna could go to medical school. It would've been the purpose she'd been searching for. But now?

Shanna was in denial if she thought at this point she could apply to a local med school—any med school—for next year's enrollment. The spots would be filled by now. Her choices were Wake Forest or a year's delay, nothing else.

Which meant that Jill would have to move to Winston-Salem to help or else her grandchild would be raised by babysitters—ones Jill would have to finance.

Raise them or pay for raising them? Her choice, her decision.

"Mom?" Tori called softly from outside Jill's door. "Can I come in?"

Jill slipped her diary into her nightstand drawer. "Of course."

Tori had barely spoken during the evening, adding few memories, but still laughing and crying. She looked more like Jill's little girl now, dressed in old flannel pajamas. She'd showered but hadn't dried her hair. Her cheeks were rosy from the warm water. She looked healthy for the first time since she'd come home.

"I need to talk to you," Tori said, hesitating after she'd closed the bedroom door.

Dread blanketed Jill. This was not going to be good. "Come sit down," she said, patting the space on the bed beside her.

Tori sat, facing Jill, making eye contact for a moment then looking toward the window as she spoke. "I flunked most of my classes."

The second cannonball of the day hit Jill in the stomach. "What? How? You're smart! You've always been an excellent student."

"I know." She wrung her hands. "I don't know. It all just got away from me, and then I was so far behind I could never catch up, so I gave up."

"When you say 'most,' what do you mean?"

"I'm flunking three. Getting D's in the other two."

Jill closed her eyes and rubbed her forehead. Tori had

had five days to break that particular news but had saved it for Christmas Eve. Some Christmas. "What do *you* want to do?" she asked, exhausted.

"Oh, fine." She shoved herself off the bed. "Fine. Shanna, as usual, gets all the love and support she needs, while I, as usual, get sarcasm."

"I wasn't being sarcastic. I'm asking you a question."

"No, you're not. You're pissed. If Daddy was here, he would understand."

"Well, he isn't. You're stuck with me." Jill stood, too, bringing herself eye to eye with Tori.

The door opened, and Shanna peered in. "What's going on?"

"I'm flunking out of college. Mom doesn't care."

"I care! What are you talking about?"

"Then where's the hug for me?" Tori shouted. "Where's the sympathy for me? I lost my father. I can't think straight about anything."

"I understand that—"

"No, you don't."

"Tori," Shanna said, coming into the room finally.

"Butt out. This is between Mom and me. She's the one with the fun, new life. Wait until you see her loft. She's living great. She's happy."

"I'm *trying* to be happy. There's a difference. And I want you to be happy."

"She's dating," Tori tossed out to Shanna. "Did you know that? Internet dating. Already. I saw her profile in the computer. She can get herself a new husband, but we can't ever get a new dad. She— Oh, forget it." She raced out of the room.

"She's wrong," Jill said after a minute, staring at the empty doorway, panic rising inside her. "I care more than words can say. She caught me off guard, and after your news, I didn't react well." She started toward the door. "I'll go—"

"Mom, don't. Leave her alone. She'll calm down. She'll see she was wrong." She hugged Jill. "Get some sleep."

But she wasn't wrong about everything, Jill thought after Shanna left. Although nothing could or would replace Wade, she *could* have a second chance. Hearts were amazingly accommodating. A new love wouldn't diminish the old love, but add to it.

A stepfather wouldn't be the same. No matter how wonderful he was, he wouldn't be Dad. If she married again, she needed to choose a man who would love her daughters, too.

Jill grabbed her diary and climbed back into bed. To her what-I-need-to-know list, she added, *What Tori* ~~wants~~ *needs from me*.

She set it aside and rubbed her face, then leaned into her pillows and closed her eyes. Her aloneness hit her full force and for a moment, just a moment, she hated Wade for leaving her to handle everything by herself.

You don't have to.

She blew out a breath and picked up the phone.

"How's it going?" Alan asked.

It was quiet on his end, so Jill decided he must be in his hotel room.

"Tori's flunking out of college."

His cursing made her eyes tear up. "Thanks for saying what I wanted to," she said.

"I'm getting a flight out in the morning. You don't have to deal with all of this alone."

Just the fact she knew he would do that took away a lot of her tension. And she suddenly felt stronger, more in charge. "You are not leaving your sons on Christmas Day to tend to the neurotic Townsend girls. You're wonderful to offer, but really, Alan, we'll be okay. Enjoy your vacation."

"Call whenever you want."

"I will. Thank you."

A minute later she turned out the light and burrowed into bed.

Well, Iris, she thought. What would you think of my perfect life now?

CHAPTER 20

Friday, December 28
1. Who needs a pet when you've got a baby on the way?
2. Never sleep with anyone again. Ever. Who needs any more complications?
3. Cheryl coming by at 7:00. Do I really want to know what she has to say about Wade?

It was probably just the calm before the storm, but Jill decided to embrace it. She'd made appointments for herself and the girls for next week with a grief counselor, having shelved her issues in order to discuss them with an objective third party, and the girls had agreed to go, a ray of hope for improving their relationships.

They had all come to the city together yesterday morning and would stay until New Year's morning, when they would return to Darien to spend the anniversary of Wade's death. In the meantime, the girls were shopping and seeing movies and having fun. It'd been a long time since the sisters had spent much time together, and Jill was ecstatic to see them bond again.

Now she waited for Cheryl. Wade's former administrative assistant was on her way up. Ever since the open house, when Cheryl had hinted about knowing something about Wade that Jill didn't, Jill had been curious. But now, on top of everything that was happening with Shanna and Tori, did she want to add a new issue?

The knock on the door sounded more like a battering ram. She welcomed Cheryl into her home, offered her something to drink.

"John's waiting in the lobby. I didn't think I'd stay long." She looked around. "It's just like the photograph, isn't it? Not the décor, but the construction elements."

"Yes. Exactly. You said he was excited about it?" She gestured toward a chair in front of the fireplace, which she'd started, then took the chair next to hers.

"Incredibly. But in a bittersweet way, too."

Here it comes. "Why, Cheryl? I don't understand why. When I asked you at the open house if Wade had seemed different toward the end, quieter, you didn't want to answer."

"I still don't know if I should. I thought …"

"You thought what?" Jill leaned forward. "You can be honest. At this point whatever I imagine would probably be worse."

Cheryl laid her hand on Jill's. "I thought you knew, but I decided you didn't. And maybe you should."

"Well, that's crystal clear." She forced a little smile.

"Did you know Wade had a heart condition?"

The room spun. "No. No, I didn't."

"He was supposed to undergo surgery. He put it off so that he could take the ski trip."

The ski trip that killed him.

"It was supposed to be his last adventure for a while."

Pain assaulted Jill. He'd known he had a heart condition, yet he'd gone on that trip? At that elevation? In the cold? Exerting himself? How could he? How *could* he? "Well, it certainly ended up being that, didn't it?"

"He didn't expect to die, Jill. He didn't have a death wish."

She couldn't talk about it with someone who supported Wade's decision. She needed someone to understand her pain, her fury. Alan? It struck her that Alan must have known. He'd been part of the deal, and he kept secrets well. She'd come to understand why he'd kept the secret about the loft—that was, in the end, a good surprise. But not this. He shouldn't have kept this from her.

"Was I wrong to tell you?" Cheryl asked.

Jill had forgotten she was there. *Yes, you were wrong. Who needs this kind of pain?* But she said, "No. No, you weren't wrong."

"I think I should go."

Jill agreed by standing. She followed Cheryl to the door, hugged her goodbye. They would probably never meet again.

Ilene. She needed to talk to Ilene. She hurried upstairs,

wrapped a blanket around her suddenly cold body and called her friend.

"It's a kind of suicide," Jill said on the phone. "He knew he could die, yet he risked it all anyway. What does that say about me? About Shanna and Tori? That he didn't love us enough to stop his stupid athletic pursuits so that he could be there with us? For us?"

"He was driven, Jill, not suicidal."

"In this instance, it amounts to the same thing."

"Yes, the end result does, but he couldn't have known that."

"He must've had a good idea."

"What are you angriest about? That he had the problem yet went anyway? Or are you angry that he didn't tell you?" Ilene didn't wait for an answer. "He knew what would've happened if he'd told you. You would've tried to talk him out of it, maybe been successful. And he would've held that against you. It was something he had to do. Period. He took a risk and failed. That's life."

Jill closed her eyes. She pictured his desk drawer stuffed with all the sentimental mementos. A quick slide show ran in her head of joyful moments, compelling evidence of his love and devotion. And then there was his final gift—the loft—confirmation that he not only loved her but that he understood her, and had anticipated a different life for her, one she might have spent years trying to find without the jump start he'd given her.

How could she stay mad at him? No, he hadn't wanted to die. He'd just been realistic about the possibility he might.

"Thank you," she said to Ilene, exhausted from the roller-coaster emotions. "You're another gift from Wade. I wouldn't have met you without him."

"Amen, sister."

After Jill hung up, she went to sit by the fire again. She made the decision not to tell the girls about Wade's heart condition. She wouldn't even pursue the question herself of what kind of condition. It would change nothing. She'd already forgiven him. Shanna and Tori might not forgive him as readily, not only for keeping it from them, but for taking such a risk—his final risk.

The question remained whether she should confront Alan about it.

Which would also accomplish nothing, she decided. If Wade had confided in Alan, he'd been asked to keep it quiet. She needed to respect Alan for keeping his promise, if the promise had been asked.

Time slipped away. Shanna and Tori came home from an evening out and were lively and animated about a movie they'd seen.

They were starting to move on, Jill thought, watching them. She wouldn't disrupt that process. Ever.

"I don't think the end of the party season could come soon enough for you," Jill said to Rose three days later in the middle of the organized hubbub of New Year's Eve preparation for three parties. Jill was grateful for the distraction of work on what would've been her twenty-fourth wedding anniversary. "You look beat."

Rose leaned close and whispered, "Morning sickness."

"Oh! That's wonderful. Congratulations."

"Thanks. We've been trying for four years." Tears sparkled in her eyes. "I thought it would never happen."

"I'd hug you, except you apparently want to keep it quiet."

"For another month or so. I would like to talk to you in private, however. Can you come to my office sometime today?"

Jill eyed the New Year's cake she was decorating—a clock face with colorful icing fireworks exploding out of it. "I'm at a good place to stop." She wanted to make her pitch about staying on full-time, anyway.

Rose closed the door then sat behind her desk—her spotless desk. Rows of binders were within reach on a shelf behind her, information at her fingertips. Her file cabinets were in order. "I can't tell you how much I've enjoyed being organized. Thank you again."

"My pleasure." Should she wait for Rose to talk first, or bring up the issue of permanent employment herself?

"I'm thinking about cutting back on my hours," Rose said.

Jill frowned. This couldn't bode well. A reduction in hours would mean less business, therefore less need for staff.

"I was wondering if you'd like to pick up the slack, Jill."

"Me? In what way?"

"I'd like to be involved on the food level, creating the recipes, setting menus, that sort of thing. I was hoping you'd like to be my manager."

"Which would mean what?"

"Hire and fire. Meet with clients on everything except the menus. Keep control of the paperwork. Handle the parties."

It sounded like well beyond forty hours a week. "Would I have to attend all of them?"

"It would be physically impossible, since we often do more than one. Maybe the most important ones? Anyway, you would be responsible for making sure everything is handled and the clients are happy. It takes organization and follow-through, and follow-up. You're so good at that."

"Would I continue to do the cakes?"

"Absolutely—unless you want to stop. I've already had a few calls from guests at recent parties asking about just the cakes. I can see that becoming a big business for us—specialty cakes. Maybe you could continue to design but at some point hire and train someone to do the work?"

Jill sat back, absorbing the news, but her decision came with little internal debate. She already knew what she wanted, except that in making that decision, it settled another even more difficult decision—what to do about Shanna and her baby. "I don't want to manage the business."

Rose's face fell. "Had enough, huh? It *is* tough work."

"It has nothing to do with hard work. But if I'm going to put that much time and energy into a business, I want a stake in it."

"A stake? As in a partnership?"

"Yes." Excitement seeped into Jill. She would be so good at this. She loved the business already, but didn't have the food background. Together, she and Rose would be a force to be reckoned with.

"I have to think about it. And talk to my husband. Can I call you with an answer?"

"The girls and I will be in Darien starting tomorrow morning, but I can come in for meetings or whatever."

Rose smiled slightly. "And if I don't offer you a partnership, you won't take the job?"

"I figure I'll be able to help you boost business, maybe not enough to cover all of what you'd be losing in profit to me, but enough to make it worth your while to be home with your baby much more than you could without me. Trust me, you won't regret spending that time with your child."

"Smart move, appealing to the deprived-baby angle," Rose said, standing and smiling. "I'll get back to you. Did anyone tell you you're a heck of a businesswoman?"

"You're the first." The compliment bathed Jill in warmth. She hadn't even been nervous. You've come a long way, baby, she thought.

"I won't be the last. I'm definitely putting you in charge of any negotiations we have. Now get to work."

"Yes, ma'am." It sounded to Jill as if Rose had already made up her mind and only needed to talk it over with her husband.

Rose's decision would change Jill's life forever, as had all Jill's decisions since she'd begun her trial run of living in the loft, one after another after another. She should be exhausted.

Instead she felt she could leap tall buildings in a single bound.

She could only hope now that no one tossed any Kryptonite in her path.

Jill made her way home hours later, knowing there was no one she could share her news with. Ilene had a date. Shanna and Tori were invited to a party.

But when she walked into her loft she found her daughters had put together a meal from their favorite Chinese takeout, had started the fire and lit candles. Jill burst into tears. She dropped her purse and opened her arms, and they hugged.

"We're sorry Daddy isn't here to celebrate," Shanna said.

"Me, too." Jill finally let them go. Shanna had tears on her face. Tori's expression broadcast her need for distance. Would that ever change?

After dinner, Jill encouraged them to go to the New Year's party, that she would be fine. Tori couldn't get out fast enough, but Shanna lingered a few extra seconds.

"I think I felt the baby move today," she told Jill. "I'm not sure. It was just a kind of flutter."

Jill nodded, smiling, then leaned down and kissed the swell of Shanna's abdomen. "Hey. This is your grandma. I love you." She hated that Wade was missing this incredible experience.

She felt Shanna's hand brush her hair. "I love you, too, Mom."

Jill squeezed her daughter tight, then reluctantly let her go, knowing Tori would be pacing the hallway, waiting.

After cleaning up the dishes, Jill wandered around her loft. She turned on the television, channel surfed for a while, then left it on an old black-and-white movie but paid no attention to it. Noise. She just needed noise.

As midnight approached she reached for the phone, hesitated, then finally picked it up and dialed Alan's number, needing to share her news about the potential partnership with someone. Or so she told herself.

But his phone rang four times and then his answering machine picked up. She hung up. Of course he would be out on a date. Of course.

At midnight she wished she'd gotten a dog—or even a potbellied pig—after all. Some living thing to talk to.

But there was only emptiness.

CHAPTER 21

Thursday, January 3
1. Neighbor e-mailed a picture of the kittens, the tricky man.
2. Crunch numbers with accountant.
3. Expose repressed emotions with grief counselor.

"There's not enough money?" Jill repeated to Bob Armstrong, the family accountant for more than ten years. Her excitement at Rose's call the night before offering her a partnership faded. She could hardly catch her breath. "How can that be?"

"There's enough to support you in the manner to which you've become accustomed, but you're asking about changing your base needs. If you want to keep the Darien house, pay Shanna's and Tori's college expenses, and also Shanna's baby expenses—you can do that comfortably. But as for paying what's left on the TriBeCa loft, including huge taxes, and a partnership in the catering business? Your money's not going to stretch that far."

She'd known it somehow. Had delayed finding out.

But wasn't a sheltered woman who'd been making huge changes in her life allowed one denial?

She looked hopefully at her accountant. "Even with the income from my job?"

"Your income probably won't cover your daughters' expenses. I worked up the numbers after you e-mailed me everything this morning. Take a look."

Jill studied the report. When she'd learned how much the loft would cost, she'd been staggered but had still figured it was feasible, even though fully renovated, prime real estate in the city cost a lot, not to mention the small fortune she'd spent decorating it. She'd never had to worry about money, so she hadn't.

"What *can* I manage?" she asked Bob now.

"If you sell the Darien house, you'd be okay. Or if you don't buy the loft."

She didn't like that answer at all. "I don't understand. How can there not be enough money? There was life insurance, and Wade's trust fund."

"Jill," Bob said kindly. "Your lifestyle went well above Wade's wages for years. Forever, really. Money came out of his trust fund every month to help. Then there were the big extravagances, like for climbing Everest. Do you know how much that cost?"

"I knew it was expensive, that's all."

"That's an understatement. As I said, you can continue on as you were, but not as you want now."

Jill stared at her lap, mentally sorting the information. Living in Darien and commuting to the city for her job wasn't an option, as far as she was concerned, not when she would be working odd and late hours. But sell the house? Shanna and Tori would never forgive her. They were just starting to heal as a family. How could Jill do that to them? They still needed a place to come home to, to feel safe.

But, for herself, how could she not sell? She couldn't go back to her old life, now that she'd seen a different world.

Bob handed her another sheet of paper. "Here's what your situation would be if you sell the Darien house and move into the city."

She took her time reading the material. "This looks doable."

"More than that. You won't have to stick to too tight of a budget, and your financial situation will only improve over time. College expenses will end at some point, and the partnership should pay off, although that's a tough business to succeed in. Which reminds me, I want to see their books before you agree to the deal."

"I already told Rose you would be contacting her accountant."

"Good."

She sat back and tried to smile.

"A little overwhelming?" he asked.

"This situation wasn't on any of my lists," she said, feeling lost. She needed a plan.

She should discuss it with Alan, since he was involved, but she was reluctant. It was time for her to stand on her own, to make these life-altering decisions herself. He would want to make things easier for her—not a bad thing, just not what she needed. She needed to prove to herself that she could manage.

Jill folded the paperwork neatly into quarters and slipped it into her purse. She drove home and honked the horn. She and the girls made it to the grief counselor at exactly their appointment time.

"I wanted to see you all together first," the counselor, Pam, said. "Then we'll schedule individual time as necessary. I understand that you've all been together for about ten days, and that there was a great deal of tension in the beginning that seems better now. Is that right?"

When neither of the girls answered, Jill said, "It's only better now because we've avoided talking about the important issues. We've made the effort to just be together, to have fun."

"Is that how you two see it?" Pam asked.

"I agree," Shanna said. "But Mom was right about us needing to just have some fun together for a while. We had to figure out how to be together again. Ever since Dad died, we've hardly talked."

"Not because I didn't want to," Jill said. "I'm not patting myself on the back here, but it's true. I tried again and again to get them to open up. I was afraid for both of them."

"Tori, would you agree with that?" Pam asked.

"She drove me nuts, always wanting to talk about it. I just wanted to be left alone."

"Why?"

She fidgeted in the chair. "Because she was bugging me. I couldn't breathe."

"What do you think she should have done?"

"I don't know. Just not what she was doing."

"What, being your mom?" Jill asked. "Being worried for you?"

"I was handling it."

Jill faced her. "You handled it by turning your bedroom into a cave. By not talking to me. By staying out past your curfew then being belligerent about it."

"Yeah, so? You should've grounded me."

"I cut you some slack. What's wrong with that? You were in enough pain."

"You didn't care."

There it was, the accusation that mattered.

"I don't see how you can say that," Jill said, crushed.

"You didn't even cry," Tori said, her voice like sandpaper.

She looked lost and scared. Jill wanted to drag her into her arms. "I cried all the time. I cried myself to sleep. I cried every morning in the shower. I cried in the car."

"You didn't cry when you left me at college."

A loud silence descended.

"Everyone else's mom was crying," Tori went on, accusation in her tone. "Not you. You smiled."

"For you," Jill said, horrified at how Tori had misinterpreted the moment. "I thought it would make things easier for you."

"Well, it didn't. It hurt. It was bad enough that no matter what I did, Dad didn't want to spend any time with me, didn't care about all I accomplished, but then *you* were so happy to see me leave."

"What? Dad? *What?* You're wrong. You're so wrong. He was proud of you. He loved you. And I was *not* happy to see you leave. I hated it. I cried for most of the drive home. I've missed you every day."

"I know he *loved* me, Mom, but I wanted him to put me first sometimes."

"I get what she means about Dad," Shanna said quietly. "I didn't even know him."

Jill sat back, stunned. Where was all this coming from?

"Tell us what you mean by that," Pam said.

"I mean I can't ever remember spending time with him, just the two of us. When he was home, which wasn't a whole lot, we did things as a family sometimes, but never just us. I got over it. It was just him. He needed to be going places and doing things."

"Is that why you're denying your baby its father?" Jill asked. "Because you don't think he would take an active role in his child's life? That your child would get over it, like you did? Because it doesn't sound to me like you're over it."

"These are different circumstances, Mom. I'm not married. He never proposed marriage, or even said he loved me."

"Do you love *him?*"

Shanna squeezed her hands together and looked at her lap. "Yes."

"Are you sure he doesn't love you? Has he said he doesn't?"

"He's obsessed with me, that's all." She ran her hand down her slightly rounded belly. "I don't want a custody battle or anything."

"Oh, you're so stupid, Shanna," Tori said.

Shanna's eyes widened. "Excuse me? Are you some kind of expert in these matters?"

"You've always been this cool, calm, *logical* person. Nothing flusters you. You follow the rules, and life is good. Now you broke the rules, and you have to pay, like everyone else, but you don't think you should pay. You think you're above the rules, somehow."

"What rules?"

"You got pregnant. There are consequences, big sister. And that consequence is all warm and safe inside of you. But in a few months, it's gonna be in the big, bad world, and you've decided that it doesn't need any help but yours. And Mom's. You're wrong, and you're selfish. That baby deserves its father."

Jill was stunned by Tori's defense. If anything, Jill would've thought that Tori would support her sister.

"What do you know about it?" Shanna asked, her voice shaking.

"I know my father isn't here anymore. And I would give anything to have him back. What if I'd never had him at all? Okay, so he wasn't perfect. He was still my dad." She hesitated. Her eyes filled with tears. "And I wish he was here."

Jill reached for her daughter, an automatic need to comfort this child of her heart. Tori moved into Jill's arms, finally, and took that comfort, sobbing, her body shaking. Then Shanna joined them, and they cried together, pain and love starting the long process of healing them.

"You have to tell the father," Tori said to Shanna minutes later. "Promise you'll tell the father."

Shanna nodded as she wiped tears from her face. She flashed a shaky grin at Jill. "Out of the mouths of babes."

"Yes. Wisdom." Jill kissed Tori's forehead. "You know how much your dad loved you, right? Both of you? You don't really doubt that?"

Tori nodded. Shanna said, "I felt guilty for being mad at him for the time we lost and the time we should've had. I've held that in for a long time. But I do know he loved me, Mom."

"Okay." Jill sat back, exhausted. She wasn't naive enough to think that all their problems were solved now, but communication had been established. They could talk things through and find solutions, in time.

And she needed to be the one to start, by being honest with them about her own needs and plans.

Shanna made another appointment with Pam. Tori headed straight out to the car.

Pam asked Jill to wait a moment after Shanna left. "Work on getting Tori to come back on her own, okay? She's an angry young woman, but once she forgives her father for dying, and you for living, she'll come around."

Pam's words resonated in Jill's head, enough that she decided to take the girls out to lunch instead of going home. They would let the tension settle over hamburgers, mounds of fries and a shared hot fudge sundae.

A shadow came across the table as they battled with their spoons for the bit of fudge remaining in the dish.

"Hi, Shanna," a masculine voice said, stopping the laughter cold.

Jill recognized him—Darryl Michaels, the young man she'd thought was ogling her at the gym. The young man Shanna had ordered Jill not to talk to again. She glanced at her older daughter, whose face had pinkened.

"Hi, Darryl," Shanna said.

Something tangible passed between them, turning the air hot and thick. He's the one, Jill realized. The father.

"How are you?" he asked Shanna.

"I...I'm okay. How are you?"

"I could be better."

"Me, too."

Hope flickered in his eyes. "Can we talk?"

"Yeah. Can you come by the house in a couple of hours?"

"Why not now?"

"There's something I need to do first. I'll be there, Darryl. I promise."

"I'm holding you to that." He strode straight out the front door, then got into his car and drove off.

"Well," Jill said.

"He's the one."

"Geez, sis," Tori said. "You picked Dad."

Shanna laughed. "I know. Rich, conservative and obsessed with his job."

He loves her, Jill thought. He wasn't obsessed with her, as Shanna had said earlier. He loved her. It was written all over his face. And Shanna had said that she loved him.

"Why did you put him off for a couple of hours, sweetie?"

"Because the three of us need this time together."

"And you need to find some guts," Tori said.

"That, too. It's not going to be easy, telling him."

"You know, if you wear the right clothes, he won't notice you're preggers. Guys are stupid about that stuff. Maybe he'll tell you what you want to hear before you tell him about the baby. Then you'll know."

"Know what?"

"That he was marrying you for you, dummy, not just the baby."

Jill squeezed Tori's hand. "You're very wise." Except, of course, it could backfire and Shanna may not hear that he loved her, only that he expected her to marry him once he knew the truth. Jill had a good feeling about him, however…

"I'm glad you think so, Mom," Tori said. "And I hope you keep on thinking it, because I've got something to tell you."

Jill consciously stopped herself from frowning. "Okay."

"I'm not going back to college."

While Jill wasn't overly surprised, actually hearing the words silenced her.

"Please don't be mad," Tori said, misinterpreting the silence. "I'd like to live in the city. Not with you," she added in a hurry. "With friends. I'll get a job, but what I really want is to enroll in acting classes. Would you help with that instead of paying my tuition at college?"

"Let me think on it," Jill said. She decided that a public place was a good choice for announcing her own news. "I've been offered a partnership in A Rose is a Rose."

"You have?" Shanna asked, her voice strained. "But what about me? I'll need you when the baby comes."

"We'll figure out something. You told me to find something to do," she reminded her daughter gently.

"I guess."

"If things aren't going well for me by May," Tori said, "I'll go to Winston-Salem and help Shanna until she graduates."

"Really?" Shanna asked.

"You're my sister," Tori said, as if wondering why Shanna was so stunned.

"Um, I have more news," Jill said. "I have to sell the house."

Shanna and Jill went silent. Both sat back.

"I know it's a shock, but let me explain." She'd decided to be honest with them about the money situation. She'd spent her entire married life not knowing about the family finances. She wasn't going to let her daughters be ignorant, too. "In order to do a good job, I need to live in the city, and the loft is more than I can afford on my income alone. Plus it's going to be expensive to buy into the business. I need the cash from the house."

"But…our home," Tori said.

"I know. Believe me, I know. It won't be easy for me, either. But here's the deal. I need this job, not just financially, but because it makes me happy. Tori, you need to find your path, too, and while a little struggle is a good thing, I'd rather you not have to work two minimum-wage jobs while also taking lessons and going on auditions. That much ease I can give you. And I'm talking about helping you, not fully supporting you financially.

"And Shanna, you absolutely cannot drop out of med school, which is what would happen if I didn't pay for it. You need my financial help more than ever. And I know you're realizing that this means I can't babysit. Not that I don't want to, but it just won't be possible with us living so far apart. You need to do your first year of med school at Wake Forest as planned so that you stay on target, but maybe you can get a second-year transfer somewhere close. Then I can help out some."

Shanna's expression was blank.

"Also, I wouldn't miss being with you the first week after my grandchild is born, but that's probably all I can manage at the time. I'll come as often as I can, however. As often as you want." Although Jill fully expected Darryl to have a say in the entire matter. "I know this is a shock. It's all happened so fast. I'm just now making sense of it myself as I'm talking to you."

She looked from one daughter to the other. She remembered her conversation with Jacob after a support group meeting almost two months ago when she'd been trying so hard to figure out how to help her daughters. She'd wondered how she could ask them for help, when they needed more help than she did. And he'd reminded her that she was the role model. So she needed to show her own vulnerabilities sometimes too. Like now. She didn't have all the answers, and they should know that.

"Well? What do you think? Am I on the right track? I'd like your help in deciding."

"Mom," Shanna said after a moment. "I am so proud of you."

Tori seemed to nod, but maybe it was wishful thinking on Jill's part.

"Are you scared?" Shanna asked.

"A little," she admitted. "There have been so many changes. But my confidence has grown. And I like the woman I've become. I'm glad I make you proud. It means so much to me."

"Well, duh," Tori said as if she thought Jill were crazy. "I just wish you'd lose the lists, Mom, and do a little free-falling once in a while."

"Maybe I will."

"Don't hold your breath," Shanna said to Tori.

They all smiled tentatively, tension still binding them, just not with the same stranglehold. Jill decided it was nice that her daughters knew her that well. "Let's go home," she said, a bittersweet request, knowing it wouldn't be home for much longer.

They'd opened the family's Pandora's Box today, letting out all the problems while leaving hope still inside it. It boded well for the future.

Now all that was left for Jill to do was to tell Alan her decisions. She would have almost a week to build up to it, since he'd decided the book needed a major revision after he'd thought he was done with it. He'd buried himself in his office.

Which was just a convenient excuse, and Jill knew it. She could interrupt him long enough to tell him the decisions she'd made.

But first she needed time to accustom herself to moving away from her very best friend in the world—an even harder task than selling the house, she realized.

CHAPTER 22

Wednesday, January 9
1. Neighbor is getting devious now. Showed up at my door holding a little orange tabby. One more week until she's weaned. I'm in love.
2. Stop thinking about sex.
3. Support group tonight, but am I welcome there?

"I can't believe you let that Iris woman scare you off," Ilene said over an early dinner at Jill's loft. "You have every right to be at the meeting tonight."

Jill kept looking at her watch, aware that the Musketeers would be gathered at the Church of Personal Identity without her. This would be the third week since she'd attended, since she'd learned the truth about Iris. "She didn't scare me off. I was stupid and insensitive, and I don't deserve to be with them. I don't want to upset Iris by going back."

"I thought I'd beaten that kindness crap out of you."

Jill smiled. "You've certainly given it the old college try."

Ilene toasted her with her wine, then took a sip. "So, the engagement party is this weekend."

"Yes. Shanna has to be back at school on Monday. You'll be there, right?"

"With bells on. Did you invite any single men?"

"Darryl's parents are in charge of the engagement party. The guest list we gave them didn't include any single guys over age twenty-two."

"And your point is?"

Jill laughed. "I guess I didn't have one. The wedding's on Valentine's weekend. I'm telling you, Ilene, the speed at which this is all happening is staggering. I barely have time to breathe anymore."

"You like him? Darryl?"

"He adores Shanna and will treat her well. That's what matters to me. His father is letting him telecommute from Winston-Salem. That makes me like his father, too."

"Did you ever find out how they met?"

"While they were in high school. He was two years ahead of her. She had a big-time crush on him that never went away in the six years that followed."

Which was the condensed version of what had happened, but Jill would protect her daughter's privacy about how Shanna, a sophomore, had thrown herself at Darryl, a senior, who didn't want to get involved, because he was headed to California and Stanford University after graduation. But they'd slept together that summer before he left, then had broken things off when he moved. He'd tracked her down after he graduated, they'd had a short affair that summer, but she'd ended it when he hadn't told her he loved her. He'd been pursuing her ever since. She'd been rebuffing him, not wanting to get hurt further. Then right after Jill had run into Darryl at the gym he'd gone to Winston-Salem, and Shanna had "used him to help deal with her grief," as she put it, but when he still hadn't declared his love, she told him she didn't want to see him again.

But love her he did, as she found out before she'd broken the news, as Tori predicted, about the baby.

Jill was still shocked that all this had happened without her suspecting anything. Shanna hadn't even hinted at a relationship, with Darryl or anyone else. She guessed it was true—that the parents were always the last to know.

Ilene snapped her fingers in front of Jill's face. "You in there?"

"Sorry. I do that a lot these days. Too much on my mind."

"When do you break the news to Alan?"

"When I go home for the party this weekend."

"How do you think he's going to react?"

"I get the feeling he would like to keep the loft himself. But a promise is a promise. He would never break his word. I hope he'll continue to come in and work with Wendi." *Stay with me. Have Sunday morning breakfast together.* She'd come to love that.

Her front doorbell rang. "Who could that be?" she

wondered aloud. The girls had their own keys, but they were in Darien, anyway. She was stunned to see Mrs. Q., Birdie, Wendi and Iris huddled on the doorstep.

"Hi, everyone," Jill said as cheerfully as the lump in her throat allowed.

"Can we come up?" Wendi asked.

"The lynch mob is here?" Ilene asked, coming up beside her.

Jill elbowed her as she pushed the unlock button. "It's open," she called out.

She watched them until they were out of camera range, but she couldn't see anyone's expression enough to know what to expect.

"Should I take off?" Ilene asked.

"I don't know. I may need a witness. Or a bodyguard."

"I've got pepper spray," she said, reaching for her purse, which hung on the coat rack.

"Have you ever used it?"

"Once. I debilitated a guy so that I could have my way with him."

Jill laughed. "You're incorrigible."

The ping of the elevator ended the conversation.

"Seriously. Do you want me to leave?" Ilene asked.

"I would say let's play it by ear, but I have the feeling they'll all clam up with you here and I'll never find out why they came."

"I didn't want to ruin my manicure doing dishes, anyway." She grabbed her coat and purse.

Jill opened the door. The Four Musketeers stood like

a wall in an obstacle course. Ilene said hello and goodbye then maneuvered past them.

"Come in," Jill said, backing up and holding the door open.

They shuffled in as a group. God, she loved them. All of them. And had missed them terribly. She swallowed hard.

"Can I get you something to drink?" she asked the group at large as she cleared the dinner dishes and set them in the sink. "Coffee? Tea? Soda?"

"Sit down, please, Jill," Mrs. Q. said.

Mrs. Q., Iris and Birdie had made themselves at home on her sofa. Wendi pulled up a dining room chair for herself and one for Jill and indicated she should sit. Her hands clenched, Jill sat.

"How was your Christmas?" Mrs. Q. asked.

Why were they stalling? "I got offered a partnership in the catering business. I'm selling my Darien home. My older daughter is four months pregnant and unmarried. And my younger daughter announced she was flunking out of college."

"So. Just another holiday," Wendi quipped.

Jill laughed. "Yeah. It's working out, though. We're gonna make it okay."

"I wouldn't have doubted it for a second," Birdie said. "Do you have any brownies?"

Jill jumped up. "Anyone else want one?"

Wendi raised her hand.

"How's your love life?" Birdie asked.

"Nonexistent." She brought brownies to Birdie and Wendi then took her seat again. *Come on, come on, come on.*

"I suppose you're wondering why we're here," Iris said.

Jill considered several sarcastic retorts, as if Ilene were channeling her. She discarded them all. "I'm curious."

"We missed you," Birdie said, earning a glare from Iris. "Well, it's true. We all agreed. Even you." She used her brownie as a pointer toward Jill. "We don't want you to stop coming. Frankly, you need us."

Emotions welled up in Jill, making it hard to focus. "I wasn't sure of my welcome anymore. I stepped way over the line."

"It was probably the best thing that happened to me," Iris said, her voice strong and sure. "I didn't think so at the time. I was pretty angry, I can tell you. But I'd never told the truth to anyone, and it had festered until everything inside me was ugly. I'm never going to date, mind you. But I'm going to live again."

Jill put a shaky hand to her mouth. "Oh, I'm so glad, Iris."

Iris nodded. Jill hadn't expected a hug, but maybe someday.

"I'd like to hear about all of your holidays, too," Jill said.

"I had everyone over to my place," Mrs. Q. said. "My children and my grandchildren, my two sisters and their families. I hadn't done that in a long, long time."

"I had sex," Birdie said, drawing surprised looks. "I

never would've guessed Louie had it in him." She finished off her brownie with a flourish. "I hope I don't have to wait another three years."

"My brother called from Florida," Iris said. "He invited me for a visit. I'm going next week."

Everyone made a fuss over Iris, who smiled tentatively. She locked gazes with Jill and nodded very slightly a few times, as if to say thank you. Jill's chest tightened.

"Alan's agent agreed to represent me," Wendi said, beaming, and everyone whooped and hollered. "He said the manuscript will be making the rounds starting next week."

The phone rang. "Don't say anything important until I get back," Jill said then picked up the phone and said hello.

"Is there something you forgot to tell me, Jill?"

"Alan?"

"I'm on my way up."

"Now? This minute?"

"Oh, yeah."

Crap. She could tell from the sound of his voice that he was angry. Somehow he'd found out. "Um, I have company."

"Kick him out. Or I will." He ended the call.

She set the phone down carefully and tried to smile. "I'm sorry to cut this short, but I'm going to have to ask you to leave."

"Are you all right?" Wendi asked, standing.

No. "I'm fine."

The women exchanged curious glances as they put on their coats and gathered their purses.

"I'll see you next week," she said cheerfully. "Thank you so much for coming." She didn't see how they would avoid seeing Alan. Did she need to come up with an explanation?

The front door opened just as Iris reached it, the others forming a kind of conga line behind her.

"It's Alan," Wendi said, surprised. She looked back at Jill.

"Ladies," Alan said, his jaw like granite. "It's starting to snow. Take care now." He continued on, until he was out of sight.

Jill shut the door behind the women. She'd waited too long to talk to him. She'd never seen his eyes look so cold, so angry.

She found him standing in front of the fireplace, his hands open to the heat, his hair damp from melting snow. The last time she'd seen him, a week ago, he'd had dinner with her and the girls. He'd made Tori laugh, and Shanna had sat next to him on the couch, her head against his shoulder. Jill had forgotten how much her daughters adored him. She believed that Alan's sons felt the same way about her.

Tenderness swelled in her for this man who'd been a part of her life for so long, as a friend to Wade, as a kind of second father to her daughters, and as something she couldn't define to her. It was more than friendship. He was confidant and advisor and cheerleader.

Somehow he had become the yardstick by which she measured every man she met. That list she'd made in her diary about the qualities she was looking for in a man—smart, fun, funny, sexy, loyal, successful, available—were the very definition of Alan Haggerty.

"I was going to tell you this weekend," she said, coming up beside him. "How did you find out?"

"I saw a For Sale sign in front of your house this afternoon. I thought someone was playing a prank, because I knew you wouldn't make such a big decision then not tell me." He finally looked at her. "It wasn't a prank, though, was it."

"No. The sign wasn't supposed to go up until next week. I'd decided to let you finish your book without bothering you...."

He met her gaze. He had lines on his face she hadn't seen before.

"I know. It was lame," she said, then explained about her partnership and her financial dilemma.

"You could have come to me for help," he said, low and harsh. "I could've acted as a banker for you. I could've given you a loan so you could keep the house, too."

"I don't want the house anymore, Alan. That part of my life is over. Not forgotten, but over."

He stared at her until she squirmed. "Okay, Jill." He took a step back and turned away then headed toward the front door.

She trailed him, panic setting in. He should be talking. He wasn't talking. "Where are you going?"

"I can't stay here with you."

"Why not?"

"You don't need anything from me. You've taken your last big steps—alone. Maybe I'll see you around."

"Alan!" She grabbed him before he opened the door. "You can't just walk out like that."

"Why not? I've served my purpose."

"You haven't begun to serve your purpose. I need you."

"You have an odd way of showing it."

"I thought it would make you happy, seeing me become strong and independent." He didn't look at her, but he didn't leave, either.

"I don't have to transfer the deed to you," he said.

Her heart began to thud. When had he become unpredictable? "You wouldn't do that."

He finally faced her. "Tell me something, Jill. What do you think it takes for a relationship to last?"

"Besides love? I think you have to find each other interesting. That's what sustains you in the long run."

"You stopped being interesting to me at some point—"

"Stop," she said, putting a hand over his mouth. She knew he was angry, but she didn't need to hear this.

He pulled her hand away but didn't let go. He came a step closer. "You stopped being interesting and became fascinating."

Her heart, body and soul responded, infusing her with heat. *Yes. It's Alan. It's only been Alan.*

"I've been waiting for you," he said. He framed her face with his hands. "Waiting more patiently than I should have, maybe. I knew you needed time to find yourself, the woman you were going to become. I felt I needed to honor Wade's memory, too, and wait until a year had passed."

"Since when?"

"Since when, what?"

"How long have you been waiting?"

"Since the night in the pool. It struck me like a lightning bolt."

"Like your swim trunks," she said, smiling, happy to know it had started at the same time for him.

"We're good for each other," he said softly, a little unsure. "And we have history. We went through the worst times in each other's life."

Her heart thumped. "What are you saying?"

"That I've been waiting a long time to do this."

And then he kissed her. And it felt right and good and exciting, everything it was supposed to be. He was both friend and stranger. There was a lot left to discover.

Thursday, January 10
1. Get a man.
2. Get laid better.

Jill ran her finger across the entries she'd just posted in her diary. Night was easing into day, and all was right with the world.

With a great deal of satisfaction she ceremoniously

drew a line through each entry, written for the sole purpose of doing so, then with a smile she closed the book and turned to the man sleeping beside her.

She kissed his shoulder.

He'd slept long enough.

* * * * *

True Confessions of the Stratford Park PTA

by Nancy Robards Thompson

The journey of four women through midlife; man trouble; and their children's middle school hormones—as they find their place in this world...

Available October 2006
TheNextNovel.com

There's a first time for everything...

Aging rock-and-roller Zoe learned this the hard way...at thirty-nine, she was pregnant!

Leaving behind the temptations of L.A., she returns home to Louisiana to live with her sister. Despite their differences, they come to terms with their shared past and find that when the chips are down there is no better person to lean on than your sister.

Leaving L.A.

by
Rexanne Becnel

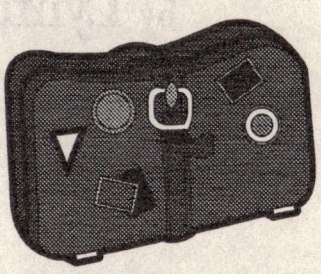

Available September 2006
TheNextNovel.com

A stunning novel of love and renewal...

Everyone knows sisters like the Sams girls—three women trying their best to be good daughters, mothers and wives. Then in one cataclysmic moment everything changes... and the sisters have to uncover every shrouded secret and risk lifetime bonds to ensure the survival of all they love.

Graceland

by Lynne Hugo

Available October 2006
TheNextNovel.com

There's got to be a mourning-after!

Saturday, September 22

1) Get a ~~dog~~ cat
2) Get a man
3) Get adventurous (go skinny-dipping)
4) Get a LIFE!

Jill Townsend is learning to step beyond the safe world she's always known to take the leap into Merry Widowhood.

The Merry Widow's Diary

by Susan Crosby

Available September 2006
TheNextNovel.com

REQUEST YOUR FREE BOOKS!

2 FREE NOVELS TO INTRODUCE YOU TO OUR BRAND-NEW LINE!

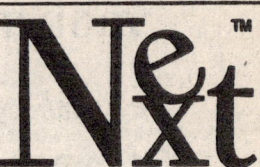

There's the life you planned. And there's what comes next.

YES! Please send me 2 FREE Harlequin® NEXT™ novels and my FREE mystery gift. After receiving them, if I don't wish to receive any more books, I can return the shipping statement marked "cancel." If I don't cancel, I will receive 3 brand-new novels every month and be billed just $3.99 per book in the U.S., or $4.74 per book in Canada, plus 25¢ shipping and handling per book plus applicable taxes, if any*. That's a savings of over 20% off the cover price! I understand that accepting the 2 free books and gift places me under no obligation to buy any books. I can always return a shipment and cancel at any time. Even if I never buy another book from Harlequin, the two free books and gift are mine to keep forever.

156 HDN D74G 356 HDN D74S

Name _____ (PLEASE PRINT)

Address _____ Apt. #

City _____ State/Prov. _____ Zip/Postal Code

Signature (if under 18, a parent or guardian must sign)

Order online at www.TryNEXTNovels.com

Or mail to the Harlequin Reader Service®:

IN U.S.A.	IN CANADA
3010 Walden Ave.	P.O. Box 609
P.O. Box 1867	Fort Erie, Ontario
Buffalo, NY 14240-1867	L2A 5X3

Not valid to current Harlequin NEXT subscribers.

Want to try two free books from another line?
Call 1-800-873-8635 or visit www.morefreebooks.com

* Terms and prices subject to change without notice. NY residents add applicable sales tax. Canadian residents will be charged applicable provincial taxes and GST. This offer is limited to one order per household. All orders subject to approval. Credit or debit balances in a customer's account(s) may be offset by any other outstanding balance owed by or to the customer.

NEXT05

Who knew Truth or Dare could have such unexpected consequences...

Suburban Secrets
by Donna Birdsell

Opting for the Dare, Grace, who has let her Day-Timer rule her life, suddenly finds herself on an undercover assignment cooking for a Russian mob boss. Suddenly, her old life as a suburban soccer mom looks like heaven!

Available September 2006
TheNextNovel.com

Just like a blue moon, friendship is a beautiful thing

Hoping to rekindle a sense of purpose, Lola resurrects a childhood dream and buys a blue beach house. When she drags three of her fun-loving, margarita-sipping friends out for some gossip and good times, they discover the missing spark in their relationships.

Once in a Blue Moon

by Lenora Worth

Available October 2006
TheNextNovel.com

It's all a matter of perspective

Grace Campisi has lived her whole life according to plan. But when her sister runs off, leaving behind a six-week-old baby girl, Grace's plans are thrown a curveball.

So in order to stick to her plan, Grace could either

a) track down her wayward sister
b) put her niece up for adoption
Or c) formulate a new plan?

Which End Is Up?

Patricia Kay

Available October 2006
TheNextNovel.com

Every Life Has More Than One Cha...

Author **SUSAN CROSBY** believes truth is usually crazier than fiction and uses her own life experiences to weave her exceptional stories.

Saturday, September 22

1. Get a ~~dog~~ cat.
2. Get a man.
3. Get adventurous (go skinny-dipping!)
4. Get a life!

She'd been the pampered and protected wife. Now she was a widow with both daughters off at college and she was suddenly desperate to fill her empty nest with something—*anything*. So when Jill Townsend finds a mysterious key in her late husband's office she sets out to find the door it opens.

Saying so long to suburbia, she heads for the wilds of Manhattan, where new friends and career opportunities loom—and sexy men are hitting on *her!* But will Jill ever be able to step beyond the safe and secure world she's always known and take that leap into merry widowhood?

ISBN-13: 978-0-373-88108-6
ISBN-10: 0-373-88108-8

TheNextNovel.com
$5.50 U.S./$6.50 CAN.